no place to call home

a novel

JJ BOLA

Arcade Publishing · New York

Arcade Publishing books may be purchased in bulk at special discounts for sales promotion, corporate gifts, fund-raising, or educational purposes. Special editions can also be created to specifications. For details, contact the Special Sales Department, Arcade Publishing, 307 West 36th Street, 11th Floor, New York, NY 10018 or arcade@skyhorsepublishing.com.

Arcade Publishing® is a registered trademark of Skyhorse Publishing, Inc.®, a Delaware corporation.

Visit our website at www.arcadepub.com.

10 9 8 7 6 5 4 3 2 1

Library of Congress Cataloging-in-Publication Data is available on file.

Cover design by Erin Seaward-Hiatt

Print ISBN: 978-1-62872-887-3
Ebook ISBN: 978-1-62872-888-0

Printed in the United States of America

part I

chapter 1

Jean's smile stretched wide like arms opening for a hug. It was warm and inviting; a beautiful house with an open front door, it compelled you to come in and welcomed you to stay. It did not happen often though—his smile—but when it did it was spring after a long winter; a sunflower blooming or some bright light. His arms also stretched long and wide, as if he had spent his entire childhood reaching for things he could not have. His hands were disproportionately large, so when his parents held him as a baby and noticed them, Papa said "maybe he'll grow up to be a goalkeeper; they have big hands, you know," to which Mami replied "or maybe he'll simply know how to keep holding on. He'll need it."

He arrived at his new school at 8:15 a.m. and waited for his tutor in the reception area. Jean, never before having seen his tutor—because he missed the induction meeting due to vomiting all night from the nerves of starting a new school—smiled at everyone who walked in his direction. After fifteen minutes of waiting his face grew tired. His tutor finally appeared.

"Hello Jean, I'm Mr. David." A dishevelled man introduced himself—top button of his shirt undone, tie slightly loosened, creased trousers, worn shoes with an attempted dreadlock hairstyle that looked as though it should be on someone else's head rather than his. He looked rough, more so as if he had finished a working day than started, but he was a pleasant man; his face was always held hostage by a smile. Jean walked toward this man who towered over him, only to stand awkwardly; he was unsure how to greet him. This man was neither his Tonton coming home for dinner, or Papa's mechanic best friend, who he was either best friends with because he always fixed the car or he always fixed the car because he was his best friend, or even the postman who delivered presents they got from their *Tantine* in France—the only adults he knew. Mr. David patted him on the back and directed them along the corridor and up the stairs into the main school.

There was an unusual quiet along the corridors as Jean and Mr. David walked through, a morbid dullness that more so resembled a hospital wing for the terminally ill than a school full of bright and hopeful children. Nonetheless, starting at a new school— Jean looked at it with fresh eyes: it was food and he had gone hungry for weeks, water to quench his thirst, color to his gray.

"This is the library—if you like books, you'll love it here . . ." was the only commentary of Mr. David's Jean had heard. He wished they had gone inside and given it a look, for the faithful cannot walk past a temple without saying a prayer.

"*Boni class, eleki bien?*" Papa asked about school when Jean arrived home after his first day. At home they spoke mostly *Lingala* and English; they would joke and called it *Linglish*, or if it was French and Lingala it was called *Frangala*, and on rare occasions when they mixed all three languages together, they created a new hybrid yet to be named. Their conversations were always a song and dance, a mix and match, a jumping up and down to a song moving side to side, on a record going round and round.

Jean lived at home with his Papa and Mami, younger sister Marie, and Tonton, his uncle, in a three bedroom flat on the seventh floor of a red-brown brick twelve story estate building in North London, past the house near the bridge with a large yellow snail painted on the side that nobody knew the origin of. He shared his room with his Tonton—him on the top of a bunk bed, his uncle at the bottom. Whilst Jean slept, he could always hear something coming from the bottom bunk: a low whispering of late night conversation, movement shaking the bed, and the slightly foul stench of alcohol, which was confirmed when he woke in the morning and he would accidentally knock over a badly hidden can of beer as he got ready for school whilst his Tonton was fast asleep. However, the cans would always be gone by the time he got back from school.

"*Elekaki bien,*'" Jean replied, not adding any extra detail, his answer satisfying Papa's curiosity, He responded with a smile.

"Congo . . .!" Papa would boldly remind the children where they were from, as if they faced an impending amnesia. He would say it is Congo and not *Zaire*, because "Zaire was not the name our ancestors gave," whilst he sat them down and told grand stories of village chiefs, brave warriors in battle, medieval kingdoms, and royalty. Jean found them entertaining when he was younger. Particularly the story of the young village prince, *Mbikudi*, who, after his village was attacked and devastated by a surprise war, single-handedly built a perimeter wall to defend and protect his people by laying one rock down every day around the outside. The villagers looked at the small princely boy as if he had thrown his senses into the river, and given up his mind to be eaten by the night wolves. But, as he got older and stronger, the village prince was able to lift the rocks to create a second, third, fourth, fifth layer, until the surrounding wall became as high as the huts. Thousands and thousands of days, and thousands and thousands of rocks later, when *Mbikudi* succeeded his father and became King, he would protect his people from a surprise attack similar to that which his father had fatally fallen victim to, and be remembered as the greatest visionary King ever to rule the land.

Little sister Marie having her own room still upset Jean, even though it had been long enough for him to be used to it by now.

"It's not fair. It's only because she's a girl." He would protest, as if he had been a victim of a great wrong.

"Yes. Correct. It is because she is a girl," Mami would reply sternly.

Jean, confused, would look at Papa for male solidarity, whose face was completely fixed on not risking showing allegiance to either side. Marie, triumphant, would flash her tongue at her older defeated sibling, a display of victory.

Marie was always told, "you have your mother's face." She was the exact likeness of her mother, in both image and character. She tied her tightly coiled, jet black, silky smooth hair in two symmetrical buns. Just like her mother had done as a child, as she had seen in old photographs. She was loud, but not like an unruly child; much like her mother, she always had something to say.

"This is no child," guests would comment upon meeting her and hearing her speak. She commanded the floor and absorbed the air of any open space.

"Boys will not like her," was another common comment, particularly among all the married African aunties.

"It is okay." Mami would reply, "my husband did not marry me because I was quiet," while she smiled quite smugly, particularly at those who were still unwed in spite of their carrying themselves quietly, for so long, in hopes of finding a husband

The family ate dinner together, and though not often, this itself, in a new house, after coming to a new country, a new city, a new life, was an act of remembrance and celebration of their journey together—from security to uncertainty, status and identity to fingerprints, signatures and profile photos in front of a stone cold wall, fluency to heavy accent, norm to other, to finding peace, away from the conflict they carried deep inside of them.

Papa worked, and worked, and worked. It was his duty, he felt. He would, if possible, work every hour of the given day, abandoning his sleep, and his favorite pastime of resting his feet on the sofa to listen to live recorded cassette tapes of the classic Congolese rhumba music of *Franco & OK Jazz*, or *Zaiko Langa Langa*. He was not interested in much else, not the drinking, or other women, as so many of his counterparts were. For a different reason, however, he loved the music with all his heart; it was all the memories of home it evoked, how the music was able to transport him to a special moment in the past and bring it back to life in the stillness of a melodic memory. The only time Papa needed was for work and family. It was not always like this. Getting a job came difficult to him and for a time longer than Papa would have chosen, the family had to rely on the *buku*, benefits, which never lasted as long as it was supposed to.

After stuttering through interview after interview—the weight placed on his tongue of speaking fluently was too heavy for him to pick up this new language—he found a job. He worked first as a cleaner. Five mornings a week he would leave the house, before the sun would break the skies, to clean the offices of a company where he was rendered invisible. Most of the tired faces standing beside him, shivering in the cold of the bus stop in the morning, told a story of journey; a longing and searching for hope of a better life. Then came a second job, which, as the rest of the country was barely beginning their day, he would make his way across town to start as security guard of a popular shoe store in Finsbury Park, the disregarded part of North London. A store where people came in empty-handed and left with bags full.

Mami, on the other hand, initially stayed at home taking care of their two children, and often Tonton. Nurturing, looking after house and home, and preparing the food is a thankless occupation. Even worse, it is a payless occupation. Mami would argue women have been working for free for centuries, and deserve more than their fair share of the pie.

Eventually, when Jean was confident enough to make his way to school by himself, as well as Marie, who inspired confidence through her cryptic knowledge of London bus routes, Mami would start her first job in this new country, and get her piece of the pie; even crumbs are considered food when you haven't eaten. She started working part-time as a dinner lady in Marie's primary school, partially because of the convenience of working in a nearby familiar place and the NOW HIRING DINNER LADIES vacancy sign printed on an A4 sheet of paper stuck on the reception window, which encouraged such confidence she felt there was no way she could be denied, even if she barely spoke the language. However, she mostly started working there because although Marie had shown such maturity through her proficient knowledge of the local transport system, Mami was still not quite ready to let her go by herself. At least this way she could keep a watchful eye on her, letting her sometimes walk to or from school on her own, but mostly, under her scrutinous observation as she watched from a distance, blending into the background.

Mami was nurturing, in a tough-love, these-hands-could-slap-you-or-soothe-you, kind of way, but in the end it was always about you. Her love was self-sacrificial. If she had her last loaf of bread to eat, she would not split it in half and *share* it with you. She would split it in half, give you one half to eat, and wait until you were hungry once more to feed you the remaining piece.

She was a devout woman; she believed the love she gave was only a drop in the ocean compared to the love she received—the love shown to her.

Mami and Papa would find time in the quietest moments of their day to give each other peace in the storm of their daily struggles, through conversations about rent payments, arrears, bills, final notices, and other responsibilities. This is how they showed they were there for each other. They carried the burden of not only providing for their own family here, but also providing for their family back home. At the end of the month, their meager salaries were never sufficient to cover all they needed. They would barely scrape enough together for themselves, let alone for everybody who was dependent on them. *Koko's* medication for high blood pressure and swollen feet, school fees for the nieces and nephews, cheap designer clothes (replica Nike t-shirts, or Adidas with the four stripes—because an imitation designer was a better defense against social exclusion than no designer at all), and the older men who had become too accustomed and dependent on receiving money—to the point where they no longer sought to work. Papa knew why and understood. He gave anyway.

In spite of their day-to-day struggle, to the family and everyone back home, Mami and Papa had made it; they were living the good life. Europe, *poto*, to them, was the Promised Land, which they mostly called *lola*, heaven; the streets were paved with gold and the rivers flowed with honey; life was the finest champagne, sparkly and sweet, or so it was imagined.

To Mami and Papa, there was not a single day where they were not *adding up their lives*. At his security job, Papa's manager Steve, the kind of man who was presumptuous beyond his secondary school education, was consistently condescending. He called Papa "boy," referring neither to his youth (because it was Steve who was younger) nor to his gender because they were both men. It was more so a declaration of his superiority; he felt he was above Papa even when stood face to chest, neck arched up to look at him.

One day at work, Papa was on the phone as he had found a quiet moment to speak to Mami. It was lunch time. He had gone barely two minutes over when Steve and his pop-belly, shirt-cannot-tuck-into-jeans, comb-over-hairstyle-to-hide-receding-hair-line, came bursting into the kitchen, took the phone, hung up the call and blasted "Boy!" in his ear. "Can't you tell the time or something?! Get back to work." A volcano of rage erupted in Papa's heart, but he let the anger spill and settle once he thought of his family, his wife and children, his loved ones back home.

"Sometimes you have to add up your life," he told Mami as they lay in bed that night when she asked why he had hung up on her so abruptly. His philosophy: in the face of danger, be sure to evaluate your entire life and make the decision best for not only you, but for everyone around you. This was their love; a sacrifice. She calmed him down, and he lifted her up—a river flowing back into itself and never drying. It was a kind of reda-mancy; a love returned in full.

chapter 2

"**A** GIRL'S NAME?"
"No! My name is Jean!"
"Yeah, so why is it spelt J-E-A-N?"
"Because I spell it J-E-A-N."
"You mean you spell it how girls spell it and you're even saying your name wrong, why are you pronouncing it *John*, but spelling it *Jean*? You don't say you've got a new pair of *Johns*, you say you've got a new pair of JEANS."
"What?"
"Or, how in the Michael Jackson song, he doesn't say 'Billie *John*'s not my lover.' it's 'Billie *Jean*'—everyone knows this."
"My name is JEAN."
"Your name is Gene, accept it."
"I see on the register . . . we have a new student joining the class today. Is Jean with us today? I need you to raise your hand." The teacher spoke authoritatively.
"Yes, sir." Jean slowly raised his hand. "It's Jean sir, pronounced John."
"Well it looks like Jean to me!"

James burst out with uncontrollable laughter, prompting the teacher, who was peering over his glasses, to urge the boy to silence with a vociferous pointing of the finger.

"Sorry, Sir." James replied. "See, I told you Gene," he whispered to Jean whilst finishing the rest of his of laughter silently.

Jean and James were so close, they assumed the status of brothers by adoption. James was a bright enough boy, though incurably lazy. He had an attention span so short you would even need to remind him what class he was sitting in. He was a quintessential working class English boy, with an Oliver Twist *"please sir, can I have some more?"* accent, size eight trainers with a miniature Union Jack flag stitched onto the side and a matching pair of tracksuit bottoms with the three stripes. The only child to parents who spent their Saturdays at their equivalent of a religious institution, the Tottenham Hotspurs football club— proud season ticket holders—and their Sundays at the Pub for Sunday Roast. Dad, a plumber, who said "you've got yourself a little African friend, eh," to James when Jean first came around for tea, was pale, built round and hard, and resembled a peeled potato. Mum was a very sweet, docile lady, who, after many years of being a stay-at-home mum, was getting back into work looking after children. The pair looked more ones than twos. Nonetheless, James learned how to carry his mother and father in each step.

Jean's ears could not listen as fast as James' mouth could speak. So keeping up with James' enthusiastic storytelling and "banter" at break and lunch times was no easy task. James could gather a crowd and keep them entertained as if it was his livelihood.

"Lads, come round and listen, yeah." The group of boys, including Jean, gathered on a sunny autumn lunch time, at the top of the playground away from the suspecting and curious eyes of teachers and the students who wanted to be like teachers. They were a curious bunch: Ola, who didn't look at you when talking but past you into the distance—it was difficult to tell whether he was cross-eyed or indifferent; Ahmed who followed Naseem around; Naseem who was always trying to get away from Ahmed; Danny, who they called BBC because he always had the latest news; Chris, the mathematics genius from China who had yet to make any true friends; and Jamil, who always brought in an endless supply of chocolates and sweets—no one knew where they came from.

"There's this new bird in Mrs. Seresa's form class. She's proper fit . . ." James continued talking, words spilling out in a wild flurry. Jean listened intently, but as his ears failed to keep up with the speed of the conversation he resigned himself to remaining silent and laughing when they laughed. This was a skill Jean would learn to perfect in the years to come: the fine art of not understanding what someone had said, but reacting in the masterfully scripted way as if you had all along.

"Right, you got the plan, boys?" James concluded his sermon to the congregation who, including a confused Jean, cheered rapturously in confirmation.

"Tomorrow, lads. Tomorrow." James finished, walking off in a kind of hasty, bow-legged waddle, arms flailing by his side, not looking back but in full confidence he was being followed by his entourage.

The next day Jean sat in the middle of his Math class, next to Chris, who he often copied from in an attempt to catch up to him, with a note being passed to him from behind: *Meet at the boyz toilets at brake time.* Jean enjoyed Math (he found the challenges really engaging) so he didn't appreciate the distraction, but not wanting to be made into a social pariah and knowing too well who the message came from—James—he feigned interest and acknowledged he had received it.

The group burst out of class and ran past the "no running in the corridors" voice of the ubiquitous on duty teacher (who was heard but not seen), prompting them to race-walk as if it were the Barcelona Olympics. The boys huddled together in a scrum, and walked toward the canteen. Opposite were a group of girls, and amongst them was the new student who James had so excitedly mentioned. Her name was Jasmine, she was tall as the heavens, her skin shone something between bronzed copper and shining gold and her jet black hair curled like the Fibonacci sequence. Jean stared in wonderment. All of the boys did.

"Told you!" James exclaimed. "Ah, she's proper fit." The boys stared, nudging each other with excitement as James broke barriers and went to speak to the girls.

"Alright, ladies? It is a pleasure to be seeing you today."

"Go away James . . ." replied Ayesha—who was to Jasmine what Carlton Banks was to Will Smith—with a feisty tone layered with suspicion.

"Not you, though." James cut his eye and returned.

"What happened?" the boys asked with unanimous curiosity.

"Nothing, don't worry, it's a minor." replied James, not wanting to bring attention to his defeat.

"Oi, BBC, you gonna do what we planned yesterday, yeah?" He pressed on. Danny, became hesitant and anxious.

"Oh, come on, mate!" The group piled the pressure on him; Jean too, though he was not really sure what he was endorsing. Danny broke with nerves and refused.

"You can't chicken out! Well, someone's gotta do it." They were still behind the girls, edging ever forward in the queue. They tried to grab Danny's hand and force him to act but he squirmed and squiggled his way out of it. Jean, realizing the plan, saw his moment of glory, of inclusion and acceptance, and stepped up to the plate.

He walked out from the group of boys and reached slowly forward with his hand and grabbed the new girl Jasmine's bum. Time slowed. He held it for only a split second but it seemed an eternity—the same length of time it feels for Papa to tell his stories when he'd rather be outside playing football.

Jasmine let out a high pitched gasp and turned around. He didn't realize how tall she was, how much she towered over him and how her face lit up to him, though her eyes stared at him with fury and were endless and deep like the dark sky. He was enthralled, and filled with regret for breaking *that* sacred covenant with his dirtied hand. Visibly upset, she reached for the bag around her shoulder, hit him with it and shrieked, "WHAT ARE YOU DOING?!" before running past the "no running in the corridor," voice of the ubiquitous on duty teacher (who was heard but not seen). Jean fell and lay sprawled out on the floor, but was lifted to his feet in a parade of victory from the boys.

"You're sick! You're sick! You get ratings!" they exclaimed. Ayesha came back from the girls, her face was more screwed up than a crumpled piece of paper. She pointed her finger menacingly at Jean and roared "WATCH!" snarling as she stomped off. Jean stood confused, in a mixture of emotions, both excitement and fear.

Triumphant for now, Jean had been finally granted inclusivity to the in-group. Regardless of how his accent had been a thorn on his tongue and forced him to listen more than he would speak, or how he was not decked in the latest sports gear, or how he was not allowed to play outside after it was dark whilst the rest of the boys hung out on the streets. None of this mattered. For now, he was in; he was one of them. The terror was that he knew he had done wrong, and the voice of a young girl had struck a chord of fear. It resonated deep in his heart. He contemplated apologizing; he did feel genuine regret for what he had done. But he knew too well, to say sorry was to be exiled from the in-group, as well as showing weakness, so he kept a face of stoic indifference whilst trembling inside.

It was now the end of the day. Jean had sat in a daydream through the dry-hoarse dull voice of Mr. Pastorini's double, cloud-centered, Geography lesson; which he ignored because *when would anyone ever need to know about cirrus and cumulus and so on? They all rain the same.*

The class had finally been dismissed and Jean had left with a gloomy feeling, as if one of Mr Pastorini's dark clouds lingered above him, a change in forecast from the clear skies before. He walked alone, not even seeing his group of boys and, luckily, not the girls who must have, by now, calculated their revenge whilst throwing sharp darts at a blow up poster with his face on it. Instead he went to the top of the playground to retreat and eat his sandwich. It was meant for lunch, but his stomach had still been rolling with fear from the earlier drama of the day. He also wanted to read his new book, *Things Fall Apart* (chosen from the library because the face on the cover looked like his), away from the suspecting and curious eyes of the teachers and students who wanted to be like the teachers.

As Jean turned the pages he felt a change of temperature, the bright sun above him had cooled and a shadow loomed over him. He kept his head down only to see two immaculately clean all-white size eleven *Nike Air Force 1* trainers with the laces tied in a loop. Behind the trainers was a forest of legs so deep, he could not even see the playground beyond them. He wished he had seen them coming; they'd appeared like creeping ninjas. That, or he had been too lost in his book. Jean was grabbed by two hands the size of baseball mitts, and lifted into the air leaving his feet dangling.

"So you're the likkle rude boy who thinks he can touch up my little sister?!" He heard an ugly-aggressive sounding voice growl ferociously. It was Jerome. Jerome had a reputation; no one really knew what for but everyone knew it was bad. He often paraded around the school as if he were a student, though he was never seen in class or in a uniform. No one knew if he even went to school, and if he did, which one. He was never alone, always had an entourage around him like a Rock Star or an underground Rap sensation on his way to record his latest music video. The crowd had followed him and added hype to the occasion as if they were ringside spectators at a title fight.

"Huh?!" Jerome growled once more, hoisting him higher. Jean shook his head vociferously left to right, as if it expressed everything his muted voice from fear could not say. His heart was beating so hard it jumped out of his chest and got stuck in his throat; he tried to gulp it down. He had no idea what to do when, with a loud god-like presence, he heard his father's voice in his head and remembered the advice Papa had given him the first time he was bullied in school, '*soki obeti ye te, ngai nako beta yo.*' It now echoed in Jean's head: 'if you don't beat him, I will beat you.'

Jean feared going home and telling Papa he had been beaten up, and so he found the courage to open his eyes and stare at the face of his avenger. A broad-faced brute with scruffy hair, grey tracksuit bottoms and a woolly hat; a face uglier than the voice he spoke with. This was the first time he had actually looked Jerome in the eyes. No one *ever* made eye contact with him, unless you wanted a fight and if he walked your way, you kept your eyes on the floor or to the skies.

In a split second Jean lunged forward, grabbed Jerome's throat with the full force of both hands and kicked him, forcing Jerome to immediately let go. The roar of the crowd had erupted so loud to screams of "Fight! Fight, Fight." All Jean could hear was the voice of Papa in his head and his pounding heart. Jerome was enraged. He ripped off his jumper to reveal an endless push-up induced, from several sessions at the local boxing gym, semi-muscular body in a white singlet and threw down his bag. What was meant to be a light warning had turned into a full battle. He was ready to charge like El Toro loco, but Jean had steeled his nerves like a matador, trying to disguise the trembling of his legs. Jerome leapt forward in a beastly motion when, in a flash, a thunderous fist cracked through the corner of the sky as if by divine intervention and landed square on Jerome's face, dropping him to the ground. It

was James. The two looked at each other, and then, with the
same mind, started kicking Jerome as if it was football practice
whilst he lay on the floor trying to protect himself. The crowd
was stunned to silence. Jerome stood and the crowd erupted
again with chanting, "Fight! Fight! Fight!" Jean and James
looked at each other once more.

"LEG IT!"

"James!"

"Jean! Leg it you muppet!" They ran. They ran so fast covering the distance of the playground and out of the school gates
they could have qualified for the Olympics. There was a huge
roar coming from behind them. Jean did not look back once.
Looking back meant slowing down, and slowing down meant
getting caught, and getting caught meant facing a fate much
worse than the one he had narrowly escaped—certain death, or
certain humiliation, and for school students, sometimes humiliation was worse than death.

James was very fast for a skinny boy whose diet consisted
mainly of fish and chips. He kept waving Jean forward to keep
up. James ran with his tongue out and had a wild crazed look in
his eye, a deer caught in headlights who still charged toward the
car. At one point, Jean thought James would stop and run back
to take on the chasing mob by himself. *I'll keep running though;
every man for himself.*

They both ran. Dodging and weaving past the passers-by on
the high street, they turned a corner and eventually reached
the bottom of the road. It was silent. They had lost the crowd
chasing them.

"James, are you crazy?" Jean asked with a quiver in his voice,
he felt as though his lungs were going to explode

"Probably, yeah!" James laughed. The boys leant over, hands
on their knees trying to catch their breath. "Anyway, it wasn't
your fault, it was mine." James continued, "It was my stupid idea,
I had to step up."

"You didn't have to. I was going to . . ."

"Going to do what?"

"Jerome, man. It was Jerome!" Jean panted, out of breath, gasping for air.

"Don't worry mate, I got your back."

chapter 3

JEAN ARRIVED HOME IN A STATE of panic, nervously jangling his keys in the door as he opened and slammed it shut behind him. Marie was the first to see him. Quick to respond to the disruption, she watched him suspiciously from the end of the corridor as he leaned on the door trying to catch his breath. Jean looked and immediately straightened up when he noticed her standing there. Marie did not say anything, however, her facial expression was filled with questions, questions Jean felt pressured to answer until he remembered she was his little sister and bore no authority over him.

"What?" he asked, not a question, more a statement.

"What? I didn't say anything," she replied.

"So why are you standing there?"

"The same reason you're standing there."

Stalemate. Frustrated, Jean gathered his bag and jacket he had thrown frantically on to the floor, and walked past his little sister who had her eyes locked on him, as if a suspicious chastising parent. He walked into the living room, and to his surprise, saw Papa sitting on the sofa watching television. Mami had gone to do the shopping. Tonton was out.

"Hello, Dad." Jean quickly greeted.

"Ah, you are home. Get changed. We are going out." Jean's heart jumped. *Out?* He did not want to go out. Not back out there, the only safe place for him was at home, in his room, underneath his covers. No one would find him there, but he knew he could not say no.

"Dad, I don't feel well . . ."

"Your mother is not home, so you have to come with me. You have ten minutes. Get ready," Papa replied. Jean released a huge sigh of defeat and went into his room to get changed, "*Sala noki,*" Papa added, after he noticed Jean was moving with the pace of a man carrying a reluctant burden.

A very short ten minutes later, Marie and a begrudging Jean dutifully left the house. Jean was no longer in his uniform and instead he wore a hooded jumper to cover his head, which Papa kept pulling down. Going down the stairs of their building—Papa had a fear of enclosed spaces so taking the lift was masked as being 'lazy'—they bumped into one of their neighbors; a mother and two sons. They were from Bosnia, they lived on either the floor above or the floor below, it was uncertain because each time they met it was always on the stairs. Papa did not know her name but exchanged pleasantries as if they were on better terms than the occasional asking to borrow sugar and waving from a distance.

Jean knew the older son from around the way. He did not know what school he went to, but they had sat and traded stories in their broken English of things they had seen too wide for their eyes and too heavy for their hearts. Jean noticed how the boy's voice was much deeper, and broken, as if worn from endless screams; maybe that was how his voice sounded to others, he thought.

Papa walked fast, so fast they would have to jog to stay beside him. Whilst Marie attempted (and failed) to keep up, Jean abandoned any effort and lagged behind. They waited at the bus stop. The children knew Papa did not feel comfortable leaving them at home alone, and so they had become accustomed to being dragged around to unknown places.

On the bus, Marie sat next to Papa near the front on the top deck whilst Jean sat near the back as if he didn't know them. As they passed the busy high street with all its shoppers, passers-by, and students in different school uniforms, Jean was startled back into fear. He sunk into the bottom of his seat not wanting to be seen through the window. Eventually they got off the bus and switched on to an unfamiliar train; just like their not being left at home alone, Papa and Mami did not allow them to travel far on their own without permission. For Jean and Marie, it was simply a case of follow where led. Jean tried to remain as unassuming as possible, however, each time he saw a group of young people with faces he did not recognize, he shifted and became so uncomfortable even Papa noticed and looked at him with serious eyes.

They were sat on the train, all beside each other; father, daughter and son. Papa staring out into the empty in front him, Marie deeply focused on the book she was reading, and Jean, headphones in ears, listening to his Walkman playing a cassette tape recording of his favorite rapper Tupac Shakur—"it's time to fight back, that's what Huey said, two shots in the dark, now Huey's dead"—nodding his head in rhythm, not even knowing who Huey was.

They arrived at the stop neither of the children knew they had arrived at, but moved once they heard Papa say, "*Tokeyi,*" and got up to leave the train. Jean read the station sign, *EAST CROYDON*. He did not know the area, or even what part of London he was in, but it was so far he had already decided he would not endeavor to come here on his own. They left the station and followed Papa as he power walked up the road, past idle people, past a greyness unfamiliar to the one they came from, past buildings which Jean did not know the names of, "To McDonald's?" Jean quietly whispered to himself in hyper-confusion as they walked in.

"Wait here." Papa sat them down and then returned approximately five minutes later with food—two Big Mac meals.

"I have to go. I will be back in ten minutes. Do not go anywhere. It is better for you to wait here until I return okay?" There was silence, neither Jean nor Marie replied, neither of them knew they were supposed to.

"Okay?!" Papa added, insisting, to which they both quickly replied "Yes, Dad," in chorus. Papa then left with the same power walk he had brought them there with.

"Where are we anyway?" Jean asked.

"In McDonald's." Marie replied matter-of-factly.

"You know what I mean, what are we doing here?"

"Dad obviously has something to do, and we couldn't stay home alone, so we had to come."

"I know all of that," Jean scoffed, "I want to know *why* we are *here*. Where did Dad have to go?"

"You're asking the wrong person. Let's just sit here and wait."

"Aren't you going to eat your food?"

"No. I do not like McDonald's. Are you going to eat . . .?" Marie asked, and before she could finish her sentence and peel her eyes off the pages of her book, she saw Jean scoffing away at the burger with a little bit of mayo lingering at the corners of his mouth. "Yeah," he replied with a full mouth. They sat waiting impatiently.

"*Tokeyi*," Papa said in a frustrated tone, as he returned to the McDonald's much later than he said he would, and found Jean and Marie where he had left them; Marie still reading, Jean's head laid in his folded arms, headphones in, listening to the Walkman that had now run out of battery and was slurring like a drunken man. He walked straight back out. Marie smacked the book over Jean's head and he awoke confused and startled, gathered his bearings and followed them out. Papa power walked them back to the station, which seemed much closer than it was on the way there. When they arrived, it was a long wait until the next train. "Argh, twenty minutes," groaned Jean, which prompted looks of disapproval from both Papa and Marie. They sat in silence between the three of them, in a cold grey train station, in a cold grey place, patiently waiting.

After passing the same few stops as before, there was an echoing voice from the end of the train carriage; "Tickets please." Papa's heart jumped as he looked over and saw ticket inspectors accompanied by British Transport Police, with their bright jackets, radios, and handcuffs on their waist. With so few people on the train, they quickly moved closer and closer towards them. Papa's breathing became shallow. He looked over at Jean and Marie, who were headphone nodding and deeply reading, respectively. They were in between stations. The authorities were now too close for Papa to get up and move down the carriage, but not yet close enough to ask him for their tickets. One of the police officers looked over and made sustained eye contact with Papa as though he were reading the fear written on his face. Papa broke eye contact and looked away. The train slowed. There was only one person left now between the authorities and Papa.

"Ah, mate, you know what, yeah, I don't have a ticket but . . ." the dishevelled man spoke. The train pulled into the platform screeching as it slowed to a halt. The doors opened. Papa stopped, stood and rushed Jean and Marie off the train.

"Why did we get off?" Jean asked.

"We will take the bus from here."

"But it's going to be sooo long."

"Quiet!" Papa snapped. "We are taking the bus."

"Bowumeli." Mami said to Papa as they walked in, shocked they had taken so long. She hung up the phone wedged between her shoulder and her ear. It was late. Marie and Jean went straight into their rooms and slept early from the fatigue.

"Where were you? You were supposed to stay with them." Papa asked.

"I know. I'm sorry. The bus took a long time to come."

"It doesn't matter," said Papa flustered.

"Is everything okay?" Papa did not answer. He fell into a silence deeper than his worry.

"What happened?" Mami sensed there was something not quite right with Papa.

"Nothing happened. It was just an appointment at the Home Office, those people have no soul," he sighed deeply, indicating a mental exhaustion as if his mind was out of breath, "and on the way back, there was *ba gando* on the train, *ezalaki ya ko banga*."

"Do not be scared." Mami reassured him. "We have come so far. We take each day as it comes."

In a quiet moment they comforted each other, jumping forward into the future, away from all of their present troubles. During times like this, they would often choose silence for it meant there was no news of things getting worse.

"A letter came for you today." Mami passed Papa the brown enveloped letter. Papa looked at it curiously, fearfully. Reaching for a knife as if it were a weapon to defend him, he slid it in between the flaps, cutting the envelope smoothly open. He pulled out the white paper which had the insignia and "Her Majesty's Government" written across the top. It made Papa's heart thud before he started reading. Anything official did: letters, phone calls, police. He always feared the worst, as if it was the final moment and they had come for them to be deported, and so he avoided them all. He calmed his nerves and slowly but very carefully read the letter, paying attention to every detail.

"What is it?" Mami asked.

"Oh, it's nothing. It's . . ." Papa hesitated, "it's not important." He gave a stuttered response, folded the letter and stuffed it into the side pocket of his dark blue cargo jeans. Mami looked at him with eyes carrying questions but Papa did everything to reassure her into silence.

chapter 4

JEAN AND JAMES BECAME MORE LIKE each other during the first few months of school; it was a mimicry of sorts. Jean now started to fit in a lot more, he had the confidence to capture the boys' attention through stories and witty anecdotes whilst James occasionally played the sidekick. They operated in tandem, swapping roles to suit the occasion. They walked home together, but would often take a diversion through to the high street or even on the long bus into central, to the arcade to play video games, the supermarket, often to help themselves to a five finger discount, or the sports shop, where they sold the matching tracksuit bottoms, with the stripes and trainers with the tick, which cost the same price as keeping the electricity on in the house for a few months.

Everything in these places reminded Jean of James—for it was through him he discovered them—even the mannequins on display in the window, so much so, it was difficult to say who was imitating who. The best part for them was being able to play computer games together. They would go around to James' house and, for hours, play Street Fighter or Pro Evolution Soccer up until the terror of realizing how much time had passed would strike Jean, and he would run all the way home.

When Jean arrived home later than usual, he would be accosted with a barrage of questions, mostly from Mami, asking him where he had been; "homework club," "open evening at school," "football practices," he would answer, which was often met with Mami's secret-intelligence interrogation level suspicion, and Papa's unsuspecting aloofness. Jean had to become more creative with the excuses, which only made his stories less believable; "someone tried to rob the bank on the high street," "I got chased by a fox," "my friend was bleeding."

James, on the other hand was barely noticed at home when he walked through the door. No questions were asked. He would often be met by the loud blast and bright glare of the TV holding his parents' hostage in a zombie state.

Jean and James were stood outside a local petrol station on the same road as their school. A lot of the students would go into the shop because it was the nearest place with chocolates and sweets.

"It's so bait."

"No, it's not, they won't see you."

"The camera's right there!"

"Yeah, but it doesn't even have batteries though. It's not real, it's for show, to scare us . . . wait a minute, are you scared?"

"No!" Jean replied unconvincingly. They plotted between them. The CCTV camera had effectively stopped many of the children from stealing, but there were always a defiant few. Neither getting arrested or the scolding he would receive at home if his parents found out, was enough of a deterrent to prevent Jean from succumbing to the heavy weight of peer pressure at this moment.

"I'm not scared," Jean added, trying to convince himself more than James.

"Prove it," James replied. The gauntlet had been thrown down.

"Look, this is the plan," he continued, with yet another elusive endeavor, "open up the side pocket of your bag, we'll go up to the counter together and I'll distract him and pay for one of them 30p chocolate bars. Whilst I'm up there talking to him, you fill up the bag, and then we split. Got it?"

"Got it."

They walked into the shop and waited in line. There were two more students in the queue in front of them. Jean's heart began to beat through his ribs, he felt the flow of adrenaline in his blood. He looked at James whose face was calm and collected, as if he had done this a thousand times before; Jean believed he had. They arrived at the counter.

"Alright, boss?" James greeted with a chirpy cool innocence. "Can I get this?"

"Hello. 30p please," replied the heavy-accented man who wore a plain white turban and had a silky jet black beard, with single strands of silver running through them. James fumbled into his pockets and noticed Jean had stood there frozen the entire time. He nudged him to action. He took the money and handed it over, first dropping it onto the counter. Jean began to fill the side pocket with as many chocolate bars as he could, sliding them in one by one. It was seemingly endless, a giant chasm, never filling up.

"Boss man, 'ow much are those?" James asked, distracting, adding time.

"50p." The man replied stern-faced.

"Alright, these lot?"

"20p."

"And this?"

"10p."

"Is it?"

The man did not reply. Instead, he stared at Jean whose sticky fingers could not be seen. Jean felt as though he had THIEF stamped across his forehead.

"Alright, see you later boss man yeah," said James.

"Thank you. Come again."

Jean flung the bag over his shoulder as they moved clumsily across the shop to the exit like two clowns on skates. The zip of the bag flew open and all the chocolates spilled out onto the floor.

"Hey! You!" the man shouted. Jean's body stopped, held statuesque in fear.

"Who, me?" Jean replied but before he could finish his words, he was pulled forward by James.

"Leg it!'" James shouted. They sprinted out of the shop and down the road. They turned the corner, and slowed to a fast walk so as not to raise suspicion. James had a grin of excitement on his face, but Jean, overwrought with paranoia, felt as though he was a criminal at large and had already been put on the most wanted list.

He looked up to the sky, saw a helicopter and for a split second imagined a huge spotlight coming on them with a booming voice shouting "STOP! Drop the chocolates! You are under arrest," as he had seen so many times in the movies. The very thought itself evoked such fear, Jean's legs trembled and almost gave way under his own weight. He wanted to put his hands in the air immediately and lie on the floor.

"What happened, mate?" James asked, bursting with laughter as they reached a quiet safety far from the fear of getting caught. "Were you scared?"

"No. You flopped, that's what happened!" Jean replied with indignation.

"How?!"

"And how much is this? This? What about this one?" Jean mocked James. "You made it too bait. Obviously we were going to get caught."

"ME BAIT?!" James burst out still in hysterics. "You're the one who *actually* stopped and said 'who, me?!' Why did you stop?" His braying hysterical laughter was starting to irritate Jean, even anger him, partially because he knew James was right. He was scared, but also, he had done something he did not want to do, and was being mocked for it.

"So, are there any chocolates left or what?"

"No. They all fell out," Jean replied despondently.

"THEY FELL OUT?! ALL OF THEM?!" said James—*still* laughing. Jean shoved him, hard enough to show his frustration, but not too hard so he would fall over. He really wanted to push him into the ground, through the ground if he were able to.

"Whatever, man. I'm going home . . ."

"Ah, come on mate. I was only joking."

"Nah, I'm just tired."

Jean walked home with the slow heavy steps of a condemned man going to meet his fate. He was certain Mami and Papa would know, he wasn't sure how but he knew they would know. Maybe it was because of another saying Papa would always repeat to him, "*Matoyi ekoyokaka oyo misu emonaka te.*" Jean contemplated this, "the ears hear what the eyes do not see" and repeated it to himself.

"What does that even mean?" he said aloud to himself walking down the street. He eventually arrived home, opened the front door and walked in dragging his feet.

"*Biloko ebeli!*? Mami announced dinner was ready in a high pitched yell as if it was for the whole neighborhood. Papa was at work, so it was just Jean, Mami and Marie. Tonton was out.

"*Owuti wapi?*" Mami asked curiously.

"I was with some friends." He could feel Mami's scolding eyes as he walked into the kitchen to serve himself.

"*Te wana te. Wana ya Papa,*" she pushed his fork away as he tried to reach for the big piece of chicken reserved for Papa; another crime onto itself. He had already committed one today so far, he was not going to commit another.

Jean began to sweat, and couldn't tell whether it was because of the *pili pili* in the food or the fear of being interrogated further and caught. Why had Mami not asked any more questions? Maybe she was waiting until Papa got home because usually, on serious matters, he was the designated chief disciplinarian. Jean went to his room much earlier than his usual bedtime, claiming "sickness"; the less he spoke with Mami, the less chance there was of her interrogating him or of him making a gross faux-pas and letting the secret crime slip.

Before he went to sleep, he sat on the chair to unpack his bag and in the side pocket he found one last remaining chocolate bar; a *Twix*, his favorite.

chapter 5

MR. DAVID WAS CONCERNED OVER JEAN's behavior both inside and out of class. Jean never missed a day of school though; his attendance so far was 100%. He was also never late, nor was he disrespectful, in any particular way, toward the staff, much unlike many of the other students. Nonetheless, Mr. David still held his reservations. Mr. David had kept Jean after registration had finished.

"You're not in trouble . . ." Mr. David insisted whilst trying to explain, "I'm just keeping you behind because I know you didn't have a good day, and I don't want anything worse to happen."

Jean did not respond. He sat sulk-faced reading the copy of *1984* by George Orwell he had stumbled across in the library. He loved books for the adventures they took him on, how they didn't just answer questions, but filled him with more, and were able to take him to worlds outside his own.

Mr. David was working away on his computer. His fingers flashed across the keyboard typing as though he was playing the piano; a contemporary Beethoven. Jean was no longer reading, instead he sat there staring into the distance. Mr. David looked over whilst still typing and noticed Jean.

"Is everything alright, Jean?" asked Mr. David, fingers still tapping rhythmically. Jean did not reply. He continued staring into the distance with the pages of his book wide open.

"Jean?" Still, there was no reply. Mr. David squatted next to Jean so he was eye-level.

"Jean?"

"What?" Jean answered, quite rudely out of character.

"Is something the matter?"

"No," Jean replied, with a kind of grunting sound, as if Mr. David had asked the most preposterous question.

"Jean, you do know you're not in trouble, right?"

"So why am I being kept behind for?" he pulled a caricatured facial expression of confusion.

"You nearly got into a fight today . . . again."

"But I didn't, did I?"

"Well, you were going to if I didn't stop you."

"It wasn't even my fault."

"And it wouldn't be the first time would it?"

"What do you mean?"

"I know about your other fight, the one after school."

"What?! It wasn't even me, man," said Jean, in a tone insinuating this false accusation was a gross injustice of the world—civil rights, the Bengal famine, Jean being wrongly accused of fighting. "Are you going to tell my Dad?" he asked in mixed voice of concern and fear.

"Jean, I'm concerned about your behavior. I don't want you going down the wrong path so I've been thinking what I should do . . . I *was* just going to put you on report."

"Ugh, Sir. Why man?" Joan let out groan of protest; more so, a whine.

"It's not a bad thing; think of it as a positive reminder. Just so you can make the right decisions. And you'll have to get it signed by Mum or Dad at home, at the end of every week."

"This isn't fair, Sir, I haven't even done anything . . ."

"Listen, as I said, I was just going to put you on report . . ." he continued, "but I also want to give you something." He walked back to his desk drawer, opened it, and brought over something he held as if it were a sacred object.

"What is it, a book?" Jean asked inquisitively.

"Well, kind of, but not quite. It's a diary." Mr. David replied and handed it over. Jean held the diary and flipped it around, taking a look at it from every angle, with a face of confusion and fascination; confusion, for he never really received anything as a gift unless it was his birthday, and fascination from the sight of this sacred object. It was made out of brown leather, a deep brown, resembling the rich soil of the earth after rain. Bound by ropes, the pages were a beige-cream color, but not paper, more so a canvas, as if whoever was going to write in it was expected to create art. It did not look store bought, rather it looked as though it had been crafted by an old man with hands able to feel your soul and eyes which had seen all the beauty of the world held in a single moment.

"What's the sign in the middle? It looks like a 3 and a 0 . . ."

"It's the symbol for *Om*, it's written in *Sanskrit*."

"*Om* . . . .?"

"It's a mantra in Hinduism and Buddhism."

"Oh, Sir, my family is Christian; I don't think my parents would really . . ."

"Don't worry, it's nothing religious, it's just so you can write in, you know, some of your thoughts; it's more about asking questions and finding peace."

"Where did you get this from?"

"India."

"You've been to India?" Jean replied, sounding more shocked Mr. David had ever left the school, let alone traveled to another country.

"Yep." He replied nonchalantly, "on my gap year from university."

"So why are you giving this to me?"

"So you can write in it."

"I'm not some girl to be writing in diaries you know."

"See this is why I think you should have this, diaries aren't just for girls, plenty of boys have one, and lots famous men kept a diary too, Mark Twain, Beethoven, Picasso . . . Tupac Shakur."

"You know Tupac?"

"I see no changes, wake up in the morning and I ask myself, is life worth living shall I blast myself . . ." Mr. David attempted to rap.

"Please don't." Jean requested, unimpressed. "Did *you* keep a diary?"

"What do you think I'm giving you?" Mr. David replied, "and if calling it a diary makes you feel too uncomfortable, you could always call it a journal instead."

Jean was surprised but did not want to seem impressed by the gesture so he resisted any facial expression at all.

"Fine. Can I go now?" Jean asked when he remembered he was somewhere he did not want to be, diary or no diary. Mr. David nodded. Jean stuffed the diary into his bag, stood quickly from his seat, and was about to shoot out of the door when Mr. David added, "Don't forget your report card," in a kind of amusing lullaby voice and pointed to the card on his desk. Jean returned, grabbed the report card from his desk and left knocking the chair onto the floor as he stormed out.

As he walked home, Jean thought a lot of his grandfather, *Koko Patrice*. He was the only person who he felt he could be himself with. He would lift Jean high into the air and sit him on his lap. He spoke to Jean. *Koko Patrice* spoke *to* him, not *at* him like everyone else. He did not tell him stories of kingdoms, and myths, or biblical parables to make him contemplate life, he did not have expectations, he simply spoke *to* him, told him about himself, and made him feel as though he was always there for him, and although they were decades—and eventually continents—apart, in those moments they were together and ageless, for the years count not when an elder sits with the youth.

Jean did not feel he had to be a different person, he just had to *be*. There. Present. Still. So when *Koko Patrice* passed away after they came here and Jean was not really told, let alone told why, he could not understand. It felt as if a piece of his own warmth was escaping from within him and he got colder inside. A lot of things stopped making sense that day.

He remembered the people who gathered for the *matanga* and how many of those people did not know *Koko*, not the way Jean knew him. No one expects a child to have memories with an elder who passes because connections are often based on time; the longer you have known someone, the closer you are to them. And because Jean had spent such little time with *Koko Patrice*, no one knew how each moment was in itself an eternity. He did not want to be in the same room as those who had gathered for the *matanga*, so he retreated and found some quiet. A full moon shone brightly through the high window, it sent a beam of silver flashing. Jean felt as though the moon was speaking to him; it was the voice of *Koko Patrice* telling him he would follow him wherever he went, and one day everything would be alright.

chapter 6

TONTON WAS A *sapeur*. "WAS" IS the questionable word here, he would argue in his mind, but he felt he did not have to argue because it was self-evident, he still is. A *sapeur*, though taken from the acronym s.a.p.e; société des ambianceurs et personnes élégants, has no official definition (it cannot be contained); it is a collective culture. A way of life incorporating a dress sense of individual style and unique eccentric expression embodied in a person, regardless of their profession, education, class or status. To *sap* is the verb, when you put this way of life into action. For instance, attending a wedding and making sure you are the best dressed so more people pay attention to you than the bride and groom, or wearing an outfit so good that you stay out longer than you intended, even though you have nothing to do, just so more people can see *you*.

Sapology is the school of thought, the philosophy and ideology itself. Essentially, it is a way of making your presence felt and creatively expressing yourself, through dress, but also a personal embodiment in a world which otherwise ignores you and forces you out of your own body.

Of course, as with most trends, there are unspoken rules and one of them was of the age limit; just as how no one wants to see a skater-boy still wearing shorts and carrying a skateboard in his mid-fiftiess, a *sapeur* man at the same age is equally frowned upon because by that point, they should have embraced the responsibilities of life—started a family, and reneged this irk-some pseudo-playboy life style which had been merged into the culture.

No one knew exactly how old Tonton was, not even Mami who was the first to meet him; though his tired eyes, receded hairline, worn skin from years of discoloration and bleaching, and the beach ball belly that sat over his belt, was not deceiving anyone about how his youth had evicted him long ago.

In Kinshasa, Tonton had a reputation. His name would always be mentioned in the same vein where parties, alcohol and women were concerned. Particularly women, he surrounded himself with women either by force or fantasy. There was always a woman held hostage on his arm and when there wasn't, he was talking about what he had done or would do to one. He had curious hands, and they always sought to traverse a woman's body as if he were an explorer navigating new land which only began to exist the moment he arrived. To say he treated women as objects would be to raise their status in his eyes.

"Objects have a purpose, a tangible use—what use do women have?" Tonton would say usually when surrounded by alcohol and other men, "They take your money, your car, your house, and leave you with nothing."

He was always the bringer of *loyenge*—the hype, the life and soul to the party. This reputation followed him across the waters, which part of him felt pressured to maintain even though he had the opportunity to form a new identify. Yet, Tonton did not enjoy the reputation; he enjoyed the attention, the respect it gave him in the community. His barely secondary school level education was not enough for him to be known as a doctor or a professor, both professions which he spoke highly of. However, what was less than his education was his motivation and willingness to work. Whenever he was given an example of how someone had overcome the odds to achieve a goal, he would find a reason as to why they succeeded and an excuse as to why he had not.

Papa was frustrated by Tonton, "What kind of man is this?" he would indignantly express to Mami during their quiet moments, "What kind of man, at his age, would choose to share a room with a boy in another family's house than to actually look for work and live on his own?"

Mami always stayed quiet when Papa ranted over Tonton; she knew that if it were not for her, Papa would have long ago kicked him out to live with which ever woman he was wooing at the time.

"I am worried he will have a negative effect on Jean."

"It will be fine. It is only temporary; not for much longer," Mami's attempt to reassure Papa was loosely strung. Temporary was the length of time you had a replacement car after a crash, or the length of time a person filled a job role whilst the main worker was off sick or on maternity leave. Temporary was not the same length of time it would have taken Tonton to earn a degree to get a job so he could pay for a place to live away, on his own.

When Mami and Papa first arrived in the UK, they did not know anyone but the government officials who interrogated them and *they* were not the kind of people you would invite around for tea. However, when Tonton showed up, no one knew exactly when or where from, he opened up a new world of familiarity to them. They called him Tonton because of an unspoken rule; any male friend of a married woman was immediately given the position of family male relative; because why would a woman need an unmarried male friend who wasn't her husband, or her pastor? Jean came to understand this way, which he found bizarre, when he was told Tonton wasn't really his uncle. However, he had already figured it out because every male elder visitor to the house since his arrival was called Tonton, in one form or another, and there was no way *Koko ya Mwasi* could have physically had so many children.

Tonton was the first Congolese person Mami met when they arrived in the country. Mami was shopping in Dalston Market, Ridley Road, surrounded by the honking sounds of the busy traffic, and the "come 'n' 'ave look please," "a'right love" colloquialisms of the market sellers. Mami was buying food to prepare for the boxing fight they would watch as a family later in the evening. Even though they had no guests, and she was not a fan of boxing herself, she took any opportunity to celebrate something together as a family. Also, Papa loved boxing; it brought back the nostalgia of the rumble in the jungle and reminded him of a youth left long behind. Jean accompanied Mami, carrying the shopping bags as a dutiful son does.

It was a spring afternoon, yet the skies were grey and it rained only light enough to inconvenience them, however not strong enough for them to stop and seek shelter. Mami was at a stall buying *makemba*, which she pointed at not knowing what they were called in English.

"These? The plantains, love?" the market seller hollered back.

"Yes. Five." Mami held her hand up with five outstretched fingers in case she was not understood. As she fumbled through her large all white leather hand bag with the Gucci buckle, bought at the same market, to find her purse the deep unfamiliar voice of a man came from behind her.

"*Boni Maman,*" Mami was startled; no one, outside her home, had spoken to her in *Lingala* in this country before. It felt surreal to hear even a word in such an unfamiliar place; among a sea of white faces, drowned by foreign languages.

She knew Papa's voice too well to know it wasn't his; this voice was deep and hoarse from a destructive combination of whiskey and cigars, a combination she knew well, as it was also her father's affliction. Mami stood still in a stunned silence. Ordinarily, she would ignore unknown men who approached her; if this was Kinshasa she would continue her ordinary activities reducing them to background noise. She eventually turned around to see what would become a familiar face, Tonton in a slightly younger form than what they would come to know. He dressed well, recognizably well, too well for someone who was simply going to the market; he wore a colorful ensemble, with large sunglasses to protect his eyes from the not shining sun, while carrying a large bag.

"*Boni, toyebani??* Mami asked, trying to find out who this man was, and how he knew they were from the same people who had journeyed from the same far and distant place.

"*Olati kintambala.*" Tonton replied, pointing to the silk scarf covering Mami's head. He explained how he saw her in the distance and noticed the scarf first, worn uniquely in the style of Congolese women, so he walked by and when he saw her face, he instantly knew she was of his country because she reminded him of every woman in his family. His words were flattering flowers and rose petals to her ears. Mami was elated. She introduced him to "*Mwana na ngai,*" her child, Jean who was more concerned about the numbness of his fingers from carrying the plastic bags in the cold, than meeting this strange man he did not know who was speaking to his mother.

Mami instinctively invited Tonton to come around in the evening to watch the boxing match. She thought it would be a great opportunity not only to get to know another Congolese person in the country, but also for Papa to have a male friend who he could watch the boxing with. Also, he wouldn't have to tolerate her commentary about how violent boxing was, and that it shouldn't really be a sport. They spoke for a little bit, and shared stories of their arrival. Tonton was more elusive with his; choosing to listen rather than share, speaking not of how he had arrived or when. When Mami said how excited Papa, her husband, would be to meet him, Tonton's behavior shifted slightly like an obstacle had been placed before the path he ran freely on. Nonetheless, he most willingly obliged and accepted her invitation. She wrote her address and telephone number, 0171 926 4230, and told him to arrive at 7 p.m.

Tonton had changed clothes and this time arrived dressed in all black; an obscure attempt to appear more formal. He wore a black cowboy-esque hat, with a leather jacket with leather strips hanging from the elbows, a black shirt, and black boot cut stone-wash jeans with a pair of pointy black crocodile shoes. Mami opened the door for him before he could knock as she saw him from the seventh floor of their estate wandering around as if he was the lost shadow of another man.

"*Bonsoir*," he greeted Mami, with two kisses on each cheek, *right-left-right-left*, as is custom. He came bearing gifts; alcohol—a six pack of Heineken beer in one hand and a bottle of the finest supermarket label wine in the other. Visiting a family home without a gift of one kind or another was worthy of condemnation; at best it allowed you maybe only one hour visiting time, and at worst to be not allowed in at all.

Mami walked Tonton through the hallway, where Jean and Marie were waiting. Jean was ordered to change from his tracksuit bottoms to a chequered shirt and the jack-up trousers that swung above his ankles. Marie wore a pretty flower dress. They both excitedly greeted Tonton assuming he was someone of importance—which Tonton played up to—rather than recognizing Mami's overzealous desire to impress.

Papa waited in the living room. He stood as soon as Tonton walked in and they greeted each other, with a hug and bumped foreheads right-left-right-life, as the men do, as though they were prodigal children—long lost brothers who had finally returned home.

chapter 7

"*Vanda*," PAPA PROMPTED TONTON TO TAKE the seat behind him. Mami asked what he wanted to drink. Tonton obliged, and she returned with drinks; Coca-Cola for Papa, and a can of the Heineken Tonton had brought. For any other family, drinking Coke was a regular activity, but for this family it was saved for special occasions; it was simply too expensive for regular consumption. Mami returned to the kitchen to continue to prepare the food for the evening. Papa and Tonton hit it off at first. They laughed raucously at each other's jokes and spoke as if they had known each other since their Kinshasa days, left without hope of seeing each other and had miraculously found each other once again in a distant land.

"*Okolaki wapi?*" Tonton asked Papa where he had grown up.

"*Ngai na za mwana ya Bandal.*"

"BANDAL," a roar of excitement and surprise echoed through the house. Tonton was surprised and elated to find out they were raised in the same neighborhood.

Bandal was the neighborhood in Kinshasa that never slept; full of parties and women; *Bandal c'est Paris*, where the bars stayed opened all night and people lived life to the fullest and drank to forget all of their problems, for which there was never enough alcohol. It was no surprise then, for Tonton to have turned out the way he did, the surprise was in how much different Papa was.

Tonton, in his hurried excitement, began throwing out a flurry of names of the people he thought they would both know: *"Junior, Fiston, Phelix, Claude, Herve?"*

"Phelix?" Papa interrupted, *"Le petit?"* and placing his hand low as if to indicate a short person. Tonton was not sure, so he shrugged and continued. Each name was met with a shake of the head by Papa, as he did not recognize most of them. Tonton stared in confusion, and then the idea came to him: nicknames!

He continued: *"Moto? Vieux Goss? Train?"* Nonetheless, regardless of how much Papa now wished he knew the names, they all remained unfamiliar to him.

An awkward space of silence rose in the air, tainting the now fading tone of brotherhood once present at the beginning of the conversation. Soon enough, and in the timeliest manner, this space of silence was filled by Mami who brought out the food and called the children to come and eat.

The men ate the same food, but sat separately from the rest of the family as if they were having their own private meeting. They were on the lower table, where the special china was neatly laid out for the grandiose occasion. Papa ate respectfully, taking care and attention; he wanted to make a good impression, there was a lot to be said about the way someone ate around guests, particularly if it was the first time.

He always reminded the children of this; "elbows off the table," "fork in left hand, knife in right, chew with your mouth closed." Tonton, on the other hand, ate messily. He defied these rules as if he had heard them before and rebelled against them. He did not even touch the cutlery, but instead grabbed the *fufu* and *fumbua* and mixed it with all the passion in his fingertips. Each mouthful was followed by a sucking noise of his fingers, ensuring he took in every last drop. Papa looked at Mami with concerned confusion, *we're in poto now, why is he still acting as if he is in the village.* He would have said it out loud had he and Tonton known each other longer, but it was too early in their supposed friendship for him to be making such harsh comments.

Tonton opened another can of beer as they finished eating and awaited the boxing match to start. The children were sent to sleep as it was getting late. Jean protested and was finally given permission to stay and watch, but Marie was sent to bed as it was deemed too violent.

It was an epic battle of two titans, George Foreman vs Michael Moorer, for the heavyweight title, embellished by the loud roars of the men in the living room, echoing through the house, loud enough to lift the roof off. They supported Foreman for the nostalgia, and, in him they saw what they thought everybody should be given: the chance to redeem themselves.

Papa had always thought about America, in the narrow distance of his mind, he wondered how Black people were treated there, and having heard the stories—the police, the riots, the shootings, it amazed him how quickly Black people were accepted in sports but not in society. To him, it seemed, Britain had a much kinder face; a softer hand, a velvet touch compared to America's callousness.

Jean watched the entire fight with his mouth open from the shock; the most shocking image was the loser's swollen eyes!

"Papa, can he still see?" Jean asked, mouth ajar, to which Papa and Tonton laughed at his youthful naivety, "He is okay," Papa replied.

There were now six empty cans of beer on the table as Tonton stood to leave. Papa showed him to the door. The smell of alcohol seeped out of his skin like sweat on a hot day. It was late, deep into the night where neither man nor beast, save the foxes, roamed. The sky breaking into dawn. Papa enjoyed Tonton's company for the most part. He showed him out, and bid him goodbye stepping back for a handshake rather than a brotherly hug. Papa did not know if he had driven, or taken the train, but he preferred to believe this grown man would be able to take care of himself and so he let him wander out into the streets to make his own way home.

Tonton became a regular feature in the lives of Papa, Mami, and the children. He would often arrive unannounced, usually in the evenings, whilst they were gripped by an episode of *EastEnders*—the hard-headed plot twists of the Mitchell brothers—or a crucial Football Champions league fixture, usually ceremoniously watched by the men. Tonton would also visit during the day whilst Papa was at work and the children were making their way back home from school. His presence in the household was becoming more familiar, however, to Papa it was more so in the way a rash makes itself known—irritating and then there all at once.

Tonton opened Papa and Mami up to a new world, where once before, they were alone in this new country, with unfamiliar faces and places to be made into memories, now they were slowly being welcomed into a new community of people who shared a story similar to theirs.

Sunday morning Mami and Papa went to Church, as invited by Tonton. They left Jean and Marie to look after themselves at home, which was a privilege they were slowly starting to earn. There were strict instructions, however: never open the door to anyone, do not turn on the heater (Papa would dramatically warn them it may explode from overheating), and to do all the cleaning. The last reminder as they left the house was they were always watching, no matter what; *matoyi eyokaka oyo misu emonaka te.*

In the church Tonton seemed to know the people present by the subtle head nods of acknowledgements they gave as he walked in late halfway through mass; Patricia, the slightly older woman, not by appearance but assumption, whose unmarried status besieged her, she prayed for marriage more than anything and anyone else; *Mama Mapasa*, whose name meant the mother of twins, because this was what she was; *Pitchou*, a handsome single man who did not pray for marriage or much else; Mama Nadège, who most people kept their conversations short with for she could talk a door off its hinges; and many more.

It was a room full of people who reminded them of people they already knew and who they thought they had left behind. There was an elderly woman who had been in the country many years. Her name was Mama Nana, she was much unlike the others though; she walked with a stick and her back was bent over from all the weight of the burdens she had to carry throughout her life. Mami noticed, when they met and began speaking to each other, that she did not speak French. She would reply to your *bonjour* with *mbote na yo*, and neither did she speak English, she would similarly reply to a *hello* with *sango boni*; she refused to speak either language saying they did not belong to her, and nor she to it. Not because of her lack of education, it was an act of resistance—her way to fight back. When asked about it from those who insisted she learn, she would reply, in her strongest *Lingala*, "Look at my back, if it is this bent from all the things imposed on me, how bent do you think my tongue is? I am simply trying to straighten it out. I cannot do this to my back, I can to my tongue."

Why learn the language? Is it to enjoy the poetry of Chaucer or Keats? Most who speak the language do not even read it. Is it only for moments of servitude, when you are at work and must follow instructions of how to stack a shelf or clean a toilet, when you can calculate quadratic equations or recite epics in your own tongue? Or is it to be included? So you can clearly understand the hate and prejudice fashioned against you? For before it was in a language, you only saw with your eyes, but now you hear it too; even more, you feel it. And when you do learn, you are told to speak it properly; you are constantly reminded how you do not sound the same. Mama Nana was too old to resist, too old to fight back; this was the only way she knew how.

The Church wasn't in a church, it was in a bare and empty hall, with plain beige walls, worn and dusty red wooden chairs organised into makeshift rows of five across and five back, to go with a makeshift podium, where a clean shaven brown-skinned man with a neat moustache and peaked, mountain-shaped hair, dressed in a bright colored makeshift suit two sizes too big, and spoke in *Lingala* with a passion and vigor to the single-hand claps of the few people in the bare and empty hall. It was a surreal moment for Papa and Mami, for different reasons though. Back home, Papa avoided religion, apart from the special occasions; Christmas, Easter, the odd wedding here and there which he did not enjoy attending, and the occasional family christening. He never attended a Congolese church regularly; in Congo, all churches have Congolese people, but not all churches are Congolese. What differentiates them are the practises in the church; if one follows Congolese traditions, the music, the singing, and dancing, only then is it a Congolese church.

Koko Patrice used to try to force Papa to go to church when he was young but never quite had the energy to match Papa's tactical stubbornness of conveniently disappearing right before they needed to go, and returning so conveniently when it was too late for them to arrive on time. This act, and other creative means of evasion, would continue for years until *Koko Patrice* would accept Papa was a good enough child without needing to go to church for moral reinforcement.

Mami, on the other hand, went to church every Sunday; and even the days in between. Every week you could find her, hands together in the pew, looking above as if the ceiling would open and a ray of light would beam down upon her. She attended a Catholic church with Congolese people; they sang hymns in a high pitch Latin and played the organ. Papa and Mami both avoided Congolese churches, although for different reasons. Here, however, they rushed to them, finding comfort in a place where they saw other people who shared the same story. It was less about the church, and more about having the familiarity of what they once knew in close proximity—the language, food and culture they had been missing; it was as though their entire country was filled into a bare and empty hall. They would eventually come back, and keep coming back and also bring Jean and Marie until the thin line between a need and a want was indistinguishable.

After the extravagant service led by the self-appointed Pastor Kaddi, reverend of the church, had finished, Tonton introduced Mami to Patricia. He imagined this would do them both well. He knew Mami had yet to meet other women and make friends, and Patricia often came and left on her own, sometimes without saying hello to anyone.

Mami quickly warmed to Patricia, "*Aza nzu-nzu.*" Mami later described her to Papa: she is feisty, and a go-getter. Patricia referred to Mami as "sister" every opportunity she could in all their conversations. Each passing Sunday, they either sat next to each other during service, or quickly gathered to speak with each other afterward to catch up if they were not able to speak on the phone during the week, and often regardless.

chapter 8

J EAN AND MARIE WERE ALWAYS HAPPY when Tonton came over.
Often he came bearing small gifts; chocolates in the form of
Twix bars for Jean and little sweets for Marie. He would often sit
her on his lap and she would read to him. He was the only adult
in their life who was not their teacher or parent, or an authoritative figure to whom they would have to report their behavior; he
gave them a freedom to be themselves wherever and whenever
they couldn't.

Papa and Tonton had a shared tolerance for each other though
they were two different kinds of men; Papa was not understanding of how a man Tonton's age—whatever age he was—did not
work, or at least try to, and had not yet started, or showed little
interest in starting, a family. And Tonton was equally bewildered by Papa's seriousness; how he had yet to open a can of
beer or even go dancing to a bar with him as the other men
did. Nonetheless, Mami kept a balance and peace between all
parties, for she bore the responsibility of bringing them together,
and she was determined to make it worthwhile.

Tonton did work though, it was just not the kind of job he

would choose to broadcast. It was uniformed; a dull, lifeless color as if two different shades of grey had dripped onto each other. A loose fitted rectangular shaped cloth hung over his body resembling a child in a costume, and large dark grey steel-toe boots to match. He worked as a picker-packer or a "warehouse operative," to those he was obliged to inform. And unlike the other staff that came into work already dressed in their uniform, Tonton would arrive head to toe in *sapology* mode with his uniform in a large cumbersome bag.

"You're always dressed as if you're going to a party, mate."

"Life is a party." Tonton would reply. He spoke English rarely, and reluctantly.

If he could, he would avoid the language altogether. They called him Eddy; hisname was "Eduardo dos Santos Ferrera."

"It's Portuguese in'it. Ain't you from Portugal?"

"Angola."

"But the name's Portuguese, ain't it?" repeated Tom, Tonton's young, naïve colleague, whose would-be fresh face was made old by the binge drinking he did "only on days ending with Y." They should have had at least this in common, the drinking, but Tom was truly an annoyance; a constant test of Tonton's patience.

It was on a rainy afternoon when Papa came home to a corridor full of suitcases and large plastic bin bags full of clothes and various personal items belonging to Tonton, he knew everything was about to change. His heart rose for he had already read the story written before it was told to him. Mami met him at the corridor to explain, and pleaded with him, knowing full well he would have to oblige. When Papa walked in and saw Tonton and the children sitting either side of him, his heart slowed. The look they gave each other was one of silent acknowledgement. An exchange of gratitude and thanks for the conversation avoided because of the presence of the children; a conversation Tonton felt too proud to have with another man, and a story Papa knew he would not believe no matter what was said. The explanation Tonton had given Mami, who did not even know he had a job, was his patience had been severely tested and he was a man who could not allow another man to forsake his honor.

They put Tonton in Jean's room. Jean had to move from the bottom bunk-bed to the top, a small adjustment, which he was delighted to make as he saw having Tonton in the house the same as having an older brother, though much, much older.

Marie excelled in school; her brilliance far surpassed her peers. She would often be unofficially promoted to teaching assistant to help the other children who struggled with their work. No one knows how she came to be so far ahead of her years in terms of smarts as well as maturity. Papa would testify, it was God's gift from above and Mami would vehemently argue saying it is tradition for a girl to follow her mother. Nonetheless, the only consistent factor was how she was always nose first in a book regardless of the occasion; long trips on the bus to shop at the market with Mami, weddings and funerals, christenings and birthdays; even her own. She had the demeanor of a university student trapped in a Year Six Primary school student.

Marie despised being the younger sibling. She felt Jean was an inadequate older brother and she made sure he was constantly aware of this with her sarcasm and witty clap backs.

"Well, technically . . ." if Marie started a sentence in this way—and left a long anticipatory pause—it was nothing to do with technicalities, it meant someone was about to be served humble pie with some tea to drink it down, meaning, they were to be lowered a peg or two, and perhaps even in so far as it was required, have the ignorance knocked out of their cerebellum.

"You're not even my older brother . . ." she continued to Jean as they were in the middle of a sibling antagonism session, fixing some snacks after school. Papa was at work and Mami was on the phone. Tonton was out.

Jean did not reply. He did not want to encourage her. He looked at Marie with a face daring her, *finish what you started; I want no part in this nonsense*, which, for Marie, was encouragement enough.

"You're not. If anything, I'm the older one, or at worst we are twins."

"Ugh. Imagine us as twins, it'd be a nightmare."

"I know, right? We would actually have the same face. It's bad enough being your younger sister, but imagine having your face. I might as well be the older one. I mean, girls do mature at least five years earlier than boys do, so technically, we're at least the same age or, really, you're my little brother. I mean, I am more mature than you anyway. If Mum or Dad weren't here, I would run the house."

"Oh, whatever."

"I'm just going to call you little brother from now on."

"Oh, you're so annoying."

"Hey, little brother. How's it going, little brother? Would you like some bread, little brother?" She grabbed a slice out from the loaf of bread and dangled it in front of him, taunting him with it. "Maybe some chocolate spread little brother?"

Jean was frustrated by Marie's attempt to annoy him, not because she was right but because it was working. He knocked the bread out of her hand and it fell on the floor. Mami walked in whilst still talking on the phone lodged between her shoulder and her tilted head.

"*Nini ko?!*" Mami exclaimed. "*Lokota.*"

"It was Jean," Marie replied.

"*Eh!* Call him *ya* Jean please; he is your big brother. Show respect."

The siblings looked at each other in heated opposition. Jean did not move. After a few moments, Marie eventually picked up the bread and threw it in the bin as Mami had ordered her to.

"*Kobebisaka bileko te.*" Mami said in a harsh tone.

"Yeah, Marie, don't waste food," Jean repeated.

"'Allo! Eh, boni?" Mami shouted down the phone. Jean figured it must have been a long distance call, most likely from
someone back home because of how loud Mami was speaking,
or more so, shouting. Phone calls from back home flooded in
when money was needed, or when someone passed away, which,
in any case, money was still needed. Jean stayed in the kitchen
partially because of the wonderfully enticing smell of the food
now cooking; *pondu*, *kwanga* and *makayabu*. He would sometimes pack some of the food in a container to take to school for
lunch, and his friends would always curiously ask, "Er, what is
the green stuff?"

"The green stuff is *pondu*. It's a stew. It's really nice."

He'd wrap his fingers around a lump of *kwanga* and mix it
into the *pondu*, eat it whole and lick his fingers loudly after it
was done. "You want some?" Jean would always offer, holding
the container up to his friends, much to their disgust as they ate
their fish and chips wrapped in a newspaper bag.

"Are you eating banana too?"

"It's plantain."

"And what's the other thing?" they would move closer in,
particularly James, inspecting the container.

"This?" Jean would hold up the container, causing all to move
back again as if the food was going to jump out of its box.

"This is *makayabu*. It's fish."

"Fish? Doesn't look like fish. Who eats this kind of fish for
lunch? You're a proper *freshie*, you know." The food was so enjoy-
able for Jean he was able to ignore the comments, no matter how
upsetting they were.

Other than the enticing smell of the delectable food, the real
reason Jean stayed in the kitchen, while Marie, on the other
hand, had made her escape, was because he knew the routine.
Every time Mami was on the phone to someone back home, she
would pass the phone to him to greet a family member. And this

time was no different. Mami thrust the phone into Jean's hands, who took it, not knowing who it was.

"*Dit bonjour,*" Mami commanded. This time it was his aunty, *Tantine* Marthe, which, although he enjoyed speaking to her, did not make much difference to Jean because the conversations were always the same regardless of who he was speaking to.

"*Allo Bonjour,*" Jean answered. Mami prompted him in the background to speak louder; it was, after all, a long distance phone call.

"*Boni classe? Okokisi age nini sikoyo?*"

"School *eza malamu.* Er . . . *na za* . . ." Jean would try to reply, in a broken Lingala, his mouth drowning in an ocean, words struggling for air. It was less about the questions and more about familiarity—every interaction was a strengthening of a connection, a bond reminding you of where you are from, reminding you there are people out there for which you are a symbol of faith; they have planted in you seeds of hope and every moment shared is a watering and watching them grow.

Mami took the phone back from Jean mid-way through his conversation, which he happily obliged. She interpreted his struggle to communicate as indifference. Mami remained on the phone for the rest of the evening, and when Papa arrived home from work, he found her laughing raucously on the phone whilst sitting alone in the kitchen where she had banished herself after realizing she was being too loud and disturbing the children whilst speaking to Patricia.

"Men are useless." Patricia said, "How will I marry? When they cannot even take hints? They cannot even take clues? Too busy trying to be righteous, trying to be men of God."

Mami laughed in the background as she listened. She saw parts of herself reflected in this woman, perhaps this is who she would have been had she not met Papa.

"*Wani nani?*" Papa asked as he opened the kitchen door and popped his head in.

"*Eh?*" Mami replied caught up in the conversation, indifferent to his arrival.

"Who is on the phone?" Papa persisted.

"*Eza* Patricia." Mami replied, covering the phone. Papa nodded.

"*Otindaki mbongo?*" He demanded, halting her conversation.

"Yes. I sent the money. $150."

"Okay." Papa replied, then closed the kitchen door and made his way to the living room where Jean and Marie were watching TV, but not together, and joined them.

"Who is it they are trying to impress?" Patricia continued, "Is it not women? Or will they marry God? They are useless. *Baza na tina te.*"

"Not all of them, some are okay."

"You, sister, are lucky. You should also play the lottery, maybe your luck will multiply; you will be rich and married."

"It will happen for you too." Mami replied. Patricia could never reconcile her desire to be married with how frustrated she was with men, it was a hole being dug deeper and deeper; the longer she remained unmarried, the more frustrated with them she became.

chapter 9

IT WAS PARENT'S EVENING. JEAN WALKED nervously into the
school reception with Papa where teachers welcomed the students and their parents. The expectation of the evening was
evident from the body language and interactions of the child,
and the parents too. If it was the child who greeted the teacher
first, followed by the parent, the expectation was positive; a well
behaved child. However, if the child was disengaged, staring
mostly into the distance, or at the ground, avoiding all possible
eye contact, or even being seen, then, it was not so positive.
Papa had a big smile on his face. It was the first parent's evening
he ever attended. His first time meeting the staff members who
took the responsibility of educating not only his son, but "the
future of the world," he would say. It was a long time since he
had walked intently through the halls of an educational institution, not since he had studied in Brussels in his younger years.

"I finished the top of my class," was another frequent procla-
mation of his. More so, it was the statement said by almost every
African parent. Papa and Jean walked to the reception table
where the receptionist, Mrs. Butler, who always remembered the

name of every child in the school but so easily forgot the little things like where she placed her glasses or her lunch at home, handed out A4 white envelopes with the student's behavior report enclosed.

"Good evening . . . Jean, can I have your surname please?" Mrs. Butler said, in her high pitched, receptionist voice.

"Ntanga," Jean replied.

"Tanga . . . ? I can't seem to find it."

"It's spelt with an N. The N is silent."

"Oh! N-Tanga."

"Ntanga, yes."

"Oh, that's an interesting name. What does it mean?"

"I'm not sure."

She pulled out a white envelope, with a wry smile, and handed it to Papa. Jean, feeling even more nervous, took it from Papa's hand, "I'll hold it; it's nothing to worry about."

Papa, head in the clouds, and in a state of absolute awe of the school building, walked around with a happiness beaming from his face. They walked along the corridors full of life with the many families who attended, families who, looking from parent to child, often proved the adage "the apple does not fall far from the tree" to be true.

Mr. David appeared out of nowhere, looking tired, and disheveled as usual; top button undone and tie slightly loosened, but Papa overlooked this, which would have otherwise made him take someone less seriously, as he introduced himself as Jean's tutor.

"Hello! You must be Mr. Ntanga." Mr. David spoke with a forced enthusiasm in his voice. "We've spoken on the phone, I'm Jean's tutor."

"Ah, yes. Hello. Hello." Papa replied. He kept his responses brief.

"Hello, Jean. How are you? Did you sort out your appointments?"

"Yes, sir," Jean replied, mirroring Mr. David's heightened enthusiasm, knowing full well he did not sort out any appointment.

Mr. David walked them to the hall where all the teachers were sat by their tables with their properness; smiles, enthusiastic, high pitched voices and special occasion suits sophisticated enough to hide the fact they would be heading to the pub to drink themselves into amnesia and count down the weeks until the holiday.

"Papa, let's go and see Mr. Johnston, he's the P.E Teacher."

"Okay." Papa willingly obliged.

They sat at Mr. Johnston's table. A large burly man whose crossed, furry eyebrows resembled two rabid dogs attacking each other. He greeted Papa's quiet hello with a roaring laughter.

"Jean is a fantastic student. He is a natural athlete. Super talented at sports, I would encourage him to pursue athletics or football. He is a great student to have in the lesson; he encourages other students to get involved and is really supportive."

Mr. Johnston continued with the praise, which left Jean beaming, and Papa indifferent, as if he had heard it before.

"Do you have any questions, Sir?" he asked Papa.

"Okaaaay. No tenk you." Papa's accent always came on heavy when he was frustrated or reluctant to engage. He shook hands with Mr. Johnston, and stood to leave. Jean quickly followed.

"Shall we go and see the Music teacher now?" Jean asked suggestively.

"No. What subjects are these? P.E. and Music?!" Papa's accent became heavier. "Take me to a real subject. Let us go to the Mathematics teacher."

Jean's heart sunk to the ground. Although he did not dislike Mathematics, he did not like the teacher or, as Jean lamented to Mr. David who questioned him after receiving several detentions, "He doesn't like me. He always picks on me in front of the whole class." Jean recalled, as the teacher once said "You are the laziest African boy I have ever taught," when Jean did not complete his work one lesson.

The Mathematics teacher was Mr. Okala, "O-KA-LA," he would say as if coughing out a hairball with each syllable. He was from Cameroon, but grew up in the *Bans-Lieu* of Paris. He spoke with an accent which blended the experience of the immigrant, inner-city French youth, and the vocabulary of the educated, middle class of West Africa. He wore two badges on the lapel of his blazer, either to remind others or even himself of where he came from; one of the French national flag, and the other of Cameroon.

Jean spotted Mr. Okala in the corner of the room finishing his appointment with another child; it was Chris and his parents. Jean was surprised and filled with doom; even they looked unsatisfied. Papa was looking in the opposite direction.

"I don't know if my maths teacher is here this evening . . ." Jean tried to stall, and lead towards a quick escape.

"Aah, there is mathematics!" Papa bellowed, seeing the sign on the table, and marched over.

"Hello, Sir!" Papa was ecstatic to see a Black man teaching at the school. Not only a Black man, but an African man; a rare face among the many he had seen so far, and for such an important subject. Papa greeted Mr. Okala, who reciprocated with a brotherly hug as if they had known each other and shared a fictive kinship, a secret brotherhood of fellow African men. The other parents and teachers stopped to stare at this peculiar exchange whilst Jean drowned in embarrassment.

"Hello, Jean!" Mr. Okala stuck out his large manly hand, which Jean shook limply.

"Hello, sir." They sat. Jean trembled. He looked up at Papa who was now looking at Mr. Okala with rose-tinted glasses after noticing the two badges he wore on his blazer. Papa showed a smile with all of his straight teeth, exuding joy.

"What can I say about Jean? He is a good boy, very able at

Mathematics. He does do good work when he can . . ." all his comments were met with proud nods from Papa. "BUT . . ." Mr. Okala paused, "he is LAZY!" Papa's head slowly stopped nodding.

"He is always talking in class and not paying attention. I have to constantly remind him to work. Since he came to this school he has been hanging around and copying this English boy with his nonsense behavior. He cannot afford to do these nonsense things. You know how hard it is for us. I am from Cameroon, and I have had to work hard EVERY DAY to get to where I am now. Where is your family from? If you do not mind me asking . . ." Mr. Okala asked Papa.

"It's okay. We are from Congo . . . Kinshasa," Papa replied.

"Oh! *Ali Bomaye! Ali Bomaye! . . .* and *Ndombolo.*" He laughed boisterously trying to ease the tension building on Papa's face.

"*Vous parlez Francais, alors?*" Mr. Okala enquired.

"*Oui, bien sur!*" Papa replied.

"*Oh, fantastique! Ce que je voulais vraiment dire est que . . .*" Mr. Okala continued speaking to Papa with the kind of French rolling off his tongue too fast for Jean's ears to keep up with. Jean's French was in its infancy; still on training wheels compared to the speeding conversation of his father and teacher. Nonetheless, there were some words flashing before him; "*paresseux . . . bavarder.*"

Did he call me lazy and chatty? I don't even speak in class, and when I do it's usually to him. I don't understand . . . ?

Jean continued to look back and forth between Papa and Mr. Okala as if he was court side watching Sampras vs McEnroe. Jean saw Papa's face transform slowly with each word spoken, from an ecstatic, straight teeth stretched-smile to an apoplectic, simmering rage; twitching right eye and throbbing vein on the temple of his forehead. The sacrificial ceremony had ended. He watched Papa stand and shake Mr. Okala's hand with a firm handshake much unlike the hug he had greeted him with before.

"Let us go," Papa spoke, with a seriousness shaking Jean to his boots. He took the envelope from Jean's hands, and walked ahead without looking back. As Jean was leaving, James was walking in on his own. He came jogging over, noticing the despondent look on Jean's face.

"You alright mate?"

"No. I'm in trouble. My Dad is proper angry, man." James heard the fear in Jean's voice. "Where are your parents? Aren't they coming?" Jean continued.

"Nah. I came by myself. I made up some excuse; I told my tutor about my ol' man and his dodgy 'eart, a proper sad story, but he's only at the pub ain't he? I only came in so I can get my report and not get a detention."

"You're lucky." Jean noticed Papa had walked off into the distance, still not looking back.

"Look, I've got to go, my Dad has gone." Jean ran off to catch up with Papa.

The front door slammed shut with a bang once they arrived home. Papa stomped heavy footed into the living room where Mami and Marie were sat on the sofa watching TV.

"*Nini?*" Mami asked shocked by the dramatic entrance. Papa threw the torn open white envelope on the table.

"LOOK!"

Mami opened the envelope and read through Jean's behavior report. She instantly sent Marie to her room telling her it was bedtime. Marie obliged, even though she knew it wasn't, she could feel the heaviness in the air.

"*Eh! Mama na ngai! Jean! Aza wapi?*" she called for him "*Jean! Yaka'wa.*"

Jean had already retreated to his bedroom, in the dark, and was under the covers pretending to be sleeping, shoes off, but still fully dressed. Tonton was out.

"*Jean! Lamuka. Tika ko kosa.*" Mami came barging in and switched on the light.

"I'm not lying Mum, I was sleeping."

"*Lamuka! Lamuka!*" Mami reached up and pulled the covers off. She yanked him by his ear and pulled him down all the way to the living room where Papa was waiting, sat on the sofa, hands together, TV switched off, in absolute stillness.

"*Vanda,*" Papa commanded. Jean listened to Papa's grumbled instruction and sat on the furthest seat away from him on the adjacent sofa.

"*Oyo nini?!*" Mami bellowed in a high pitched voice holding the white envelope.

"It's not my fault mum."

"Not my fault mum . . ." Mami mocked, "English: poor. Maths: poor. Science: poor . . ."

"It's not my fault. I did good in P.E. though."

"In P.E.!" Papa roared tearing down Jean's frail defense. "You want to play sports?"

"Yeah . . ." Jean replied, not seeing how it was best not to reply at all.

"Jean! *Nabetayo?!* We did not come to this country so you can play sports or be stupid in school! You will get an education!" Papa began speaking in English, the kind of English seemingly fighting an invisible opponent, throwing punches into the thin air but not landing any.

"We came to this country so you can get an education! Your mother and I are not stupid. We are smart people. We went to school, but we come to this country, and we sacrifice for YOU!" Papa was animated, pacing up and down, arms flailing, his heavy finger thrust towards Jean's face, "If you carry on behaving this way, we will send you back! So you can really learn."

"But Dad . . ."

"Is it because I am a cleaner you think your father is stupid— *Hein?!* Is it because you run around with the English boy? You think you are the same as him—*Hein?!* Answer me! You want to be white—is that it?!"

"No, Dad! But it's not my fau—"

"BUT NOTHING! You will listen to me!" Papa's outstretched hand flew through the air and smacked Jean's face. The sound echoed across the room. It knocked the air out of Jean's mouth, and left him gasping. He held his breath, held the side of his head up as if it would roll off.

Mami quietly left the room and closed the door. There was rage in Papa's eyes. It boiled inside him and showed on his skin, in sweats. He took off his belt and told Jean to lie on his stomach. Jean's body shook with fear; his limbs trembled like a small dog's. Papa cracked the belt. The whip of the belt came thundering down on Jean's body, blow after blow after blow. Jean felt sharp surges of electricity with each blow until he was numb. He felt no more; he was disconnected from the pain in his body. He wandered in his mind, somewhere far away but to a place getting colder and colder. The blows stopped. He knew this not because the pain had subsided, but because he could no longer hear the crack of the belt breaking the air. His tense body relaxed. He was cooled by the liquid pool flowing beneath him. It wet his trousers and dirtied the sofa. The smell of piss rose slowly through the air; it mixed with the smell of rage and fear, and lingered. Papa sat on the adjacent sofa, put his belt back on and sent Jean to sleep.

chapter 10

KINSHASA WAS A THRIVING CITY. THE two-lane streets were filled with imported cars only driven by the Belgians and the affluent Congolese men—with their wives, or mistresses, as passengers. They showed their wealth dressed in smart suits with short sleeved arms, neck scarves with matching pocket squares and weighted gold or silver watches, hung at the end of their wrists like a burden of sacrifice. The women, who were mostly held to managing household duties or worked, very few and far in between, in positions of hospitality or servitude, wore beautifully bright colored printed clothes. A *liputa* they tied around their waist, and a *kintambala*, usually made of silk, which they would fold at the corners and tie around to cover their heads.

Kinshasa was not a city you came from, it was a city you came to; for work, for business, for travel. But once you came, it kept you so you would never leave. Maybe it was whatever was in the air; the melee of languages; the formality of French, the official tongue, spoken in public spaces; the institutions, schools, universities and offices, airport lounges, and government buildings. Or the *Lingala*, which ran like a sweeping undercurrent, through the roads, with its back bent rhythm, stood on the street corners or back alley-ways, on the tongues of lovers, after the sunset, when the music would play. The music, in the language of the swaying hips of women and the watchful eyes of men; men whose eyes were their hands, and they would watch until they wanted to feel, all while the alcohol flowed until it too spilled onto the streets.

Mami came from a very strict family. In a society where women were afforded very little privileges, unlike the men, she was held to impossibly high standards, which meant there was very little she could do, never mind what she could do wrong. They lived in a large house with black metallic gates in *Gombe*. Her father, *Koko ya Mobali*, was a military man, whose position Mami was never quite sure of. He was important enough to have intricately designed multi-point badges of honor hung on the lapels of the khaki-green uniform he wore, and have someone he could tell what to do and run around after him, but not too important he could not himself be told what to do; such as disappear in the middle of the night for a mission or leave his family whilst they had dinner on a Sunday afternoon together after church. He spoke in detail of honoring the family and fighting for things Mami was too young to understand.

Her mother, *Koko ya Mwasi*, took care of house and home, raising the children, which was seen as the duty bestowed upon her by divine right of her gender. She was a quiet woman; never spoke louder than her husband, never walked ahead of her husband, never loved another man but her husband. Each day she wore the most beautiful *liputa*, whether she was shopping at the *zandu* or in Sunday mass, she looked elegant and graceful, as was expected of her. She had so much more than other women she did not dare challenge it, for if she did it meant risking losing all she had received.

Mami had four sisters, two older and two younger: Marthe, Monique, Micheline, and Marie. She carried them through their ups and downs as if she was their balancing scale. She was the reluctant mediator, the peace-keeper between the two warring clans of elder and younger. She was the voice of reason. At times she looked the oldest, not due to her appearance but her sense of style and dress. She emulated her mother; fitting comfortably into her mother's clothes, wishing for the life she had—a life of quiet abundance.

Koko ya Mobali felt disappointed when he found out their first child would be a girl; he believed a man's firstborn, as did many others, must be a boy to continue his legacy. Five daughters later the disappointment turned to damnation, then eventually acceptance as the sight of his legacy faded away. He felt he must be carrying some kind of eternal curse from a *nganga*. After Mami was born, he treated the youngest two who came after, Micheline and Marie, as if they were boys; they too would follow in his footsteps. Nonetheless, he never let his daughters know exactly how he felt. He loved them dearly, the best way he knew how a father could; over-protective, with authority and from a distance.

As quiet and submissive as *Koko ya Mwasi* was, her smile widened with each daughter she gave birth to; knowing she could never challenge or overcome the power of this man who she loved as her husband, giving him five daughters was her quiet act of rebellion.

Papa, on the other hand, was an only child. He was a quiet, observant boy who saved his words for the right moment, spoke only when spoken to but listened all the time. Papa was of slim build. He wore mostly dark colors varying between black and grey; they all blended in the same way he did. His trousers flared and collars popped out, top button always undone. He lived together with his often absent (due to work and other non-descript causes) father, *Patrice,* in a large empty house where they hardly saw each other apart from at dinner. And when father felt he was losing touch with his son, they would sit in silence, cutlery clinking, mouths chewing, Papa waiting for *Koko Patrice* to ask the usual questions: *How is school? How are your studies? Did you do your homework?* The questions always revolved around his studies and were much less questions, and more so commands. Papa only answered with enough detail to satisfy a father's curiosity, but not so much he ended up speaking more than he desired. Their conversations resembled business meetings, rather than a father and son relationship. And, in the many conversations they had, or did not have, neither of them would speak of Mother. Their tongues always felt too heavy to lift this conversation into the air between them.

When Papa and Mami first met, they were in neighboring schools in the heart of Kinshasa. Papa went to a *Iti-Gombe; Institut Technique Industriel de la Gombe*, where the boys wore jeans, smoked, played football and carried sticks in their bags where their books should be, just in case they needed to beat a lesson into somebody. Mami's school, *Lycée Dr. Shaumba*, was much more well-to-do; the girls wore blue skirts and white shirts as uniforms, and the boys wore pleated trousers, and carried books in their bags where their books should be. They were both taught in French, but no matter how well they grasped the language, it was always made to seem as if it stumbled as it walked compared to the Belgians whose French strolled freely.

As Papa walked home with his friends after school, making ill use of their time, he saw Mami standing alone in a crowd across the street. He looked at her and felt something. It was not this young love he had never been spoken to about by his inauspiciously quiet father. He did not look into her eyes and see two nebulas balancing in the vast darkness of the cosmos. He did not, when he eventually heard her speak, hear a symphony of violins played in E minor by the soft hands of angels. He did not want to kiss her lips because they resembled everything he had longed for calling him back to himself; his mother, the quiet of his grandfather's village after their house burned down, the lost peace of the morning telling him there is life again because the sun was simply a giant burning ball of fire, and all fire reminded him of the burning, and burning brings no life. He did not see the curves of her body, her long slender body, her long slender body with a *liputa* tied around her waist, and want to lay her down to run his hands through her like an artist's brushstrokes on a canvas. He did not, when he first touched her, an accidental touch, two weightless bodies crashing through space, feel an electric surge along his spine making him weak at the knees. However, he did look at her and the person inside him who was always running away stood still.

Their eyes met. Mami looked at him and saw nothing. Nothing like the vastness of the entire universe before a beginning, nothing like the space in between the words of a poem deeply felt, nothing like the moment after you breathe out but before you breathe in, or the nothing like the gap in between two hands clasped together in prayer. She saw nothing but she offered him rest, for she felt how tired his feet were, how he had been running for so long. How the heavy breathing had taken its toll on his lungs, they were always gasping for air as if each breath could be the last. It showed in his eyes. Papa quietly slipped away from his friends unnoticed and followed Mami who was now shopping for bread where *Koko ya Mwasi* would send her to fulfill her duties as a daughter.

"Bonjour," he whispered softly, with a smooth polite voice not matching the way he was dressed. He spoke in French because he wanted to show he too was well learned and educated, this is what speaking in French meant; it could make a pauper look like a professor.

"Bonjour," he repeated, this time with a slight change of tone in his voice, knowing she had heard him but unsure as to why she had ignored. She continued with her shopping. He continued with his pursuit.

"*Tu m'entends pas?*" He asked and reached for the loaf of bread on the second shelf beyond her outstretched arm. The hairs of his forearm brushed softly against her smooth skin. He gave it to her. She looked at him in the eyes, setting all the ships inside his blood to sail down the stream, as he stood over her with his slim frame and wide shoulders, and said "*Merci.*"

Papa stood still in a dazed bewilderment. It was akin to watching a predator politely ask the prey if they could be hunted, and the prey refusing. She turned to walk away and Papa placed his hand on the soft part of her arm gently and said nothing; the words he searched for could not be found. Mami looked at him with both confusion and understanding. She walked to the counter, paid for her goods and walked out of the door. Papa followed her hesitantly for a few steps and watched her leave. She did not once look back. He looked at her not looking back, hoping for a glance, a stare, a subtle sign of curiosity. So he looked away in case if she looked back, she would not see him looking, but he couldn't keep looking away for long and so he looked back once more only to see her not looking back.

They would continue to meet in this manner for many moments to come. Papa began shopping in the same shop as Mami, sometimes spending hours in there waiting for her to arrive, hoping she would be there the same time he was. In the moments they were both there, it was nothing but quiet, subtle solitude and long gazing, as if each time was the first time they had met.

chapter 11

MAMI SHARED HER BEDROOM WITH HER eldest sister Marthe. They both shared a penchant for soft things and quiet places; pillows, duvets, poetry, and libraries, much unlike the other sisters, who, in their shared room, would now be listening to loud music and paying the driver to go out and buy them snacks, and more serious things not usually allowed for them.

Mami lay on her bed one night with her eyes wide open, staring at the ceiling when she should have been asleep. Papa was on her mind. She dreamt him, in an eyes wide open type of dream, walking towards her in reverse as if he was walking back to the beginning of their journey.

"*Olali?*" Marthe asked in a tired voice.

"No. I can't sleep. Why?"

"I can hear you rolling around as if you have bugs climbing on your back."

"I feel like they are climbing in my head."

"Is something the matter?"

"*Te.*"

"Well, go to sleep then."

There was a long pause; they both knew this silence was not their last.

"Okay. Maybe 'no' is not exactly the most accurate answer. It's not something is wrong, it's just I have some questions."

"Questions?" Marthe replied curiously.

"Yes, questions . . . about love."

"*BOLINGO?!*" she yelled.

"Shh! *Bako yoka yo.*" Mami said quietening her sister.

"Love?! Why are you asking about love?! You're not having sex are you?!" Marthe sat up swiftly and turned towards Mami. She lit the candle lamp, as if they were part of a clandestine movement, passing secret messages to each other. The last thing either of them wanted was to be having this conversation in front of the other sisters, let alone their mother and father.

"No," Mami, giggled, "not yet . . ."

"*Nakobeta yo.*"

"No, no, no. I'm joking, don't hit me. I'm only curious. But come on, you must know something, you're old."

"Thanks." Marthe replied wryly.

"No, I mean you're old as in you're older, you have experience. You'll be getting married someday soon; you already have all these men who come to father and make him all sorts of offers for you; land, cows and goats . . ."

"Yeah, all those old men with their pot-bellies who have wives hidden in other parts of the country they tell no one about."

". . . real crocodile skin shoes. An actual crocodile! Father loved those. Remember the man who said he swam into the *Ebale and* killed the crocodile with his bare hands?"

"Yes, Prince. That man. Fat and rich. How I could forget?"

"Father almost gave you away instantly." Mami burst out with laughter.

"I know. It's nice we have a father who knows our worth isn't it? Sold to the average bidder." They laughed, and in their laughter, they imagined their other sisters, and how this would be applicable to them, and laughed some more.

"You will make a great wife though. You are beautiful. You are smart . . . ."

"Men don't want a smart wife."

"What? Why?"

"They want a woman who is dumb, dumb but pretty. A woman who doesn't talk. I mean, look at mother."

"What about her?"

"When was the last time you heard her talk?"

"Er, all the time. Are you telling me you've never heard mother talk?"

"No. I mean, talk, talk. Actually talk over father. Give a different opinion. Heck, even silence him, tell him to *kanga munoko*, as he sometimes tells her."

"Oh, come on. It's not that bad . . ."

"Maybe it is, maybe it isn't. Anyway, this is about you. Why do you want to know about love? Is it a boy?"

"No, I simply want to know. I'm growing up . . ."

"Is it a boy?" she interrupted, this time slower.

"No!" Mami insisted. "I want to know. No one ever talks about love. Has mother or father ever spoken to you about it?"

"It's a boy." Marthe let out a heavy, defeated sigh.

"Okay, maybe it is a boy, but I still want to know. It's just one minute you're a child packing your homework into your bag, and the next you're waiting at home cooking for a big-bellied man and his children."

"They are your children too."

"But no one talks about how we get there. You're just expected to know, you're expected to somehow pick it up as you go along. What is love?"

"Well, I remember mother saying one thing, on one of her nights where she had drunk too much wine while father was away. She said marry a man who you can tolerate, because in the end you will want to kill him . . ."

"*Trés* bizarre!"

"Though, I'm pretty sure she didn't know it was me and maybe thought it was one of her *Mamas* who come around to drink wine because it's un-ladylike for a married woman to be seen drinking at bars." Mami let out a huge sigh of frustration in reply.

"Truth is little sis, I don't know. I imagine love to be like water . . ."

"*Mayi?*"

"Yes, water. Sometimes you drink it. Other times you wash in it. But mostly, it is what you are made up of."

"I don't get it."

"Neither do I. And that, little sister is love. No one gets it. We talk about it, write poems, books, and songs about it, cry and lose sleep over it, but no one ever gets it. Now let us go to sleep, unless you have to confess you are having sex with this boy so I can slap you now and send you to father."

Marthe stared at Mami with a stern but compassionate look only big sisters know, blew out the candlelit lamp and went to sleep. Mami stayed awake for a few more hours, staring at the ceiling.

chapter 12

I 974 WAS THE YEAR OF THE great fight, from Slave ship to Championship, or, as it would more commonly come to be known, the Rumble in the Jungle: the fight for the heavyweight championship boxing title between Mohammed Ali and George Foreman. The biggest fight of the twentieth century landed in the heart of Africa, bringing with it a new wave of people from around the world, sweeping the streets of Kinshasa with an infectious electric energy, galvanizing the young Zairois—at the time—and the old alike, the men and the women, the little boys and little girls.

The chants of "*ALI BOMA YE! ALI BOMA YE!*" echoed in the streets and followed the world famous boxer around, as if he were a triumphant leader with a powerful political slogan, accompanied by waving hands and fists thrusting through the air in support of this long-awaited victory. It was as if he was bringing freedom to his long-lost people. Ali considered himself one with the people, and the people considered themselves one with Ali. There was an eruption in the streets every time he was spotted outside, when he ran they followed him as though he were the pied piper, the village drummer, and he played the beat to which they all danced.

Mami did not dance though. She was not moved. There were more important issues to consider, duties to be taken care of, responsibilities to be tended to; within school, the family, the church and at home. She despised the sporting affair and saw it as an exaggeration; to her, people were overcompensating for the failures of the national team in the Football World Cup earlier in the summer.

"*Eza soni! To polaki.*" Mami bemoaned to their family about the shame of their team's losses. When they could not watch the games, they would gather and listen to *Kin Radio*, where the presenter, *Bongadio*, a man with a fast tongue, elucidated the listeners on the latest football affairs and all things relating:

Eh, bandeko, Zaire is the first sub-Saharan African team to qualify for the football World Cup; sub-Saharan is the notable distinction because it propelled a new image of Africans onto the eyes of the world. An entire team of tall dark skinned men, on an equal playing field, doubled by the fact Haiti—the land where freedom was won—an equally outstanding sight of men, who may at one point in time have been closer related, were also first-time qualifiers. It is a historic moment, for both symbolic and political reasons, which could set a sporting precedent for the years to come.

Zaire did end up losing all of their games; so did Haiti. However, Haiti did at least have one moment of glory when they took a 1–0 lead against Italy—a victory in itself. However, the lead didn't last; they lost 3–1. For Zaire on the other hand, it wasn't so much the losing but, rather, how they lost which will be difficult to forget. After a 9–0 thrashing against Yugoslavia where the players looked like their bodies were on the pitch but had left their fighting spirits on *na ndako*, the 3–0 loss against Brazil felt victorious. After all, Brazil was considered the place where the gods of football resided and so it should have been a lot worse. A lot. This would have been a moment to celebrate, were it not for the infamous free-kick moment.

In the latter stages of the game, as Brazil lined up to take a free kick that had no bearing on the outcome, Zairean defender Mwepu Ilunga broke out of the defensive wall and booted the ball down the field. The Brazilian team looked around in confusion, whilst the referee ran to Ilunga, chastising him with a yellow card. It remains the embarrassing haunting legacy of the World Cup tournament for Zaire, ladies and gentlemen. It will be remembered as though Africans cannot follow rules; an echo of colonial legacy. But maybe one day, we will live to see Zaire be the first African nation to lift the World Cup. *Ba ndeko, mukolo moko biso mpe toko gagner.*

"*Soni!*" Mami would continue to cry shame whenever the subject came up, which was frequent enough.

"*Ah tika!*" Her father would intercede; airing his frustration, telling her to stop.

"You are a little girl. You do not know the story. The players went to represent our country. You should be proud of their fight. Instead you complain; shame on you. Ilunga kicked the ball deliberately, in protest against a government who sit and do nothing but eat the food of the people while the rest starve. These players did not get paid for their service. He is an example, we all should fight like him!' He raised his voice in dramatic fashion, and slammed his fist on the table, as if he too had been on the field with the men, and left the room dramatically.

Mami remained in stunned silence for she was not aware, but how could she be? She was a young school girl who could fit all her responsibilities in her backpack. She was not a fan of sports, and took any given opportunity to make a mockery of it. Papa, on the other hand, loved sports. Actually no, he did not love sports; he loved to *fight*, so therefore he loved boxing as it was merely a way of civilizing his violence. He earned his reputation as a young man for having a long reach but a short temper.

Mami had begun sneaking out to meet Papa with the help of Marthe, who covered all bases for her. If *Koko ya Mobali* was looking for her, Marthe would step in and say she was too tired so she went to sleep early, shooing him away from their bedroom door so he wouldn't disturb. Or, she would say Mami had been sent to the market to buy some food; Mami was even eating more so there would be less food in the house. Or she would say Mami was simply sick or unwell. And when father would want to enquire to find out why Mami was sick, Marthe would not reply but instead give him the look fathers knew all too well. After the experience of having five daughters, he understood it was not the kind of "unwell" he, as a man, should concern himself with.

If mother ever looked for Mami, which she rarely did, mostly because she felt Mami was occupied taking care of things herself somewhere, Marthe would simply reply that Mami was occupied and busy taking care of things herself somewhere. They would go on walks, Mami and Papa, long walks, in places hidden away from the city. It was by grace that this bustling city also had space full of quiet green places in which to get lost; in between flowing waters and tall trees, away from the noise and the watchful eyes.

"You are finishing school soon. What will you do next?" Mami asked, as they walked through the quiet of the green forest, crimson colored sun setting in the sky, with nothing, save for the sound of their voices, and their stepping feet over the leaves and broken branches on the ground laying their path.

"I don't know. I will go to university. I want to be a doctor." Papa replied.

"You? A doctor?" Mami responded, almost laughing, in a surprised tone of voice.

"You sound shocked . . ."

"It takes seven years, you know."

"I know."

"That's a long time."

"Also . . ." she paused and observed him, "it's just you don't look like a doctor," she looked him up and down, then down and up, and observed his sandals, wide flared dark trousers, open buttoned shirt with the spread collars and hat.

"No, I don't see it." She took the toothpick he was chewing out of his mouth. Papa looked at Mami looking at him up and down, then down and up, he then looked at himself.

"Well how else are doctors supposed to dress when they are on a long walk in the woods with their secret girlfriend?"

"Oh, so I'm your girlfriend now?"

"I'll probably go to Uni Kin, you know. But my father wants me to study abroad. He wants me to go to Brussels."

"Really?"

"Yes. In fact, he insists. He says I will be able to do more, get a better education there. But if I go I will have to do two extra years in school to get my Baccalaureate there before I can go to university . . ."

"But you will have it from here."

"Yes but, you know Europeans think African education needs extra help. Plus, I don't want to go. I have everything I need here. My father is here. And he made good of the opportunities he had, and so will I."

"What does your father do?"

"He works in a bank. He is the only Congolese there. They pay him to be seen but not to be heard. He says when a white person employs a Black person, they pay them to smile and not to speak. But one day Black people will pay White people not to speak."

"And your mother?" Mami asked. A gust of wind swept through the space between them and rendered everything to silence.

"What about my mother?"

"You do not speak of your mother . . . .?"

"My mother is not here to speak of."

"Where is she?"

"She is gone."

"*Wapi?*"

"She is dead."

Mami gasped as if the air had been ripped out from her lungs.

"Oh God, I am so sorry."

"It's okay."

"I mean, I shouldn't have asked . . . if I had known . . . I wouldn't have . . ." Mami stuttered and stumbled with her words, which was unusual for her.

"It's okay," Papa reiterated. A silence fell once more. It stretched outward like the long shadow of a stranger standing between them. Still. Moments passed.

"How did she die?" Mami boldly asked, but with as much compassion as she could.

"She died on the *masua* crossing the river. I was a young boy. She was going back to Brazzaville, to see her family . . ."

"You're . . ."

"Yes. I am." Papa paused, and continued. "Somewhere in the middle of this god-forsaken river, too far from Kinshasa, but not yet close enough to Brazzaville, the boat sank. It was swallowed up. Her body was never found."

"Oh my God . . ." Mami wept softly, as tears fell from her eyes.

"And you know how people are. Some say it was an accident, some say it was deliberate; that the boat was sabotaged. Some say it was *kindoki*; that there were evil spirits after her, because she was too young to die this way, some blame Father. Even Father blames Father."

"What do you think?"

"All I know is I don't know exactly how or even when it happened. My father protected me for a long time and always said mother will be coming home soon but I do remember there was a day when I felt as though my lungs had collapsed into themselves, and breathing was but labored sorrow. This must have been when she died. And every year at the same time, I struggle to breathe."

"You know what the sad thing about death is . . ." Papa continued "aside from such an untimely death, it is not so much the tragedy itself. You learn to cope, time heals; you learn they will not be coming back. No, the truly sad thing is there is no forewarning; no last moments, no goodbye, no last words; 'I love you,' 'remember me,' 'I'll miss you,' and no opportunity for you to ask, beg even, for them to stay."

"You were only a boy . . ."

"And the older I get, the less I remember, everything starts to fade."

"You cannot blame yourself."

"My father and I do not talk about it. We barely talk at all, only about school or his job. It was not always this way. Those who do know don't say anything though; silence is sorrow."

"I'm sorry."

"You're the first person I've ever told . . . I feel I can talk to you."

"Thank you for trusting me . . ."

He looked at her as if he had seen her again for the first time. Quiet. Still. They kissed, swift. Lips locked how time sits soft in the palms of the dying, how bright eyes lift darkness from souls crying, the tired, weighed down, burdened from the heavy of the world, finding rest. In the tenderness of this moment, they shared the same breath.

". . . I should get going." Mami said. "It's getting late, and my family will be wondering where I am. Marthe can only cover me for a short while."

"Please stay . . . it doesn't have to be for long."

"I should go . . ."

"Please."

"Okay, but only until the sun sets."

"I hope it never does."

chapter 13

"WHERE HAVE YOU BEEN?!" MARTHE EXCLAIMED at Mami in a loud whisper as she snuck back into the house through the bedroom window, "Father was looking for you! I had to stop him from coming into the room."

"What? Where is he now?" Mami panted, out of breath. There were three loud bangs on the door.

"*Allo! Tu est la?*" *Koko ya Mobali*'s deep voice echoed from outside the room. Mami gasped and froze.

"He thinks you're asleep. Quick! Get into bed . . ."

Mami leapt with cat-like athleticism into the air and in one motion, was laid in bed, eyes closed, fully clothed, under the covers. Three more loud bangs.

"*Je vas entrer . . .*" *Koko ya Mobali* announced his entrance. His head floated in first, as if it had no body, the rest of him appearing shortly after. He went straight to Mami, and sat beside her on the bed.

"*Ca va ma fille? Qu'est ce qu'il y a?*" he asked, speaking now in a softened, sympathetic tone. Mami shuffled in her bed, groaning and moaning, as if she had caught an incurable disease.

"Nothing father, I'm okay . . ." she forced two hoarse coughs from the back of her throat. Father placed the back of his hand on Mami's forehead to feel her temperature.

"Oh, you are cold! You need to see a doctor. Tomorrow you are not to go to school," he ordered.

"But . . ." Mami tried to intercede, happy she had been believed but sad as she did not have the intention of missing school. There were three loud bangs on the door.

"*C'EST QUI?*" Father asked, roaring at the interruption. The night watchman came bursting in, and stood at the foot of the door in a stiff upright salute.

"M . . . m . . . *maître* . . . *c'est urgent!*" the night watchman trembled and stuttered. Father snapped his fingers and pointed outside, to which the watchmen slightly took three steps back out of the bedroom still in salute. He kissed Mami on the forehead, and planted a kiss on Marthe's cheek, who was sat statuesque on her bed staring at the brown carpet flooring, and left the room. From outside the door there was inaudible tense conversation, followed by the pounding feet of military boots along the corridor, into the distance.

Papa had arrived home later than usual, taking the scenic walk back in the warm air of the city whilst being caught in a dream thinking of Mami. He entered the gates of the porch; shadows loomed over from the lamppost barely lighting up their house at the bottom of the street. He stood in front of the door and opened it. The floorboard creaked as he walked past the living room. Papa looked across; he knew he should not have. *Koko Patrice* was sat holding a wide newspaper covering his face. He lowered it; clear lens glasses with a golden rim dropped to the edge of his nose, and gave Papa a stare which planted his feet still into the ground. *Koko Patrice's* jaw looked swollen, as if all the foul words he were saving for someone else were growing in his mouth.

Koko Patrice took one look at the chair opposite him at the table, and then returned to reading the newspaper. Papa slowly walked to the chair and sat. There was a full plate of food in front of him. He looked at father's plate and it was empty; nothing left but bare bones. Papa picked up the knife and fork and began eating. There was silence. The air was as heavy and thick as smog; it smelled similar to the foul stench of something dead, as if a grenade of despair had exploded into the room. Father finally stopped reading the newspaper he was not reading and looked up, mouth full of questions.

"*Ozalaki wapi?*" Father asked the question, wanting to know where he was, as though it carried handcuffs.

"I was playing *balé.*" Papa replied quickly, looking down at his plate, as though his voice had grown legs and was trying run out of the room from being caught. Silence fell. Father began reading the newspaper he wasn't reading once more.

"*Ozalaki wapi?*" This time his voice was heavier, carrying more weight.

"I was with my friends." Papa replied, timid, wishing his words had not left his mouth. Father let out a low deep sound, the lovechild of a grumble and a sigh.

"*Ozalaki wapi?*"

This time Papa did not answer. He swallowed his words, letting the silence remain. Father folded the newspaper he was not reading, and placed it squarely on the table. He lifted his hand and smacked Papa across the side of his face.

"Do not lie to me . . ." his rage made itself known. "Do not disobey your father."

There was an implied message; they both knew this went beyond what was said, beyond what had transpired. As if it reached back in history, to a time even before Papa himself was born, but it was now being handed down to him.

"One thing . . ." *Koko Patrice* continued, "*remember, when you lie, the truth is always written on your face.*"

"*Lia.*" *Koko Patrice* pointed to the food prompting Papa to eat. Papa swiftly followed instructions and began eating the meal, with two streams of tears running down his earth-brown cheeks. This meal was not meant to be a sad one.

chapter 14

Papa did not get to see Mami before he left for Brussels. He was not one for goodbyes. Goodbyes meant he was not going to see the person again, and sometimes, this was preferred, but in cases such as this, he felt a goodbye was akin to handcuffing himself to something unmovable; a lamppost, a railing, a family who already told you no. He was leaving, she wasn't. She was also not yet his wife, and a girlfriend was a foreign concept—to be a girlfriend is to be half of a whole thing you need, and one cannot be half of air to breathe or light to see, love must always be whole—therefore, regardless of what either family may have known or assumed, the privilege of seeing her, on request, before he left, was not granted.

Papa did not want to leave, and he knew a goodbye could persuade him to change his mind. This was a decision he could not afford to make for *Koko Patrice's* watchful eyes and strong hand had moved him and taken him away long before he even left. *Koko Patrice* did not even take him to the airport; this reluctance for goodbyes must have been inherited.

It was not uncommon for a Congolese person to be going to

Belgium to further their studies, however, there were not many who were able to go; Papa was one of the selected few. When Papa left he did not feel the excitement as much as before, not as much as he would have liked; the energy and effervescence of the city he called home had not traveled the distance to reach him across the seas. Instead, he felt the cold wind and the dim sun of a European city. Brussels, to Papa, was a city asleep. Nonetheless, he did enjoy the scenery; the tram in the city and the gargantuan Cathedral of St. Michael and St. Gudula. That being said he never felt compelled to embrace the cold, as well as the lingering stares of the passers-by, to really go forth and explore.

Unlike Kinshasa, Brussels was not the life of the party. It was the friend you brought along when you were worried they hadn't left the house for three weeks. And, when they arrived to the party they remained standing in the corner whilst everyone else danced, but you were at least glad they came. Papa was already looking forward to going back home for the summers.

He was the only Congolese person; the only Black person, in his classes of maths-physics-biology-chemistry at the *Ecole Polytechnique de Brussels*. Conscious of the fact his French sounded different to the others; not better, not worse, just different, he rarely spoke. He was invisible for most of the classes; the professors did not ask him much nor ask much of him, unless it was occasionally at the end of class. For the last fifteen minutes, the Mathematics professor, Professor Gibeaud, a young looking middle-aged man with timely streaks of silver-grey hair, elbow patches on his blazer and thick-rimmed glasses, would open the class up for discussion, which, by his guidance, usually ended up being about colonialism in Africa and the Belgian civilizing mission in Congo.

His position was unclear. One moment, he would play devil's advocate, stating Belgium had civilized Congo, which Papa's Belgian classmates agreed with—particularly Jean-Luc, who always nodded a bit too enthusiastically for Papa's liking—and then he would ask Papa to provide a counter-argument, *"qu'est ce que tu pense?"* Papa being not yet informed on the specifics of Congolese, and African history, would struggle to offer a retort, but he remembered *ba nzembo* his mother used to sing to him to sleep before she passed. He remembered the story of *Bakanza* who fiercely resisted the colonial missionary's attempt to convert him to Christianity and held on strongly to his ancestral traditions until the moment he was killed. Or that of *Mbikudi*, the would be King who saved his village from attack. Papa thought how they must have come from time immemorial; these stories were not told by the Belgian teachers in his school; or even his teachers in Congo, who mostly taught the history of Belgium, and only spoke of Congo as if it started with the arrival of the Europeans.

There were other moments when Professor Gibeaud would rally a rousing response in defense of the Congolese people, speaking of the powerful Kingdom of Kongo, the complex civilization of the Twa, and the ancient mathematics of the Ishango. Here, he spoke as though he were one of them; as if it had been his grandparents who had had their hands chopped off in the field for not producing enough rubber on the plantations, or as if it were *he* who had lost his entire family in the genocide of ten million Congolese killed during Leopold's reign.

Professor Gibeaud's discussions on this subject always left a lingering thought in Papa's mind. He wondered why people did not react with the same visceral disgust at Leopold's name as they did with Hitler's. For if a flower by any other name still smells as sweet, then what is the smell of evil?

Professor Gibeaud was a mathematician, but more so, a philosopher; *true liberation is having freedom of thought*, he'd say and would always urge the class to think critically, before dismissing them. So Papa read and read. He read to prove him wrong, he read to prove him right.

As the months passed, Papa began to settle in this new and foreign city; it was strange for him because the familiarity of the language, which made him feel comfortable, was overridden by the unfamiliarity of the culture, people, and lifestyle. On days where he could not tolerate being stared at, followed around in the local supermarket, accused of stealing, having a banana skin thrown at him, or being spoken to really, *really* slowly (the thing he hated the most), he would choose to spend his days alone, in his room, surrounded by books, reading.

Papa also began to make friends. Although there were many young Congolese who had come to the country to further their studies, it was not easy to discover them. Many of them were the children of dignitaries; ministers and wealthy businessmen— unlike Papa who was only there because he had been one of the top five achievers in his school and therefore was granted a scholarship to study abroad. Ultimately they occupied different spaces and as they did not know of each other before, there was very little reason for them to know each other now. Or, it could have been that perhaps, when their daily treatment became insufferable, they too retreated to the safe space of their bedrooms. But Papa was quietly proud and confident, he made friends with many people beyond his own.

He met Phelix, who had also come from Kinshasa to further his studies; an aspiring engineer, a short young man with a pentagonal shaped head, which appeared as though it was too large for his body, but had a deep voice seeming to belong to a man twice his size. There was a freeness about him Papa could not quite understand, he was very studious, intelligent, bright, but he abused alcohol; he drank each can of beer as though the production was due to cease. The effects leading to slurred singing of unrecognizable lullabies and sloppiness.

Phelix loved women; exclusively Belgian white women, it appeared to Papa, as he never saw Phelix with the very few Congolese girls who were also found to be studying abroad, or any other women for that matter. It was also the way he spoke of them, as if he had discovered something he could not comprehend how he had gone so long without. This made Papa think of Mami, and how she would be if she too were here; he even thought of how they would be had he stayed. Phelix was amicable, and had seen something in Papa not many others saw. He called Papa *vieaux*; old; reflective of his actions which were similar to those of a wise elder. So Phelix stayed close, usually either inviting or dragging Papa out to embrace the world and not be stuck in the recesses of his mind. Phelix too, was a philosopher, of some sort; there is only one life, so drink, smoke, do what you will for each day we are nearing our last; *boko pekisa ngai pamba*. And although Papa learned to appreciate his philosophy, reason being it could exist and it did, he never adopted it for his own life. He knew his limits, and chose to live by them.

Whilst Papa was retreating from the world once more, Phelix came knocking, this time bringing a few more friends. They arrived at his dorm room.

"*Tock, tock, tock.*" Phelix announced his arrival; he would always announce instead of knocking which confused Papa but also filled him with anticipation, "*Vieux fungola porte.*"

Papa opened the door and saw the two tall Congolese looking men, towering behind, before he saw Phelix. He greeted Phelix enthusiastically and welcomed them all in. Claude and Paul introduced themselves warmly. They looked at each other as if they could have known each other before and felt only the kind of familiarity present in a foreign place among people of a common origin.

As they sat in the cramped room in the presence of one another, where the length of Papa's long outstretched arms could almost reach end to end, it felt as if they were back in Kinshasa. They spoke only in *Lingala* to each other now, a bit louder and more vibrantly than usual, in the way you hold on stronger to something when you feel it slipping away.

"Vieux, yaka to bima. Feti eza ko zela biso."

"Ah, Phelix, na lembi. Na za ko tanga."

"Eh! Lelo Samedi. Te! Lelo te! Naboyi. Lata sapatu, toza ko bima dans five minutes."

Papa shrugged, but obliged. Although he wasn't opposed to the idea of a night out of drinking and dancing, it was, after all, a Saturday night, and Phelix did claim he knew all the best places to go. Papa did not want to appear too enthusiastic for he worried about becoming easily influenced so he got ready slowly. He put on his brown faded jacket, his worn leather shoes more grey in color than black, and headed out.

chapter 15

THE STREETS OF BRUSSELS COULD HAVE easily been mistaken for a library, or a museum; it was quiet and calm as if everything was on display from a time before, which was what Papa liked about it. The only thing saving this dullness was the life and energy the young students carried with them. The small group commanded a lot of attention when they walked the streets. Four tall (well three tall and one who looked like their little brother) young African men, with narrow waists and wide shoulders, in an all-white city.

Phelix's short, fast-paced steps lead the way, always walking in front taking three steps to their every one, seeming as though he struggled where they strolled. They boarded the tram for a short while, eventually they got off and walked to a small bar, hidden in the back alleyway of a quiet street Papa did not know.

Papa did not manage to catch the name of the bar written in red above the door as they walked in; he did not care to know it too much either, for he already knew he was never going back there. He was distracted by the burly security guard with the shiny bald head appearing to glimmer in the darkness. He captured Papa's attention. He had not seen a Belgian man of such a size before, he was not aware there were any so large. The man looked as though he had been fed, since birth, a steady Congolese diet of *fufu* and *fumbua*. A substantial diet, only without the excess heat for him to sweat it off. Maybe he had been born in Kinshasa, there were many Belgians who were. Many were born there and never left; they stayed, married a Congolese, or not, and adopted a new identity. Papa realized this, as a child, the first time he heard a Belgian man speaking *Lingala*; it was as if the man's mouth had colonized his body; reinverting what was considered the norm, even everything else about him had changed, he was not as stiff, as upright, he spoke and vibrated as if there was fire dancing on his tongue.

Papa wondered if this burly man also spoke *Lingala*, if there was a different vibration in him too. The man looked over sternly, whilst they were finding their seats, and Papa looked away realizing he had been staring too long.

There was nothing special in this place; empty walls with no décor, poor choice of music playing in the background, nothing tempting you to leave the house and embrace the cold; there was some kind of animal busk at the counter, an antelope or a deer, Papa did not know the difference. The only mentionable quality of this place's worth was it was filled with the kind of girls Phelix adored. He was giddy and smiled ear to ear the way children do when they receive a surprise gift. Claude and Paul also seemed content; they smiled, politely, sipping their beers whilst Papa drank his glass bottle of Coca-Cola.

There was singing and dancing, partying and good times, an uninhibited atmosphere let loose by the aid of alcohol; all of the things making Papa wish he had stayed at home and continued with the book he was reading on the human body and medical discoveries; how the ancient Egyptians had used moldy bread to treat their ill and how moldy bread contained penicillin.

He looked at his watch: *8:30 p.m.*, *8:33 p.m.*, *8:34 p.m.*.. It frustrated him, *8:37 p.m.*; even more. Phelix was having the time of his life dancing with a girl who had taken his fancy, locked hips, swinging to the rhythm of the music. Papa, for the first time, noticed how he was dressed; black leather jacket, with an oversized light blue shirt—too big for him as most things were—and a pair of faded jeans. Claude and Paul remained seated with Papa, drinks in their hands, they seemed a lot more reserved, and cautious, or it may be the alcohol had not yet hit their blood stream.

A group of young Belgian men walked through the door. A raucous bunch; also students, as it appeared. They took residence on a set of tables in the corner, on the opposite side of the small room. They were four. Papa observed. There was nothing particularly outstanding about them; he tried to see if he recognized any faces, they could have been anyone from the fellow students in his class, or the shelf stackers who worked the local supermarket where he shopped for groceries and was served reluctantly. Their entitled loudness escalated but was not noticed as much as Papa and Phelix's loudness with their friends; for their loudness was seen before it was heard.

The group looked over at Phelix, whose hips were still locked with the girl several songs after, tapping each other and pointing. One of the boys in their group stood, and walked towards them and then past to the dance floor. He was frail, walked as though he was going to fall over after each step and wore a blue chequered cotton jumper, faded from the number of times it had been washed. He walked right in between and pushed Phelix and the girl apart, wiping the wide grin off Phelix's face.

"*Qu'est ce que tu fais?*" Phelix spurted out angrily.

"*C'est ma femme!*" He said, pointing to his own chest.

"*Oh, Alex, lesse moi!*" the girl shouted at him.

"*Reni!*" he hollered back.

The music halted. Alex tried to grab her by the arm, she fought herself free. Phelix came in between them, the smallest of the three, trying to separate him from her.

The boys at both tables; Phelix's group, and Alex's group, stood on red alert; a pack of hyenas ready to pounce. The burly security guard with the shiny bald head came stomping over.

"*Qu'est ce qu'il y a? Qu'est ce qu'il y a?*" he repeated. He had dealt with this many times before and was tired of being disturbed.

'*Rien, Rien.*" Alex repeated, in the same vein, letting go of the girl's hand he had grabbed. He walked away. Both tables sat. The music returned. Phelix returned to his table in a huff. He resembled a blown up puffer fish.

"*Boir.*" Claude slid the bottle of beer over to Phelix to drink, offering a remedy. Alex was sat on his table, with his group, simmering; a pot of water brought to boil. He stared, making eye contact or not at all. Papa looked at his watch: *9:45 p.m.*, *9:47 p.m.*, *9:50 p.m.* He felt an unease sweep into him like dust into an empty room. *10:01 p.m.*

"*Phelix, on y vas,*" Papa suggested they leave, he spoke with an anxious tone in his voice as he watched Phelix drink can after can in a short period of time.

"*Non!*" Phelix shouted back, slamming the now empty beer can on the table hard enough to smash. Papa had not seen Phelix act this way before, he had expected it, because he knew what alcohol did to people, but this had changed him so much from the bright boy he knew. *10:30 p.m.* Papa's discomfort grew; he felt a queasiness in his stomach he was no longer used to. He was no longer the kid carrying sticks in his bag where his books should be, in case he needed to teach someone a lesson.

He picked up his jacket, stood, put it on, and told Phelix to do the same. Phelix refused. Claude and Paul remained seated; faces blank as the empty walls of the bar they sat in. Papa, grunted, and huffed, then left the bar walking past the stares of the group in the corner, and the burly man with the shiny bald head.

Papa eventually arrived home, the home he now called home, in his small dorm room, where everything felt safe and secure. He threw his brown faded jacket on the floor, and flung his worn leather shoes across the room. He had walked, and walked, and walked, bracing the cold, not knowing the direction he took but knowing he would eventually arrive. He was tired, the only kind of tired you get from walking for a long time; how your shoulders slumped forward, your back forgets its upright position, and your feet feel a burning sensation as though it was bare on sun-beaten concrete. He laid down in a slump on his bed; the embodiment of a sack of potatoes being dropped, staring at the ceiling, angry, frustrated, and confused. Angry at Phelix, frustrated at himself, and confused as to how things managed to spiral out of his control. He lay, and slowly fell asleep; falling into a warm dream of Mami, a Kinshasa sun, and waist-swinging rhumba. Abruptly all that faded with a loud bang on the door.

"*Tock! Tock! Tock!*"

Papa sprung upright in shock, *Phelix?* He rubbed the sleep from his eyes. He looked at his watch: *2:10 a.m.* He waited, sat startled, upright; maybe he had imagined it.

"*TOCK! TOCK! TOCK!*" this time louder and more urgent than before. Papa leapt forward and opened the door so fast a gust of wind swept inside. Phelix barged his way in, open-mouthed, tongue hanging, panting, in a state of shock; eyes in a wild frenzy. He sat on the bed with his head in hands. He looked rough; the kind of rough that is not done alone.

"*Osali nini?!*" Papa enquired, asking what he had done; but really asking what trouble had he brought back with him. Papa's voice trembling with fear. He stepped out of the door to check if there was anyone behind him. Phelix did not speak, he stood and lifted his blue shirt, which Papa noticed was now torn and ripped, and missing several buttons, and revealed a huge gash on the side of his lower abdomen; the contrast of the bright red blood, on the bright blue shirt caught Papa by surprise, he wondered how had he not noticed it when Phelix walked in.

"*Yo mutu olingi ko koma Docteur, te? Yaka ko sala.*" Phelix spoke, voice broken into pieces. Papa went to the shared bathroom along the hallway, and returned with bandages and wipes to clean the blood which had now slowed to a drip, and left little red dots on the carpet floor. Papa assumed the position of Doctor, as Phelix had demanded, and began treating his wound, in a heavy cloud of silence, which Phelix eventually broke as he told what had happened.

After Papa had left, they stayed at the bar, no longer drinking, or enjoying the music, but simply sitting; silent and stiff. It was closing time. The girl, Reni, who had come with a friend, walked home on her own after they left each other. Phelix noticed Alex, the boy, following her from some distance behind, unknown to Reni, so he followed him following her. Claude and Paul were walking behind and following them. Alex eventually caught up to Reni, he grabbed her by her arms overpowering her as she let out a loud scream echoing into the empty streets and hollow buildings. Phelix charged from behind with the force of a man twice his size and pushed Alex so hard they both fell and rolled over a few times on top of each other. Reni ran off in a panic, screaming. Scrambling to get up, on their knees, they squared up to each other and tussled, brawled and scrapped on the floor. Claude and Paul caught up from behind and threw Alex off Phelix, who was underneath being pounded. It was now three to one, but Alex sneered with a crazed look on his face, ready to fight to the death; it was as if he became larger and stronger than what his frail body had previously been.

From behind came a loud blow; either Claude or Paul must have got hit with something, Phelix did not look back to see but it was something heavy because when it landed it shook the ground beneath them. They were ambushed. Alex's group, the other three boys, attacked and fought them bloody. Phelix was on the ground, face being pummelled with heavy fists, when he felt a sharp stabbing pain in his side. He did not know where it came from or even from *whom* but he remembered the cold of the blade before it pierced his soft skin like a knife into fresh fruit. Phelix mustered the last strength he had and ran, shouting at Claude and Paul to run too.

The three scattered in different directions, daring not to look back. Phelix was too scared to go to the hospital, if he did his university would find out, and he was certain he would lose his scholarship. So Phelix ran, and ran, and ran, until his little legs eventually carried him to Papa's dorm.

"*Soki ozalaki wana . . .*" Phelix said as the tears now streamed from his face, "*tolingaki ko beta bango!*" he punched his fist into his open palm. Papa did not think about this. He did not think about how they would have won the fight had he not left. He did not think about seeking revenge or getting anyone back, instead he thought about reading, and how, earlier in the evening, had he decided to keep reading, he would not have been a part of any of this. He let Phelix sleep on the bed where he could be comfortable, and could at least roll over to sleep on the side of his body that was not wounded. Papa slept on the floor, in the small space not wide enough for him to even roll over in.

For the next few weeks, Papa would carry a big stick in his bag where his books were, in case those boys showed themselves again, and needed to be taught a lesson.

chapter 16

GOING TO CHURCH WAS AN ACT of going back home. It was a miracle how the collective religious experience of attending church could close the gap of the thousands of miles it would take to make that journey. People did not only come to hear the word of God, they came to hear the word of *their* God. Their God spoke *Lingala*, their language; with their vivacity, their energy and passion; their words dancing and moving in the same way they did, words and a language they had to hide.

The church is an exiled space, a place neither here nor there, carrying hearts that both long to stay and long to return but in bodies that have been turned away by both. And if God is here, in the church, and has made this journey with them, then maybe God also knows what it means to be a refugee.

To the children, every Sunday was a journey, an adventure outside of their mundane, everyday experience, into another world unveiling itself, a world they knew only with faintness; it was the blind person learning to read braille; beginning to feel with their fingertips what was written in the world, the words coming to life in front of their eyes with each sentence; it was a deaf person slowly beginning to hear, and the first sound is the same song being sung inside them.

Pastor Kaddi spoke with so much vigor that by the time he was finished he would be drenched in sweat, forming patches in his armpits and neck area, changing the color of his shirt to a darker shade, showing an outline of the vest he wore underneath. He preached urgently, so much so you could feel the word alive inside him, as though it bounced around looking for an escape. The congregation listened, ready to receive as if their ears were landing pads for these flying words. When he prayed, everyone closed their eyes, and not only did they listen, they imagined; it was as though he was the one who carried the flame and led them through an eternal darkness.

He prayed for many things in the world; he prayed for peace for those in war, he prayed for food for the hungry, and shelter for the homeless, he prayed for love for those without, for marriage and for work. The most resonating was the prayer for citizenship; an incantation for those without papers, which was the situation for many of the congregation; their only wish, to receive their "papers" or "*mukanda*" as it was called; the right to remain in the country.

The question on the edge of everyone's lips was often "*Ozui mukanda?*" It was the climb to the top of the mountain, it was Daniel escaping the Lion's Den, or Jonah being freed from the stomach of the Whale, it was reaching the Promised Land after years of wandering the desert, a miracle on equal par, it was a sign there was a higher power who showed eternal grace and favor toward you. Conversely, if someone was deported, it was a curse, an eternal damnation, and more often than not, quite simply, a sign the person had sinned and was now bearing the consequences of their actions.

Those who had yet to receive their papers lived in a kind of perpetual purgatory. It was not that going back was bad—many longed to one day return—but not in this way. They did not want to be deported, forced to leave, like you are also forced to return; no one wishes for such volatility. For now, they lived day by day, waiting for the time when the judgment of a higher power would seal their fate and deliver their verdict. It was not just Papa, Mami and the children, or Tonton and Patricia; it was the *entire* congregation. All, apart from Pastor Kaddi and the other chosen few.

Pastor Kaddi had received his papers quite quickly compared to the rest. He had only been in the country for a few years now, and had worked every job under the sun, including none. His current day job, which he saw as divine provision, was in security at a large corporate firm working day and night shifts. It paid well and regularly. It came to him after a long bout of unemployment and being on benefits, which coupled itself with a well-masked depression.

The community, who knew much less of him then, saw it as some inexplicable unworldly possession. For days at a time, sometimes weeks, Pastor Kaddi did not clean or dress himself, his meals came few and far between, and he left the house even less so. He was not a pastor at this time. In fact, there was not a thing he was but a man unfulfilled and undefined in a land alien to him.

Pastor Kaddi felt compelled—this is the way he re-tells the story in his sermons—to pray, not ask, but demand to God there be a divine intervention. He prayed and gave sacrifice; he would sleep on the floor, away from the comfort of his bed, duvet, and pillow, he would fast from sunrise to sunset, not listen to worldly music, go dancing to bars or clubs, or even entertain women, in the way he so famously enjoyed entertaining them. He prayed and prayed and prayed. Until one day, and so timely, a few weeks into this forbearance, Pastor Kaddi received a letter from the Home Office granting him indefinite leave to remain in the UK, and shortly after he would begin the process of naturalization as a citizen. Subsequently, within a few weeks of this, Pastor Kaddi was informed by the Job Centre that he had been offered a job.

Pastor, just Kaddi at this moment, felt compelled to share this miraculous manifestation with his community. His fortune was no random act of chance but a manifestation of his faith; proof *"Nzambe azali awa,"* God is here, alive and present, and at work, for those who believed. With his passion, dynamism and eloquent storytelling, he quickly became Pastor. However, in this case, Pastor was not comparable to Professor or Doctor, it was not a title you acquired by going to school or receiving an education; it was not a qualification or training, not here. It was a calling based on the works appearing in your life. And it was only then that the community accepted you. This was his path.

Papa and Mami began regularly attending the Church Tonton had brought them to, even on the days when he was late or had not accompanied them at all. Tonton's Saturday nights were often heavy; the ooze of alcohol and sex would seep from his skin when he arrived home and send him crashing into a virtual coma leaving him sleeping for hours, sometimes days.

More often than not, Papa and Mami brought Jean and Marie with them; Jean trying so hard to stay awake, his head would frequently bounce forward during Pastor Kaddi's electrifying sermon performance, whilst Marie had her face in a book; either the Bible, or something about the Bible as though she was studying it.

Mami had grown closer in friendship with Patricia; beyond the phone calls, she began to occasionally visit the family, and was well received. They would often laugh into the night until she left again. Patricia was the notably unmarried woman of the Church, soft-natured but layered with the hardness of someone who had run many laps in life's race. Her perseverance showed as if she had started off running with shoes, but was now barefoot. Although she was actually older than Mami, she was considered young due to her unwed state. It was considered more as an affliction, a malediction than a choice. The insufferable condition of singledom, a condition women should seek to escape rather than embrace. A girl would not be considered a "*Mama*"—which was not necessarily based on motherhood, for many *Mamas* did not have children, another damnation—until they married.

For the men, the same game was played with an entirely different set of rules; it did not depend on either marriage or parenthood. Something even Marie would eventually come to notice very early on but would only speak about later once the affliction would be passed on to her.

"Today we will read . . . from Hebrew . . . Chapter 11 . . . verse 1 and 2," Pastor Kaddi captivated the congregation, "We shall begin reading in the name of the Father, the Son and of the Holy Ghost." He read as if he had an electric guitar placed in his throat and was played by the hands of *Franco Luambo*. Mami sat looking, not at him, but into him, armed with a pen and the small notepad she carried with her to church every Sunday. Marie sat beside, watching her watch him.

Now faith is the substance of things hoped for, the evidence of things not seen. For by it, the elders obtained a good report.

"My brothers and sisters, God is good. Hallelujah."

"A-MEN." the congregation replied rapturously.

"It took FAITH for Moses to lead his people out of bondage! It took faith for Daniel to get free from the Lion's Den! It took faith for Job to endure his malediction and win God's favor once more! I say it IS faith because FAITH is alive; and it will take the same faith to deliver you and I, my brothers and sisters, Hallelujah!"

"A-MEN."

"Brothers and Sisters, I am a personal example of God's endless favor. I entrust upon you today that whatever you believe, you will achieve . . . by the grace of HIS name, as I did." Pastor Kaddi continued delivering a most impassioned sermon, all the while pouring with sweat, as if the Spirit was oozing out from within him; a symbol of his hard work and dedication.

Once the sermon had concluded and the congregation had finished swimming in their salvation, Patricia approached Mami after the service, this time with tenderness in her voice as if her words were two hands clasped together in prayer, "Sister, I need to speak with you."

Tuesday night arrived and Patricia had come around to visit for dinner as they had planned on Sunday. It was her, Mami and Marie. Jean was too busy avoiding awkward conversation by hiding in his bedroom and Papa was at work. Tonton was out. They sat having dinner whilst watching the television. It was a weekday evening, which meant it was time for one soap opera or another; *EastEnders, Coronation Street, Emmerdale, Brookside, Sunset Beach, Dallas, Eldorado*, you name it, Mami watched them all. It was almost as if she was conducting an anthropological study; a field observation into the lives of the people who in real life denied her access because of the otherness placed on her which she could not explicitly articulate. However, in this fictional realm, she was given full silent participation, through which she learned of their habits, traits and mannerisms, from the food they ate to the way they spoke; it was similar to being invited around for dinner but you were a silent eater at the table.

Patricia was comfortably placed between the unfamiliarity of tonight's viewing (*EastEnders*) and the beautiful welcoming setting of a well-prepared meal, plate as full as the moon, in a loving home.

"Mami . . ." Patricia started the conversation as the pounding drums of the closing theme song to the show played in the background. Mami picked up the remote and lowered the volume. With a head nod, she signaled to Marie to clear the plates and leave the room.

"Yes, darling . . ." Mami replied.

"You are such a kind woman, with a big heart. I really need your help . . ."

"Of course." Mami felt the weight of this conversation slowly fall upon her. It is almost proverbial: big sister does not come to little sister for help, unless all her pride has disintegrated into dust.

"Please tell me what can I do?"

"Since I have come here, I have been told how life will be easier for me. I was told I will be able to provide for my family back home, and give more for them here than I would have if I was still with them over there. But I come here and I have nothing, my hands are empty. I cannot even send anything back, something small; some toys, clothes, books, nothing. I avoid phone calls because at the end of every phone call, I know they will ask for money to help them. And I cannot keep making empty promises. How can I help any of them if I cannot even help myself?"

She buried her face deep into her hands as if she was collecting the tears streaming down her face. Mami reached for the conveniently placed box of tissues on the table and passed one to her. Patricia blew her nose ferociously and wept on.

"Mama, how can I help you?" Mami asked place her arm over Patricia's shoulder to comfort her.

"I need a job. I need money. I can do anything."

"I will speak to my husband, maybe he can help you get a job cleaning . . ."

"But I don't have papers, I cannot work . . ."

"Don't worry, God will provide."

The anguish in both their voices was enough to break the foundations of the floor beneath them.

"It is one thing to not want to help, but it is another to want to help in every single way you can but not have the power to do a single thing." Mami lamented to Papa after he came home from work.

"I'll see what I can do."

chapter 17

COMING BACK TO SCHOOL AFTER THE condemnation and disappointment following Parent's Evening was no small feat for Jean; he walked as if his body hurt in new places he had yet to feel. As the months passed he avoided eye contact, with almost everyone, particularly those who knew him best. To look into their eyes, Jean felt, would be allowing them to read the pain submerged within him. He did not want to speak, his jaw felt locked and lead-heavy. It felt as though his mouth was covered with duct tape and inside it, his teeth ground together into dust. He appreciated silence more; from himself and others. Silence meant no questions were asked, and if no questions were asked, no questions had to be answered.

"Jean!" he heard a distinct recognizable voice call out to him at break time whilst he sat alone at the top of the playground away from the rest of the children. He looked up to see—a natural reaction he could not avoid—but he already knew it was James. He was running toward him with hesitant excitement; there was never energy lacking in this child, even in the sombre moments, though it was often misplaced. He would be the kind you'd find smiling at a funeral, whilst everyone else was sad at the loss of the beloved person, he would be filled with happiness in remembrance of the sacred memories shared.

"You alright?" He eventually caught up with Jean, panting heavily, trying to retrieve the breath he had lost.

"Why are you out of breath for?"

"Just tired, don't worry, mate."

"Listen, I've got a detention 'cos I didn't do my English homework, init, but wait around and I'll meet you outside after school, yeah?"

"Nah, I can't."

"Why? Where you going?"

"I'm going home."

"But you always wait."

"This time, I've gotta go."

"Why? What's wrong?" James asked curiously worried.

"Nothing . . ." Jean's eyes averted James, looking instead above his head, as if he observed something dangling there.

"Are you sure, mate? It doesn't sound like nothing."

"Leave it, yeah."

"Mate . . ." James put his hand on his shoulder showing concern.

"Leave it!" Jean snapped and pushed his hand away. He walked off at the timely sound of the bell signaling the end of break time, leaving James standing with hands wide open in confusion.

"Hello . . ." Marie answered the house phone, in her light and airy voice.

"Hi, can I speak to Mr. N-tanga please?" a quite jovial sounding man enquired.

Papa observed, attention now switched away from the TV to Marie. Papa was having a rare afternoon off; with the *Metro* newspaper opened halfway, he had just finished a huge coma-inducing meal of *kwanga, soso* and *ndunda* and was now watching the music videos of *Koffi Olomide* on VHS. Mami had gone shopping, and was somewhere unknown. Tonton was out.

Marie held the phone in the air, stretching the cord as far as it could go, for Papa to come forward and speak.

"It's for you," she whispered.

"Tuna soki eza nani?"

"Can I ask who is speaking?" Marie asked, promptly following instructions.

"Oh, of course. It's Mr. David, Jean's tutor, from Havilland School."

"It's Jean's teacher . . . Mr. David."

"Aa-argh." Papa let out an unsatisfied grunt, anticipating the bad news to come.

"Naza te."

"He said he's not in," Marie continued to mediate.

"Tell him, it's about Jean. It's good news." Mr. David replied, in a chuckle. Marie held the phone to him once more, and Papa quickly grabbed it avoiding further embarrassment.

"Yes . . ." Papa answered hesitantly, as if he were approaching a kind of threat standing in front of him.

"Hello. Mr. N-tanga, how are you? I won't take too much of your time . . ."

"Mmm hmm."

". . . I'm calling to say Jean has shown incredible improvement in his behavior in school lately, he's done really well on his report. He's been getting high marks all around. I wanted to let you know, so you can encourage Jean to continue the good work!" Mr. David spoke loudly and excitedly, in a flurry, as if he were throwing his words at Papa to catch them all with nothing but his two hands.

"Okay. Thank you." Papa replied, and ended the conversation.

"Alobi nini?" He asked Marie, who remained standing there the whole time.

"Dad, he said Jean's been doing really well in school."

Papa's smile burst forth with color as if a hand had grabbed a rainbow and threw it across a dull grey sky. It stretched far and wide, across his face, from one end to the other like the belt of the equator. Marie looked at him and noticed how straight his teeth were, and how she rarely ever got to see him smile. Papa looked at Marie, who was now also smiling, caught by this contagious thing, and whisked her into the air singing and dancing around the room. The sound of the key and the front door opening preceded Mami's entrance, *"Allo!"* she announced, and walked into the living room met with surprise.

"Boni boye?"

"Dad is happy because Jean is doing well in school . . ." Marie enlightened, "his teacher, Mr. David called."

"Oh, very good." Mama replied and placed the heavy shopping bags on the floor. *"Wapi Jean?"* Mami asked. *"JEAN!"* Mami hollered, voice echoing off the walls.

"I'm right here." Jean appeared out of nowhere from behind them. They looked at him with confusion, questions written on their faces.

"I was right behind you. You left the door wide open," he explained, "anyway, why is there so much noise?"

"Mwana na ngai." Papa bellowed. *My son.* Jean was not used to hearing this. It was usually saved for big occasions such as birthday parties, which they did not do often; at least not for him.

He was a boy; boys were expected to grow out of birthdays from an early age, and once you're a man, you're a man, nothing much else left to celebrate; not even your wedding day is yours. Age becomes meaningless, what matters after is what you acquire. Jean had long stopped thinking about birthdays, and his birthday wasn't for another six months. *My son.* It was also reserved for when something serious had happened, such as a major accident or a loved one passing, but Papa sounded too happy to be announcing the death of a loved one. *My son.*

"You have made me proud . . ." he continued, another smile broke free. Jean also noticed how Papa's teeth were so straight and well aligned they resembled a row of desks in an exam hall.

"What did I do?" Jean replied nervously.

"Mr. David called . . ." Papa paused; Jean remained still in his silence. "He told me how well you have been doing in school, and how you have improved! Well done!"

Papa hugged him, grabbed him close and ruffled his hair back and forth, messing it. Jean shuffled nervously, smiled and swept his hand forward through his hair to straighten the wave pattern in his hair he had been quietly working on with a brush and the doo-rag he wore to sleep at night. *My son.* It was also reserved for when he was to be claimed as Papa's son, a declaration to the world a worthwhile progeny had been created.

"Thanks, Dad." Jean replied sheepishly.

"Well, I'm very proud of you too," Mami added, and gave him a gentle warm embrace. "But I'm also very tired, and I now have to cook."

"No. No cooking tonight," Papa announced enthusiastically, "tonight we eat pizza!" The children cheered with excitement. "Jean, here's ten pounds. Go to the shop and buy it."

"Papa, how was it growing up in Congo?" Jean asked whilst they ate the pizza.

"Oh, my son." He burst out with a chuckle; this excitement surprised Jean. "I'm happy you ask, but you don't need to worry . . ."

"It's just you never talk about it."

"I have many stories to tell you. You know, growing up, we had a good life but not always. We did not know how hard things truly were in the country; we thought everybody in the world lived like us."

"Really?" Jean replied sounding astonished.

"I left the country twice, each time for very different reasons. The first time was before your mother and I were married.

Before Marie was born, and even before you. The second time
. . ." Papa recalled to Jean, who was sat wide-eyed on the floor
staring into this man, his father, as if they had just met; as if he
was finding out who he truly was for the first time.

chapter 18

"DAD, YOU'VE GOT A LETTER." JEAN walked back into the house to pass it to Papa as he noticed it stuck in the letterbox on his way out to play football with friends in the local park. It was early Friday evening and he had been allowed out, particularly now that he had improved and was grasping the benefits of responsible behavior. Papa took the letter from him, and remained seated on the sofa. The envelope of the letter was brown, and the paper inside was white, a bright white, as seen through the window of it. The brown envelope letters were usually more official, from the council or the government. Papa did not trust brown envelope letters at all, they made him anxious, suspicious, even more so than white envelope letters, which were usually bills, which he also didn't like but preferred.

The only letters Papa actually liked were those from family back home, which came in a white envelope with red and blue stripes, and contained heartfelt prose and family pictures, which they would gather and read together. But those came few and far in between.

Papa avoided this brown envelope letter for the time being; he threw it nonchalantly onto the table and returned to watching TV. Mami came bursting through from the kitchen to the living room, with the house phone in her hand, hollering and screaming, "*Eh! Eh! Eh!*" and disrupting Papa's watching of the afternoon cooking show.

"*Nini?*" Papa asked pleadingly, in a frustrated tone, wondering what on earth it could be causing this eruption in Mami. She did this from time to time and it annoyed him because most of the time it was about nothing he felt worthy of disturbing his peace.

"*Oyo nini?*" Mami enquired as she immediately noticed the brown envelope letter on the table and wanted to know it's contents before she could start talking.

"*Nayebi te.*" Papa replied, claiming he did not know and had not seen it. She picked up the letter and grabbed it, both hands tightly clutching the paper.

"Look!" she shoved it into Papa's hands forcing him to take a look, "*ekomi nini?*"

Mami waited nervously and impatiently, for Papa to read it and tell her.

Papa opened the letter begrudgingly. "I have been taken to court."

"*Eh?*" Mami replied, confused.

"I don't understand." Papa replied sounding even more confused than her.

"*Wapi Jean?*" Mami asked in a panic, "*Jean! Jean!*" She bellowed to no reply.

"*Aza te.*"

"*Ake wapi?*"

"*A bimi.*"

Mami grunted at being told Jean was not in, she knew he would be playing football, which she found a waste of time; it annoyed her even more.

"*Marie-eh! Marie!*" Mami bellowed out.

"Yes, mum . . . ?" Marie replied, a faded distant voice in the background.

"*Yaka!*"

Marie swiftly followed instructions, the pitter patter of feet along the corridor got louder until she appeared before the worried face of Mami who had called her.

"What's wrong?" Marie asked instinctively, seeing the looks on their faces.

"Read this letter for us, explain it." Mami asked, her voice seasoned with worry.

You have summarily been summoned to appear before Highbury Magistrates Court in regards to . . .

"It says you have to go to court. Papa, are you in trouble?" Marie sounded worried; her light, usually happy voice trembled with fear for her father.

"No." Papa replied, in a disguised comforting tone, firm and sure, "I am not in trouble. There is nothing to worry about."

Mami looked at him with a new found worry of her own, her eyes holding back the tears welling up, trying to be strong and reassured so as not to relay this new burden onto Marie or anyone else. Papa took the letter back from Marie.

"But I thought only bad people get taken to court?" Marie asked, confused.

"It is bedtime now." Papa replied trying to sound as routine as ever, as if there was no implosion in their lives, as if ignoring the boulder that had just landed upon them crushing their dreams, as if all was calm.

"Okay." Marie replied despondently. She was old enough to sense the trouble in the air, but too young to ask any further and demand to be told about it.

Papa stood from his slump on the sofa and hugged Marie, kissing her on the forehead. She was smart beyond her years; he knew she would worry, as though it were her problem, if she knew too much. "Focus on school." He added as she walked out of the room, to distract her from the burden of this problem; as if it could help here, now, as if school was the solution to their problems. Papa picked up the letter to look and pulled it close to his face to analyze it as if there was something he could have missed; maybe it was addressed to the wrong person; a case of mistaken identity, or at the bottom of the letter there was an apology for the inconvenience, a change of mind, or a prank even, anything to answer the small flurry of prayers now flying from his heart since he had seen the word "court."

Having to go to court was not the issue striking the chord of fear into Papa's heart, it was the consequences of going to court, it was the decision made afterward, and what it meant for them. Anyone in the community who had gone to court, usually shortly after were not seen again; they were deported, returned, or removed. Court was simply purgatory, where you waited until you received your fate. There were others who spoke casually of court and authorities; lawyers, policemen, but for Papa this was not the case, the authorities were heavy on his tongue, they turned his tongue to lead, he desired not to speak of them, or even to them. He did not wish to cross paths with the authorities not because he hated them, there was no malice, no disdain or anger towards them, on his behalf, it was more so because they were the ones who made the decision of whether or not they could be deported or removed, and calling them for one thing, could lead to another, so it was best not to call at all. It was best to avoid all contact, most times the family would forget and get on with their daily lives, however, every now and then, a reminder of this fate, of the sword of Damocles hanging above their heads, the decision of whether or not they could be deported, would come rushing back to strike a kind of terror in their hearts.

"What is it for?" Mami asked.

"For two jobs; something to do with tax, for not declaring two jobs." Papa replied defeated.

"What does that mean? What is going to happen now?!"

"I don't know. We will find a way."

"But what if you get . . ."

"We will find a way." Papa interrupted, not allowing her to finish. He reassured Mami who was now sat with him and visibly upset. The thought of court consumed his mind. He wondered who would be overlooking his case, and what decision they would make; most likely a man, most likely English, single or married, perhaps divorced, a father, a family man; maybe he has a little girl who he loves and a son who he worries for, maybe he lays at night anxious about tomorrow, never truly certain what it may bring, maybe he is worried about his job or just wishing for some kind of security in his life, and has a lingering fear tainting the picturesque sunset on his horizon, or maybe there is no stir in his soul, no echo in heart, no longing, no fear, maybe to him, this will be just another job, another case, another decision he has to make.

chapter 19

JAMES HAD NOW PICKED UP THE habit of smoking and it was irritating Jean. He always smelt of cigarettes; on his hands when they would shake them, his clothes when they stood close enough to each other and even his breath when he spoke. Jean did not want to be around him anymore, but he did not want to be seen as if he was the only one who was worried about the smell of cigarettes. It was something all the kids wanted to do, smoke, though only the bravest dared, and this was James in his full act of defiance. Nonetheless, it did not appear natural to him. He did things a little slower now, a little more forcefully, he lagged, appeared to be heavier; slouched shoulders, and cursed much more; a juggling of the *f*, *b*, and *c* words.

Jean did not enjoy hanging around him much anymore, however, he felt obliged to maintain a friendship, at least some kind of allegiance, for you cannot just un-know someone and terminate a friendship, particularly when you attend the same school every day. Nonetheless, he felt a distance between them which was not there before.

Jean smelt the smoke as it passed out of James's mouth and
into the air. He looked at his face, it was an unnatural calm and
collected expression as if someone had set fire to his lungs, and
he was forcefully not trying to notice. They were sat at the top
of the playground after school, hidden away from the suspecting
and curious eyes of teachers and the students who wanted to be
like the teachers.

"Here, hold this." James threw the pack of twenty Benson &
Hedges into the air and it landed perfectly onto Jean's lap.

"No," Jean replied, as if he was disgusted at the suggestion
and hit the pack away from him, which eventually caused a few
cigarettes to spill out from the pack and scatter on the grass.

"Aargh, what are you doing?" James groaned in frustration,
"you're gonna ruin them!"

Jean did not care for what a ruined cigarette was, he had
never even held one and had no intention to, and with no one
else around, he no longer felt he had to pretend. James crawled
onto the floor, cigarette still in hand, and began to pick them
up one by one. In the distance, at the bottom of the playground,
he noticed the outline of a man he did not recognize walking
toward them. He stopped and squinted his eyes to get a better
look, watching the man get closer and closer.

"Oh, shit! It's Mr. Allen."

Jean looked up and froze. He felt a lightning strike of terror run from the top of his head to the bottom of his feet.
Mr. Allen was the Head Teacher, the unhappiest man Jean
had ever met. He did not spare any smiles; they were very
hard to earn. He was bald and clean shaven, and appeared so
strongly built even his forehead had muscles. An ex-British
Army Officer, he had served in the Gulf War, in Bosnia and
in other places forming the glazed stare in his eyes no student
dared stare back into; and even adults too. He walked with
a slight limp, only noticeable with close attention, which,
according to school rumors, was caused by him being shot on

the battlefield and the bullet remaining wedged in his giant calf muscles formed from all the hill running he did in the local park every morning.

A panic-stricken James quickly gathered the cigarettes, swept them underneath Jean's bag, put out the one he was smoking on the grass and planted his right foot on it so it remained hidden underneath his shoe. Jean looked at him eyes wide open, as if James had lost his mind.

"Hello boys!" Mr. Allen spoke in staccato, at the top of his voice as if every word was an announcement in a school assembly. They both sat rigid and back straight, as if they were giving a demonstrating of how to sit with the correct posture. Even James's demeanour had changed, no longer was he defiant, body slouched with curse words.

"It's home time, gentlemen. So what brings you two out here?" Mr. Allen said, and continued to pace up and down rhythmically, 1-2-3 turning on the 4, stopping only to speak. No one responded. James looked at Jean, who was motionless, paralyzed by the fear visibly showing on his face.

"We're just hanging out, Sir?" James replied, voice rising higher in intonation, as if he were asking a question rather than answering.

"Just hanging out." Mr. Allen repeated, this time slower, still in staccato.

"And you N-tanga?" He called everyone by their surname; as if it was a roll call. Jean, underneath the frozen surface, jumped out of his skin when he heard his name. In a school of over a thousand students, the last thing either of them wanted was for the Head Teacher to know their names, especially under this circumstance; he was identified, but maybe there was still a chance of escape for James. Jean did not reply, his muted mouth could not muster the courage; instead he nodded vigorously, as if each nod was an exclamation point at the end of a sentence.

"I see. So can you tell me, gentlemen, why I smell smoke?"

"Smoke, Sir?" James replied, and began sniffing the air around, "I don't smell smoke."

"Don't crack wise with me, Botham." Mr. Allen replied harshly. James's heart sunk.

"I can smell smoke, and not the kind from a fire. Trust me, I would know," Mr. Allen continued sternly, "stand up please."

The boys followed instructions and stood upright as stiff as soldiers in a salute. "Step off the grass." Jean and James looked at each other, communicated in a silent stare. Jean stepped off first, "you too Botham," Mr. Allen insisted. James slowly stepped off the grass first lifting his left foot, and then his right foot, where the cigarette had remained crushed underneath.

"Ah, ha!" Mr. Allen hailed as if he had discovered something significant, "I thought you couldn't smell smoke, ay Botham!" James had no reply. "Ntanga, can you get your bag for me?"

Na kufi! Na kufi! Na kufi! Jean thought to himself, he imagining the consequence of being caught, he imagined too, that this would be the day he died. He hesitated but in the end did not move, acting as though he had not heard the instructions. Mr. Allen looked with widened eyes and a deep stare saying *well, what are you waiting for?* Jean looked at him, and reacted in a startled manner mumbling "sorry, I didn't hear you, Sir," as if to offer an apology Mr. Allen was not interested in.

Jean reached for the straps of his bag and lifted it off the ground and put the bag on his back. Mr. Allen's reaction was not the one of rage or anger they were so used to seeing; where his face would turn red, the veins would appear from his ripped forehead, and he would shout so loud that when he stopped, his voice still echoed for a few moments after. He simply replied with "I see," in the softest voice they'd ever heard from him, and then instructed them to follow him.

Jean and James followed Mr. Allen, struggling to keep up, as he stomped rhythmically as if marching to a voice was shouting *1-2-3-4, 1-2-3-4,* in the background. James had his head down,

staring at the floor the entire time whilst Jean stared at him as though he could take his last breath with his bare hands for all the trouble caused. They walked through the school corridors toward the Head Teacher's office, which was situated on the third floor. The click-clack of the heels of Mr. Allen's shoes echoed loud through the corridors reminding them only of how silent it was now everyone had gone home. This made Jean think of how if something were to happen there would be no witnesses. He was sure it was now they would meet their fate.

They entered the Head Teacher's office. It was the first time either of them had been inside. The main door was large and grand; it made its presence felt, however, it was much different on the inside. As you entered, there was a desk where the PA, who had the most affable demeanour, received visitors and served them with tea and biscuits in a plastic wrapper of two or three. Inside the office, it was very simple; well proportioned, neatly designed. There were ornaments around the office collected from the places he had visited over the years. On his desk were pictures of his family; he had a wife and two children, his wife had bright red ginger hair as though it was on fire, and her smile was wild, a caged bird trying to escape. Their children resembled her the most; hair on fire, and a wide smile. There was no sign of him in them. Mr. Allen was almost unrecognizable in the picture; he had hair. *He had hair?!* Jean stared at the picture with surprise and looked over at James who was doing the same; for a moment their fear subsided; Jean's anger too. They laughed together, in secret, unnoticed.

Mr. Allen motioned for them to sit as he went behind his desk and slid comfortably into his chair. There were two chairs waiting there for them, exactly two. Jean wondered if Mr. Allen always took the students two-by-two into his office when they were in trouble. A Noah's ark for children instead of animals, and only for those who had been unruly and were not going to be saved.

After tapping away on his computer, without saying a word, Mr. Allen picked up the phone, dialled a number, and pressed the phone firmly against his ear. The *ring, ring* of the phone calling could be heard by everyone in the room; *please leave your message after the beep.*

"Good afternoon, this is a message for the parents of James Botham . . ." Mr. Allen spoke once again with his staccato voice whilst leaving the long detailed message. Jean looked at James who appeared to be surprisingly calm. His calmness made Jean fearful of the phone call to his home.

"You see, Sir, my old man's ticker's got a problem . . ." James stepped in sounding confident.

"Your old what? Speak properly, Botham!" Mr. Allen replied, frustrated at James's audacity to speak, let alone speak as though he were one of his mates.

"My father . . ." James spoke, slightly condescendingly, "has a heart problem, which means he ain't . . . I mean, he isn't . . . he is not . . . able to get to the phone, when he does not feel well."

Mr. Allen did not reply. James looked over at Jean and quickly raised his eyebrows up and down, and Jean remembered he had used this story several times before, which meant James's Dad was not at home and probably at the pub, and his Mum never answered the phone. Jean did not find this amusing, James was getting away with something whilst Jean was almost certain someone would answer the phone at his house. They didn't notice Mr. Allen dialing the number and by the time they looked, the phone was already pressed firmly against his ear. The *ring, ring* of the phone was even louder this time; at least to Jean. With each ring his heart beat with fear; the ring and his thumping heartbeat seemed to be synchronized. It continued and he counted each ring: *twelve.* A voice spoke *please leave your message after the beep.*

"Good afternoon, this is a message for the parents of Jean N-tanga . . ." Mr. Allen spoke, once again in staccato, leaving a detailed message. He hung up the phone. Jean felt a great wave of relief wash over him, he could not believe his luck. He looked up at the clock; *4:30 p.m.*, maybe Papa was at work. Mami should be in, and she would have at least got Marie, who was always so eager, to answer the phone. Tonton was out.

"Well, boys, it seems you must have a couple of four-leafed clovers tucked away in your back pockets," they looked at him clueless, "the luck of the Irish? Both of your parents not answering the phone, what are the chances? You have, nonetheless, broken a very serious school rule. I do not take smoking on school premises lightly; not only is it illegal for you to buy cigarettes, but it means you've had them, and a lighter, on you all day during school, and could have endangered other students. So I stand by my two-day suspension, starting tomorrow."

Jean almost dropped to the floor unconscious in shock, *What?! Suspension?!*

"I hope this gives you an opportunity to reflect on your actions. Your parents have been informed. You can leave now." He showed them out.

Parents have been informed . . .? Jean was sweating profusely with anxiety as if the skies had opened above and rained on only him. He realized it must have been when Mr. Allen made the call; he was so relieved no one answered, he did not even think of listening to what was being said in the message he left.

"Two-day suspension, I can't believe it!" James blurted out as they walked along the corridor to leave the school.

"Oh, my God! Two days!" Jean replied.

"I know! It's like a short holiday, I can't wait."

"A holiday?! Are you mad?! This isn't a holiday, I'm dead!"

"What's the big deal? You don't have to go to school for two days," James replied.

"The big deal is I'm going to go home, and I'm going to die, and it's all going to be your fault; all because of some poxy cigarettes."

"Don't try and blame me. It's not my fault."

"Not your fault? YOU'RE THE ONE WHO WAS SMOKING!" Jean shouted in anger, as loud as he ever had; turning heads in the busy high street they had now reached.

James, now realizing how serious this was for Jean, put his hand on Jean's shoulder at an attempt to console him. This angered Jean even further, he did not want to be touched. He reacted, and threw James's arm off him quite aggressively as they carried on walking.

"Why did you do that for?"

"*Why did you do* . . ." Jean mimicked him in mockery. "You're so annoying!" Jean grunted at the end infuriated.

"Alright, calm down, mate."

"Mate? I'm not your mate." Jean turned to face James and shouted in his face, "I wish I never was. I wish we'd never met. You always get me in trouble. You're so annoying! I wish you'd just die!"

He pushed James so hard James took several steps back until he lost his balance, and landed with a thud on the concrete. Jean felt good, to his surprise, there was no guilt, or remorse. It was deserved. He felt he did a good thing, as if he had returned, a little bit, the pain inflicted on him back to the original source.

He stood over James, and watched him sprawled out on the floor, struggling to get up. Jean huffed and puffed, like a wolf, clenched his fist, cracked knuckles and all, resisting the desire to kick James, to punch him in the face, several times, and feel the crush of bones on his fists until his hands turned numb. He stood still, saw the fear in James's eyes, relaxed his fists, and walked away.

The walk home was long for Jean, but even for as long as it was, when he arrived on his street, he still wanted to keep on walking, past his house, past their block of flats with red-brown bricks, and broken windows, past the traffic lights at the end of the road, past everything before bringing him to everything today. He opened his front door, and it was eerily quiet, even though the lights were on and he could hear the TV. Jean was expecting everyone to be home as he walked through the corridor into the living room. He found only Marie, sitting on the sofa, with the TV on low, and a book in her hands. When she noticed him enter, she didn't say hello. Neither did he; they simply stared at each other. Marie looked at him as though she was the parent waiting for him to arrive home, and he must be first to greet and explain where he had been all this time.

"Where is everyone?"

"Dad's at work. Mum went out a few hours ago to meet with Mama Patricia, she said. Tonton is out." Marie replied abruptly, as though she did not welcome being disturbed.

"So you were home alone?"

"Yes, genius, why are you so shocked? It's not the first time."

Jean looked over at the house phone. A blinking red light usually appeared when someone left a message. There was no red light. He looked at Marie as she noticed him looking at the phone. They stared back and forth at each other again, in silence, both expecting the other to speak first.

"Did anyone leave any messages?"

"What do you mean?" Marie replied, assuming ignorance.

"Oh, you know what I mean, Marie. Did anyone leave any messages on the house phone?" He spoke, this time a bit louder, thrusting his hand at the phone.

"There may have been, I'm not sure . . ."

"Don't be annoying! This is very serious." he interrupted.

Even though Marie knew exactly what he was talking about, she delayed. She did not want to let him know she knew straight away, this was a rare moment where she had the upper hand against her older brother and she was not going to easily relinquish the power.

"I am being serious." She replied, noticing how his voice was starting to rise, "I think there was a message."

"Did you listen to it?" He asked sternly, with an intimidating look crushing her defiance and reminding her, acutely, of his status as older brother.

"Yes, I did." Marie succumbed.

"Have you told Mum and Dad?"

"No . . . not yet."

"Not yet?"

"I haven't told them yet."

"What do you mean you haven't told them *yet*?"

"Well, I have to tell them. What do you expect me to do? Lie?"

"Please, don't tell them." Jean pleaded, as his demeanor changed from intimidating to importuning.

"Why were you smoking for, *ya* Jean?"

"I wasn't. I swear. It's not me. It wasn't my fault."

"You know what Mum and Dad think about it . . ." She spoke as though she was the older sister giving council to her younger sibling who was losing his way.

"I wasn't smoking. You have to believe me."

"It was your Head Teacher who called, and you've been suspended. Why would he make it up?"

"I'm not saying he made it up, I'm saying it wasn't me."

"Well, if it wasn't you, then who was it?"

"It was James, some boy I hang around with. He was smoking. I was just with him, and Mr. Allen thought it was both of us. I was too scared to say anything. I didn't want to snitch."

"Well, you shouldn't have been hanging around him them."

"I know that now!" Jean raised his voice, fed up of Marie's condescending attitude, she stood to leave and go to her bedroom, and as she walked past he grabbed her by the shoulders and blocked her path, "but if you tell I'll be in so much trouble."

Seeing Jean's frustration and genuine anxiety made Marie soften toward him a little bit.

"Don't you remember how happy Dad was when my tutor called to say how well I was doing? Do you really want to end it?"

Marie sympathized with Jean, as she remembered the joy in Papa's eye, and how she had noticed his teeth, so straight, when he smiled, and how she rarely ever got to see them.

"Fine, I won't tell. But if they find out, it's not my fault. I never knew." She replied, and they both agreed. He pulled her in and hugged her, a rare moment of affection between them. It was not so much she felt sorry for him, she more so felt sorry for Papa, and did not want to disturb their happiness with bad news.

"What are you going to do about the suspension?" She asked, showing genuine concern.

"Don't worry, I'll figure something out."

They heard a key in the door. "*Allo!*" Mami announced as she walked through the door whilst also talking on the phone. She found them in the corridor, and noticed how Jean was still in his uniform, and had not long returned.

"*Boni boye ko?*" she asked.

"I had football training, Mum." Jean replied. Marie remained quiet.

"*Yo mpe!* Everyday *kaka* football training," Mami responded, disgruntled; she saw it as a waste of time as he could have been helping her with the shopping or doing his homework. She dumped her bags of groceries on him so he could carry it into the kitchen and returned to her phone call.

"Who was that, mum?" Marie asked with intrigue after seeing her mother now beaming a bright smile after finishing the phone call.

"It was Patricia," Mami replied in a happy tone. "She says *hello*. She said she will come to visit you soon and bring you presents; maybe a new book." Marie received the message with a smile and left the room knowing that was the end of the conversation.

Patricia was telling Mami how well things were going after she had recently been given a work permit and had started a new job; even though it was only cleaning, and part-time, it could lead to more, but for now, she was able to at least send some money back home, which was the difference between being able to pay for medical care and keeping someone alive, such as her grandmother, or being able to pay for her little niece to go to school and learning to read and write. These small gains were to be celebrated because in the long term they made all the difference to a life. Patricia promised to visit soon so she could truly sit down and thank Mami, and Papa too for how they had made a sacrifice—small to them, but incredibly big to her—and helped her. Mami, who was, by now, overflowing with joy, had happily accepted and was already preparing what kind of food they would eat on the day. It would be a festival; a most worthy celebration.

The next morning, Jean got ready for school as if it was an ordinary day. He often woke without an alarm, so being awake and ready early was no big deal for him, although on this day it surprised Marie. He had played the part so well even she thought he had forgotten he had been suspended. It was 7:30 a.m., Jean and Marie were eating breakfast together and watching cartoons; *Captain Planet*, "he's our hero, going to take pollution down to zero," they would sing the theme song together, and *The Simpsons*. Marie particularly loved the latter show because she saw herself as Lisa Simpson, young, bright and brilliant. She was already becoming a young social activist in the making; she felt in her element when she refused to wear a Lion costume when she was chosen for the part in her school play of *The Chronicles of Narnia: The Lion, the Witch, and the Wardrobe*. She was protesting against animal rights abuse and wanted to highlight the fact that Lions could face extinction in only a number of decades; her teacher did not think her suggestion of holding a sign saying "Save the Lions," instead of wearing a costume, while she read her lines, was the best way to transmit this message. Marie often relegated Jean to Bart Simpson; for all the trouble he got himself into—intentionally or otherwise. Jean did not see himself in the same way; he found Bart annoying and far too obtuse for his liking. He saw himself as Bleeding Gums Murphy, but only without the saxophone; a tortured soul, with his own world of pain. He enjoyed watching the cartoon shows because it helped him escape his own life and suspend his thinking, which, according to Marie, he never did anyway. Papa had already left for work hours ago, unseen and unheard, whilst the sun was still breaking into the dark sky of the night before. Mami was awake early, also in the living room arranging the house. Tonton was out.

"What are you going to do?" Marie whispered softly, as she held the bowl of Quaker oats they ate for breakfast close to her mouth to muffle the sound of her speaking so she wouldn't be heard.

"What do you mean?" Jean questioned, not understanding, his attention lost in the cartoon.

"About today?!" she replied, irritated by his composure.

"Don't worry," he knew exactly what she had asked, "I'll just hang around, and come home at normal time."

Marie was amazed at his insouciance; this calm and collected manner impressed her. It appeared as though it was familiar to him, a bit too familiar as if he had done this many times before. Perhaps he did. Perhaps he had been suspended from school several times and always got home fast enough to destroy the evidence, and act as if everything was normal. She would have believed this, Jean, the cunning criminal mastermind, however this was the same boy who washed his white clothes, including his Arsenal football kit with "Ian Wright" written on the back he bought from Ridley Road Market - a fake, though he would not have you believe it—with a red t-shirt of his he wanted to wear the next day, and was very upset when it came out pink. Marie, on the other hand, was already doing her own laundry, and occasionally his, as well as cooking to help Mami with the burden. She smirked at his boldness as he said his goodbyes, grabbed his rucksack and bolted out of the door.

The high street looked fuller than it usually was; Jean noticed a hoard of people, from the businessmen in suits to the underground rappers selling their CDs, who he would ordinarily walk past and ignore, as they rushed to work, or not. This time he did not ignore them because he scanned each face in case it was Papa's, or even Tonton's. Although he did not want to see either of them, he kept a lookout to avoid, but figured the latter, Tonton, would probably take him out for a fun day and still keep it a secret. He felt the high street was too busy and dangerous for him to be caught, Mama and her secret team of Aunty Spies who always knew what other people's children were doing, but never their own, would probably see him and report back to Mami saying he was skipping school.

Jean also saw other students walking to school and decided to take the back streets. He checked the time on his black Casio calculator watch: *8:15 a.m.* He sighed. He knew he had a long day ahead of him. He would ordinarily be arriving to school around this time, and his first lesson would be at 8:30 a.m., but he put it out of his mind whilst he walked through the back streets. He stopped, and decided to change from his uniform; he had packed a hoodie and trainers before he left the house. If he changed clothes, there would be less chance of being recognized, also, less likely to look as if he was truanting school and arouse the suspicion of adults and authorities.

Jean hung around aimlessly like a paper airplane in a vacuum; he was really getting nowhere. The sun was bright in the morning but the brisk breeze meant its warmth could not be enjoyed. *8:30 a.m. Only fifteen minutes? Aargh!* He knew he should not have checked his watched and just let the time pass but it couldn't be helped. Time went fast without him even realizing: *12:00 p.m.* It was lunchtime. Jean felt lighter. He finally began to feel the day pass but after his stomach rumbled, he quickly realized he had not brought any lunch with him.

He reached into his pocket, and counted the money he had on him: two pounds, just enough for chicken and chips. He went to the local chicken shop where the owner, Bossman, used to joke about the fried chicken being pigeon, which Jean found more amusing than he should have, but maybe it wasn't the joke he found funny rather the accent Bossman spoke with.

Jean ordered his chicken and chips, and a can of Coke to go with it; the owner wasn't there, but he was instead served by a peculiar pale-faced Bossman (they were all called Bossman) who breathed slow, lungs struggling for air, and knew little of customer service. Jean packed the food and drink into his bag, and went to find a place where he could eat it unnoticed and undisturbed.

He followed the path of the canal, walking by it on the bridge, until he found a route leading right beside it via a flight of black metallic stairs. The pathway along the canal was narrow, barely enough for two people. Though there wasn't anyone else around, this made Jean feel nervous about how anyone could walk up from beside, or behind him, and push him in. He constantly kept looking back, listening out for footsteps. Papa had told him several times not to venture by the canal alone, particularly at night. This must have been the reason why.

There were always stories passed around about what happened at the canal. Some of them sounded like discarded scenes from a badly written horror movie, stories you told a younger sibling before they went to sleep to scare them, an over-active imagination exercising itself to exhaustion, rather than real life occurrences; kidnappings on a boat, murders during full moons, floating limbs in the water, bodies rolled up in carpets weighed down with bricks and dumped to the bottom, endless needles and pipes, and canoes capsizing leaving the person trapped.

He found it bizarre, not necessarily the stories, but more so how it could happen here, in this location. But he did remember reading in the local journal about a woman who had been killed and her body was dumped in the canal, he thought he recognized her picture and had at least seen her several times on the high street.

Jean sat alone for hours until time became an abstract idea he was no longer bound by. This was the first moment where he was truly alone; he was not in school surrounded by hundreds of people, friends or otherwise, not at home where there were always people, always something happening, or he was always demanded to perform some duty. He was alone and it brought him a sense of calm and peace he had not known he was looking for. It was as though someone had walked in and turned down the white noise blasting from the broken radio bringing silence once more.

Jean arrived to find Mami at home with Marie. He greeted them as he usually did, however, this time there was a happier tone in his voice which left Marie surprised at his nonchalance. She said nothing though, choosing to honor her promise made in secret. Mami was on the phone to family in Kinshasa, Jean could tell it was long distance from how loud she was speaking.

"How was school?" Mami asked when she noticed Jean greeting her as he arrived.

"It was fine." He replied, with a placid smile on his face. She returned to her phone call, and Jean returned to breathing, after holding his breath hoping he had not been caught. Marie still did not say a word, for the rest of the evening, she looked at him with amazement.

There was a knock on the door as they ate dinner and watched television. Jean jumped up enthusiastically and offered to answer, which no one protested.

"Who is it?" he shouted, in a song, as he walked toward the door. He grabbed it and swung it open.

"Police." Jean froze, unable to speak, he felt the wind get knocked out of his lungs as if he had been punched by a heavyweight boxer. His eyes glared in disbelief. This is what real fear

felt like, not even a roaring ferocious lion, or an untamed tiger
could have got him to feel the fear he felt at that moment. There
were two police officers; one man, one woman. The man was
tall, so tall Jean had to adjust his head to look him in the eyes,
the woman was short. It was an odd pairing of sorts.

"Hello," said the woman police officer, attempting to sound
bright and cheerful. The policeman did not speak. Jean did not
respond, he was muted from fear, defeated by his heart beating
loud beneath his ribs.

"Is your mum or your dad in?" she asked, in a strong northern
accent. Jean nodded. He closed the door and went to get Mami.

"Mum . . ." he called out, as he walked back to the living
room.

"*Eza nani?*" She replied.

"Mum . . ." Jean gave his answer. Mami did not get up, she
wished not to be disturbed, however, when she saw the look
on his face, as if the color had been drained from it, she knew
immediately something was not normal.

"Can you come please?"

"Okay." She got up and followed Jean to the door. He opened
it and the two police officers were there, in the exact same position they were in before.

"Good evening ma'am, we're really sorry to disturb, are you
the tenant of this property?" The woman police officer asked
in her calmest voice, whilst the policeman remained silent, still
not having said a word. Mami looked dumbfounded. She tried
to maintain her composure but her apprehension appeared on
her skin like boils.

"*Alobi nini?*" She whispered to Jean.

"My mum doesn't speak good English." Jean attempted to
intervene. It's not so much she didn't speak good English, it was
that she did not want to say the wrong thing, the wrong thing
could land her in prison, or worse, she thought. The police officers she had known did not knock on doors to ask questions,

they came to take; either you or something from you. Maybe this time it was worse, maybe what they had feared for so long had finally arrived.

"Well, maybe you could translate?" Jean nodded in response, "we've come because there have been some disturbances in the local area; nothing serious, just lots of noise, low-level disruption, youths hanging around being intimidating, and we were wondering if you had seen or heard anything?"

Jean spent a few moments whispering to Mami, attempting to explain to her what had been asked. The male police officer still had not yet moved from his position.

"No." Mami replied herself, also shaking her head vociferously.

"What about you?" the male police officer said in a voice that did not match his appearance, looking at Jean deadlock in his eyes. Jean shook his head side to side. The woman police officer continued, "Well, if you do hear anything or if at any point there is anything you would like to discuss, please do not hesitate to call, okay?"

chapter 20

JEAN HAD COMPLETED ONE DAY OF his suspension and had one more. They sat together once again, him and Marie, eating breakfast and watching cartoons, as they did every morning. Mami was already awake sorting out everything to do with home. Papa had left for work since the dawn. Tonton was out.

"Where did you go yesterday?" Marie asked, whispering into her bowl of oats, trying not to be heard.

"Don't worry. I made it back didn't I? I'll do the same thing today."

"Oh, my gosh," she was genuinely surprised at how well he had done, she really did not even expect him to last the day let alone last so smoothly, "so didn't Mum and Dad ask you?"

"No, why? Did you tell them?!" He asked suspiciously, almost raising his voice loud enough to be heard.

"No, no, no!" Marie insisted, "I said I wouldn't, didn't I?"

"Okay, good. I believe you. I was just making sure," before he stood to leave the table, Jean turned to Marie, put his arm around her, hugged her and said "thank you." Marie felt warmed by this, a welcomed but rare feeling of her big brother being a big brother to her.

Jean went to the playground once again, sat on the same bench and began reading, this time for a shorter, intolerable time due to the sheer boredom. He looked at the adventure playground; it looked less of an adventure than the day before. It was difficult to feel nostalgic about something you did yesterday, so he did not even really bother going on the swings and the slides, all he did was sit on the other side of the see-saw down to the bottom because of his weight. Time passed slower: *10:30 a.m.* He decided to go to get an early lunch at the chicken and chip shop. The owner Bossman was there this time, but he did not recognize Jean (maybe because he was out of his school uniform) and there was no joke about the chicken being pigeon. Bossman looked more tired than usual, as if he hadn't slept for days and was saving what little energy he had left for the busy hour after school when all the students piled in.

Jean walked once more following the path of the canal until he found the same staircase as the day before. He continued walking until he found the same bench he had sat on. He searched for the quiet, for the peace he had felt only the day before but it did not come, not how it did yesterday. Nonetheless, he was happy to be alone once more for a rare moment.

He reached deep into his bag and found the diary Mr. David had given him. He pulled it out and looked at it with curiosity. It looked like it had aged, even in the short time he had it. He flicked through the pages, stopped on a random one and pulled out a pen from his bag; *maybe I should write something*, he wrote, stopped, shook his head and threw it all back in his bag.

3 p.m. Jean realized the time. He changed back into his uniform and made his way back home as if he had been to school. He walked along the high street when he saw a group of young people in the same school uniform as his walking toward him. He could not make out specific faces, but he knew he needed to avoid them at all costs. He considered crossing the road but running through the busy traffic would only bring more attention to him, he also thought about quickly turning around, but again, more attention. So in the end, he carried on walking, avoiding eye contact by looking down at the pavement busy with pedestrians, hoping he could hide behind someone and not be recognized.

Jean almost successfully passed by unnoticed when he heard a voice call out, "Oi, Jean!" from somewhere around him. It made him flinch, but not noticeably; he did not react or look up in a way suggesting he had heard.

"Jean!" the voice came again, this time closer. He felt a hand on his shoulder and it turned him around. He saw Ola standing before him. The other boys also stopped and noticed Jean. His plan was foiled.

"What's going on?" Ola asked. He showed an enthusiasm Jean could not place; it could not have been about this moment. The rest of the boys stood around, forming a kind of circle like a roundtable meeting. Ola had still not broken the habit of always looking around and behind as if there was something else more exciting going on than the conversation he was having; as if he was going to spontaneously run off into nowhere. He sometimes did.

"Nothing." Jean replied, showing a lack of engagement, as if he was not there.

"Where have you been? I ain't seen you in school."

"I've been ill . . ."

"So why are you in your uniform?" Ola asked, and pulled a confused face, pointing, as if he was trying to figure out the value of x in an impossibly difficult equation.

"Er . . . er . . ." Jean could not think of a lie fast enough, he did not even realize he was in his school uniform and was not prepared for an interrogation from anyone else apart from Papa.

"I swear you got you suspended." Another boy said, who Jean did not see. He looked for the voice and saw it belonged to

Danny, *BBC*, the current affairs correspondent. Jean forgot how quickly he got hold of recent news and information but never got involved in any of the action.

"Is it? What for?" Ola asked excitedly, as if it were a good thing.

"Yeah," Jean replied with a deflated voice. The boys cheered as if it was an achievement.

"Yeah of course, I just told you. I'm not lying. My sources are always correct. Proper HP." Danny added, much to Jean's annoyance, whose squinted eyes and screwed up face was not enough of a signal for Danny to recognize he should stop talking.

"It was for smoking, wasn't it?" Danny asked, as if to ask, but really to show he knew, "yeah James told me, they got caught smoking by Mr. Allen, he was basically texting everyone."

"He didn't text me . . ." Ola added.

"Do you even have a phone?" Danny replied, trying to mock with a joke.

"So how have I got your mum's number then?" Ola replied, which caused an eruption, a loud uproar of jeering and laughter among the boys. Jean, consumed by the noise, sank deep inside himself and wished he could escape the moment. He had not thought of James for a couple of days and already, the first thought of him since caused frustration.

"Did you hear though?" Danny asked attempting to change the subject after suffering a defeat from which he could not come back, "apparently James got beat up."

"What?" Ola replied, in shock. "What happened?"

It was a surprise because although James got himself into difficult situations, he always knew how to get himself out; he always had. It was almost his superpower.

The news left the rest of the boys gasping. Jean, on the other hand, felt indifferent. Actually, less than indifferent, he simply did not care; a part of him thought James deserved it so he remained silent; in his head he was already at home drinking tea, as he did after school, and watching TV; *Fresh Prince of Bel Air*, being annoyed by Marie. He never realized he would actually long for this.

"Basically . . ." Danny began as if he was going to tell an epic story, "he got beat up by Jerome and his boys, yesterday. Obviously it must have been whilst he was suspended, I heard he was walking around somewhere in the manor and they battered him. But not bad, it was just to teach him a lesson or something, it could have been worse."

Jean instantly remembered why. The memory came back to him like a wave crashing against the rocks. He was swept with new emotion, but tried to fight it off with the indifference he was also feeling.

"We should go see him, you know." Ola suggested. The rest of the boys agreed. Jean, mixed between resentment and rage, fear and frustration, said "I can't I've got to go home," ultimately allowing the indifference he still felt to settle the affair.

"Just come man," they urged him, in unison, but he insisted until eventually he pulled away from the group and made his way home.

Jean arrived home and was first met by Marie, who had a stunned look on her face, because he had actually not been caught, and was silently mouthing *how?* as she did not want to be heard by Mami who was settled in the living room. Jean's mind was occupied with several other things at once but mostly guilt and fear; guilt James had been beaten and he felt it was his fault, and fear he too may be sought after. He sat drinking tea and eating sandwiches waiting for dinner, whilst they watched TV. Papa was at work. Tonton was out.

As he sat, on the sofa, in a fixed position whilst the minutes passed like hours, a quiet discomfort grew within him, "Mum, can I go out?" Jean eventually asked.

"*Zela biloko ebela.*" Mami replied.

"Don't worry, I'll back before dinner's ready."

After Mami's nod of approval, Jean was quickly changed and out of the door heading to James's house. They did not live far from each other. They were separated by roughly a ten-minute walk, which depended on whether you strolled comfortably through the main street to get there or power walked through the back streets. He chose the latter, and he arrived faster than the time it took for him to leave his house. James's high rise building lived up to its name; it was so high, looking up at the top for anything more than a ten second period was guaranteed to leave your neck stiff in an uncomfortable position. It was also grey, like a long block of Lego. Jean had been here several times before, more times than James had come to theirs. In fact, Jean felt really uncomfortable bringing his friends to his house. He always felt it wasn't enough, it was as if everyone else had more and they would judge him. Jean remembered the door number and buzzed up on the intercom. It rang and rang, but no one answered. Due to a fortune of good timing, someone left the building just as Jean was buzzing up and he was able to make his way into the building. He could not remember which floor James lived on, but the number, 73, on a little broken display board, was shown to be the twelfth floor. As Jean was pressing the button to call the lift, a voice coming down the steps from behind said "Lift's not working, mate," and came and left just as quickly.

Jean knocked on the door; two loud knocks to make sure he was heard. He waited. Looked around and noticed lights on; someone was sure to be home. He continued waiting, stood on the communal balcony area looking out at the city and how the skyline resembled a heartbeat on a monitor. He knocked again, this time harder; louder. He heard steps coming from behind the door. He waited. It stopped then shuffled on what sounded like carpet. Jean's heart thumped.

"Oh, what do you want?" It was James. He groaned at the sight of Jean. He looked rougher than Jean had ever seen before;

the tiredness in the eyes was distracted by the dark bruises surrounding it.

"James . . . are you alright?" Jean asked, throat swelling with emotion, voice quivering with concern.

"What do you care?" James walked off closing the door shut but Jean managed to put his foot in the way before it could close. He walked in and followed him. There was a different air in the house this time, it was cold, as if all the warmth had been sucked out.

"I do care. I came to see you. I didn't know this happened."

"Who told you?" James asked. He spoke with a soft rage.

"Danny," Jean answered quickly, "he told me and the boys, today."

"How did he tell you if you were suspended!"

"I saw them after school, when I was going home. They said they were going to come see you."

"They didn't come, they don't care. Ugh, Danny and his big mouth, always spreading fake news. He talks too much."

"He said you told people. You were basically telling everyone."

"What?" James pulled a face questioning the absurdity of Jean's logic for not questioning whether this was true, "why would I want to tell people? Look at my face!"

He pointed to his bulging eyes, and split bottom lip with tiny bright red remnants of blood. Jean felt his pain as if it was his own; he felt it should have been, after all it was his fight.

"I'm sorry," was the only small compensation Jean could offer to alleviate the pain James felt. His hardness began to soften when he heard it, but still, it was not enough.

"Where's your mum and dad?" Jean asked, seeing no sign of them.

"They're out. You know, same old, same old."

There was still a bitter harshness in his tone; a resentment. A long silence was drawn out between them like a pencil pressed on an endless piece of paper.

"James, look . . . I didn't mean to be angry with you. I was just angry I got in trouble, and I was scared."

"So?" James replied blowing his excuse away, "don't you think I was scared?"

"You? Scared?" Jean replied in high pitched tone embellished with confused, "what would you be scared of? You love this kind of stuff. You're always boasting about it."

"What, just because I act up, you think it's all roses and daffodils, yeah?" He scoffed, and continued, "you know what my old man said after he came home and saw my face, he said I deserved it, and I should stop running off my mouth."

James was starting to turn red, brewing, as if something inside him was filling up and ready to burst, "You know, when he said this, I wanted to . . . I wanted to smash his face in." Jean watched him, as he spoke and paced the room. He had never seen James this way before; filled with so much rage yet so vulnerable.

"Who is he to talk to me about what I deserve?" James continued, as he shouted down the house, "when every time he comes home, drunk, so drunk, you can smell it in the corridors . . . He deserves a few things too!" His mouth curled from disgust.

"Do you know what he does?"

"No, what?"

"He comes home, and he batters my mum, with his own two fists, he proper lays into her and sometimes I can hear her begging him to stop."

"I mean, how could he?" James continued, "hit a woman? Hit my mum?"

The thickness of the air between them became too heavy for either of them to breathe in; the shock left Jean out of breath.

"So . . . I went and got this," James reached, with his skinny arm, underneath their faded sofa and pulled out a blue crowbar sharpened on each end, "I swear to you, next time he even thinks about trying anything . . ."

"James, wait . . . you can't do that!" Jean didn't know whether he was asking him or telling him not to.

"Why not?"

"Because . . . because . . ." Jean stuttered and stuttered, "because you'll get in trouble, you'll be arrested . . ."

"Oh,who cares?!" He replied, slowly and menacingly.

"I do. Come on. I don't want to see you go prison."

"I would happily go down for this, I'd even throw a little party in there 'n' all." James' tone frightened Jean, it was unfamiliar to him. This wasn't the voice of the friend who entertained the school playground at lunchtimes, or passed notes, with incorrect grammar, spelling, and punctuation, in class. He did not recognize the voice; he did not recognize the boy.

Jean quickly grabbed the crowbar from James's hand. James came after him and grappled for it until they both fell on the floor, knocking over the ugly flower patterned vase next to the mauve chair. The vase, broken, did not look any more out of place in the room.

"What you doing?" James asked, confused, and angered, "I thought you were on my side."

"It's not about sides, James. I just don't want to see you do anything stupid."

"It is about sides, you never cared. You're the same as my ol' man."

"I'm not!" Jean shouted back, angered at the suggestion. "I'm doing this for your own good."

He burst out of the door to the balcony and threw the crowbar over the edge down into the darkness, and eventually heard clang onto the concrete below. James came out chasing after him and saw what Jean had done. He was panting heavily as if the air had thinned, and he needed to take in all he could to stay alive. James broke down in a flood of tears; it overcame him, uncontainable like a deluge in a plastic bowl. This was the first time Jean had ever seen James cry; he did not imagine he ever did. He always thought he laughed in response to everything; the joy and the pain. Crying was never an option, it was not allowed, but he did not know why. It was a rule of the game they played along to, a rule no one had told them about.

Jean placed his hand on James's shoulder, who was now lent over the side of the balcony looking out into the distance. James's breathing started to slow. Still looking out into the distance, he climbed up on to the edge of the balcony, and sat, placing both legs on the other side facing outwards.

"What you doing?" Jean replied, in haste, worried; fearful.

"Stop panicking, man. I sit here all the time."

James's reply reassured Jean much, much less than he would have liked, much less than if he would have just put both of his feet on the floor. There was no movement around, no people and no sound. They stayed there, on the balcony, in the stillness of their solitude for what seemed a lifetime of its own; it felt as though the peace that had missed them was finally coming back around.

"Do you ever . . ." James spoke, softer than before, soft as a passing cloud over a clear blue sea, "do you ever think about what it would be like to die?"

"What do you mean?" Jean replied, knowing exactly what he meant, but wishing he could un-know; wishing he could un-know the whole evening.

"You know, what it would be like to end it all." A silence fell upon them like the moment after a tragedy. "I'm just tired of it, tired of all of it." James continued "You know, sometimes my Dad hits me too."

Jean looked at him with wide eyes as if to let him know there was more in this sentence they shared than anything else. "But I've gotten older, stronger, and so I take it now; it doesn't hurt so much . . . but I'm just tired."

"James, get down . . ." Jean pleaded with him, his voice breaking as he watched him shuffle further forward on the edge. It had started to rain, but only ever so lightly. A breeze carried each raindrop and brought it to the ground as though a lover, laying their dying partner to bed for the last time. The night had darkened; the only remaining light was the dim moon in the sky, and the brightness of inextinguishable hope still shining in their eyes. Time was lost on them, it did not exist for moments such as this; there was no rush, no slowing down, everything was frozen, silent, still. The world did not watch, but it waited; no flowers bloomed, no breeze blew, no clouds passed. James got down. Time started once again.

chapter 21

MAMI WENT TO CHURCH THIS SUNDAY morning, accompanied by Jean and Marie. Papa was working; he had been taking extra shifts whilst still working his morning job to make some more money, which often left him working seven days a week and so there was little time for him to do anything else during the rare moments he was at home but rest. Mami did not like this, however, there was no other way. Tonton was out.

Mami was sat listening to Pastor Kaddi who had his histrionics in full display whilst he preached. She sat with focused attention, listening closely and intently, but still could not help but be distracted. Maybe it was because there was so much going on at home and back home; rent to pay, no money, another phone call from Marthe, something about the sisters, everything seemed to come together as one big problem and name itself life. Or it could have been who she was sitting next to distracting her. Mami was sat next to Mama Nadège, who was notoriously known for not being able to maintain more than two minutes worth of silence. She talked so much, it made you wonder whether she was talking to you or herself. She was what was called, *songi-songi*; a gossiper. She was always so eager to speak of other people's business, but never her own. And she was almost always the first one to receive the information, as if she had a team of informants on the ground ready to update her. She was married, but her husband was a no-show, and no one ever really knew why.

"Psst," Mama Nadège tried to get Mami's attention, who was actively ignoring her even though they were sat right next to each other.

"*Nini?*" Mami replied, asking what it was hastily, showing she was annoyed.

"*Oyoki sango?*" She would always start her gossip mill this way, asking whoever she was speaking to if they had heard the news, knowing full well they hadn't.

"*Nini?*" Mami replied, this time with a growl.

"*Oyebi Maman wana Mama Patricia? Ba refouler ye.*" she whispered covering her mouth, like a pupil in class not wanting to be caught by the teacher.

"*Olobi nini?!*" Mama replied louder, from the shock, almost disturbing the sermon as others turned their heads to look.

"They deport her." Mama Nadège said, this time in English. No reason as to why, maybe it sounded harsher in this language, more loaded, consequential and violent.

Mami was no longer able to take in what Pastor Kaddi was saying; *how could Patricia be deported? They had only spoken last week,* she wondered, thoughts distracting from the sermon. After the church service was over, she looked around but did not see Patricia to catch up, as they usually do, so Mami quickly made her way home with Jean and Marie, avoiding the extra time people would usually stay behind for socializing, food, and, more often than not, more gossip. She did not want to hear any of it; not today. She did not want to fear the worst, so she left.

It was a long bus ride home; everything seemed to pass in slow motion. Papa had not returned, she expected he would be back by now but as he had not yet arrived, this gave her the opportunity to prepare some food.

Mami could not stop thinking of Patricia. Her woes and cries echoed in Mami's head. Memories of the last time they spoke to each other, the phone call of how things had gotten better, how she promised a gift to Marie, came back to her. Patricia was never one to break promises. Mami refused to believe she was gone, not like this; a fate of death would have made more sense; more of a chance at reconciliation, she would at least be able to reach her through prayer.

Papa came home and found Mami in the kitchen in tears, visibly upset, whilst Jean and Marie were in the living room watching TV.

"What is wrong?" Papa asked curiously, almost probing. He did not want to see her upset, seeing her upset made him upset.

"What happened?"

"She was deported." Mami wept.

"Who?"

"Mama Patricia."

Papa gasped in shock, but realized this and collected his reaction to reduce it to something much smaller. He knew of these things, and was the kind of person who always prepared himself for the worst.

"Are you sure? Who told you?"

"Mama Nadège."

"Hmmph." He grunted, doubtfully; he was aware of Mama Nadège's infamous reputation for spreading rumors, "*O ndimi ye?*"

"Yes, why wouldn't I believe her? She wouldn't lie, well not about something like this."

"*Aza songi-songi . . .*" Papa was dismissive of Mama Nadège's claims, "have you tried calling Mama Patricia?"

Mami shook her head in response. Papa looked over at her phone on the kitchen counter next to the leftover bits of the chopped onions from the meal just prepared. Mami picked it up and began calling.

The number you have dialed has not been recognized, please check the number and try again. The number you have dialed has not been recognized, please check the number and try again. The number you have dialed . . .

Mami hung up the phone. What she feared had come true. It wasn't so much because Mama Patricia had been deported—although it played a big part, and, of course, they were friends and had gotten closer over the course of time—it was the stark reminder of what someone around you being deported meant. That it could have been you, and secondly, most importantly, it is only a matter of time until it is. Mami was reminded how she did not belong here, that this place was not hers.

This was the reality they often tried to ignore but sometimes it came crashing back like a sailboat in a storm, fragile bones on a steep climb. It reminded them their fate was sealed by the hands of another, as though the sword of Damocles dangled above their heads, and they could do nothing but wait for it to fall.

"I am scared." Mami spoke panicky, out of breath, as if there was an imminent threat. "This could happen to us. What will we do? What about the children?" Mami asked, stumbling over her own words, with a world of worry in her voice.

Marie came rushing into the kitchen, full of joy and excitement, then asked, "Mummy, are you okay?" as she noticed her mother looking flustered; lacking her usual composure.

"Yes, my love," she bent down and gave her a hug, "Mummy is fine. Now go, carry on reading, dinner will be ready soon." Marie skipped out of the kitchen unaware, with her book in her hand.

Mami then broke down again with a flurry of tears streaming down her face. Papa brought her in, and held her close, holding her up from falling.

"Shh, do not worry," Papa tried to calm her.

"I should have told her."

"No, you did the right thing. There is nothing to tell them."

"She is smart enough to know."

"They are children; they have to concentrate on school."

"But what if *we* are deported?"

"Then we will find a way."

"But you have your court case. What about if . . ."

"Ssh, just trust me. It will be okay. We will find a way." Papa replied, unable to say no, or promise it will not happen to them, for even his abundant hope and optimism was not enough to meet this challenge.

"We will find a way." He repeated to Mami, as she wept, trying to reassure her; trying to reassure himself. Papa held her tightly as if it could be the last time he held her, as if tomorrow could take her; as if it would bring a fresh trauma to face, as if the hand sealing their fate was starting to let go.

chapter 22

THERE WAS LOUD BANGING ON THE door in the middle of night. It was heavy-fisted. It banged in threes, and sounded as though the fist wore a boot and packed a huge kick. Papa woke up from the disturbance. He looked over and Mami was still asleep. It was pitch black outside; the darkness swept into the room leaving no space light to break through. The banging persisted. Papa found the first thing he could reach for in the dark to wear to cover himself, a *liputa*, wrapped it around him and headed towards the door. He decided to pick up the metal pole end of the hoover, and carried it, as protection, waving it sideways, as if he was Thor and it was his hammer. There was no peephole on their door, so Papa had to approach with caution.

"*C'est qui?*" Papa grumbled, in a deep voice, with added baseline, almost in a growl. He could hear shuffling; movement from the other side, and unintelligible noises. "*C'est qui?*" Papa asked again, shuffling and noise continued. The fist banged on the door again, one, two, and before it could land on the third, Papa swung the door open and hoisted the metal pole of the hoover into the air, and saw Tonton standing there. He was drunk, he

151

smelt as though he had been dipped into a sea of alcohol. He stumbled into the front door, and clumsily onto Papa. The smell overwhelmed him; it was pungent, strong as if it lifted weights on steroids.

Papa pushed Tonton off him as if he carried a contagious disease. He switched on the light and watched Tonton stomp heavy-footed through the narrow corridor bouncing side to side like a human pinball in the machine. Tonton tried to go into Jean's room, where he usually sleeps but Papa stopped him, and took him into the living room and watched him crash onto the sofa. He was angry at Tonton for the disturbance and for being drunk, however, anger was a wasted energy at this moment in time because the subject of this anger was too inebriated to receive it's intended message. Papa looked at the time: *3:00 a.m.* He had to be awake and ready to go to work in two and a half hours. He went to check on Jean and Marie who were both in their rooms sleeping, undisturbed by the noise. He went back to his bedroom.

"What was it?" Mami asked, she had awakened and was rubbing sleep from her eyes.

"Tonton." Papa replied bluntly as he crawled back into bed.

Mami was swarmed by guilt. She remained silent. She did not even have to ask, but she knew it was not good. Anything from Tonton at this time could not have been. It wasn't so much she felt responsible for his actions, it was she felt responsible for him even being there, so whenever he did something good, such as offering to look after the children, take them out for treats or cooking when neither Mami or Papa were able to, she would glorify his actions as if they were extraordinary, but only because they were so few and far between. They were more so used to these moments of disturbance, and it had risen once again, this time, she felt, for the last.

Papa's alarm rang at *5:15 a.m.*, right at the crack of dawn. He almost always beat his alarm to wake, he prided himself on this, saying it would be a good day if he did. It usually took Papa exactly thirteen minutes to get ready, another thing he prided himself on, and today, when he was finished and ready to leave at 5:28 *a.m.,* he went into the kitchen, poured a glass of cold, cold water, and splashed it onto Tonton's sleeping head.

"*Lamuka! Lamuka!*" Papa shoved him at the same time whilst he slept on the sofa, telling him to wake up. Tonton was startled into an upright position, shouting "*eh! eh!*" and began half paying attention.

"Today. You leave. Pack your bags. When I come back from work you are gone."

Papa spoke, in English, with an authoritarian voice, to assert himself, as if he had been given some kind of power with a new title he now wore. He slammed the glass onto the table and swiftly left to make his way to work.

Papa left work early to make his way home as quickly as he could. There was a quiet confidence in him, a relief in his step as if he had achieved a long-awaited accomplishment. To him, with Tonton gone it would give them a chance to feel what it would be like to be a family, a normal family, in one household, as they had seen in the movies and the TV shows, the ordinary family they had not yet been given the opportunity to be. Also, it was the space that he really wanted; it was more air to breathe, more room for family.

Papa arrived home expecting to see Tonton gone; he was not interested in when he had left, how or even where he was going to. This, he could find out later. Papa opened the front door to an eerie quiet, he sensed there was no one in, not by the silence, but more so the lack of movement there was in the air. He casually strolled into the living room and there he found Tonton sitting on the sofa in the exact same position he had left him in. Not only had he not packed his things and left, he had dared to not even move from where he lay. Papa saw this as the ultimate defiance, adding insult to injury, but kept his cool, not allowing anger to bear witness just yet. He stood over Tonton until he woke from this alcohol-induced slumber.

"Wapi Mami, Marie na Jean?" Papa asked when he saw Tonton was half awake. Tonton was not surprised to see Papa standing over him with a face like a bull ready to charge. He casually, with the slowest possible movement, which only frustrated Papa further, sat rubbing the sleep from his eyes, still dressed in yesterday's clothes, and began speaking with a groggy voice, as if his throat was still gargling the remnants of the drink he had indulged the night before. Tonton told Papa he had given Mami and the children some money for them to go out and buy some "take-a-way"; their main choice was KFC, so they did not need to worry about making dinner.

This frustrated Papa; frustrated and relieved him. It frustrated him because he did not want another man, let alone this one, paying for anything for his family, particularly now as he should be gone, but the relief came in knowing his family was safe, for the fear of something worse did arise within him. He had never come home from work to an empty house before, not like this. He settled, a little, easing the tension within. He went and sat on the adjacent sofa.

"What is the problem?" Papa asked; a feeble attempt at showing sympathy and concern, however, the question came out in a harsher tone than he had intended. Tonton took his head out of his hands and looked up at Papa in bewilderment. This is the first time they had truly spoken since Tonton stayed at the house. There was an unwritten agreement, something between them that was implicitly known but not spoken; all contact is minimal, preferably, none at all. Perhaps this was why Tonton was always out, he knew although he had somewhere to lay his head, he did not have a home.

"There is no problem." Tonton replied.

"What is the problem?" Papa insisted, this time, intentionally harsher, "you are a man, you do nothing here. Ever since you come to this house, you do nothing but drink and party, you go after lots of women; *ki-ndumba ya somo*. You stay out late at night, you stink of alcohol. I cannot let you influence my children anymore, I cannot let them keep seeing this."

Tonton remained silent, he stared into the empty space on the wall in front of him as if trying to focus on something moving in the distance far away. He placed his head back into his palms, and nodded, with the smallest of head movements, agreeing with Papa, whilst taking deep breaths, really deep, as if the air was escaping or out of reach. Papa was confused; he had not seen Tonton this way before, whenever he was around, he was always so exuberant and high-spirited, today he was a man broken; a man barely a shadow of himself.

"So . . ." Papa was about to speak to stop the silence falling between them.

"I know," Tonton interrupted, "I know."

"Do you know how it feels to be a man, but to live as a child in another man's home?" He continued speaking, a lament, as though this was a plea to the skies above and a savior who was not listening, "to every day be reminded of what you had and how it will *never* come back to you?" He sobbed softly into his palms.

Papa's heart softened for this man who he had felt anger toward not long ago. He did not know exactly what Tonton meant, although they had taken the same long journey to be where they are, they did not have the same experiences.

"What do you mean?" Papa asked, this time a question of genuine sympathy.

"I mean, every day I look at your family and I see my own, and every day I see your family and I am reminded . . ." he paused, "of things I am trying to forget."

A silence fell between them which, this time, Papa was not comfortable in breaking; Papa sat and watched Tonton as if he was peeling the old from himself and bringing forth someone new, someone he had not seen before.

"What happened?" Papa eventually asked, after a long silence, when he saw the tears were starting to dry. Tonton began opening up to him, quite freely and willingly, as if they had spoken this way since the beginning.

"Do you remember *le pillage* in Kinshasa in 1991?" Tonton asked, finally looking up at Papa once again.

"Of course! It was horrible, *les Soldats*, and what they did . . . and the government . . . *Le Maréchal, Mr. Président* . . . corruption . . . a game of politics!" Papa replied emphatically, but stopped, not wanting to get carried away.

"Yes, politics." Tonton replied indignantly, with a venomous rage. "To many, it was just politics, to many it was just corruption, to many it was just the government; I can still hear their chants MPR *egale, servir, se servir, non*, serve others; do not serve yourself, such lies! Just politics! But to me, it was my family; it was my wife . . . when *les Soldats* came into my house . . . it was my wife and her dead body on the floor. To many it was just politics, it was just another riot, but it was my family; it was my little girls, who laying bleeding, bleeding in front of me . . ." Tonton reached into his wallet and pulled out a picture of a beautiful smiling woman, and two young girls as radiant as a tropical summer, and showed it to Papa.

"I have only one question. Why?" Tonton spoke. "Why take them and leave me? They made me watch everything. Everything!" He burst out into tears greater than before, "and every day I ask why? Every day, I have no answers. This is what I'm trying to forget." He continued, "You know what I will never forget; the smell . . . the smell of death is the same everywhere. I smell it even here; inside me."

"Please . . ." Papa intervened; he felt the pain as though it were his own, like it was a seed planted and started to grow wildly in him, "you do not have to go."

"No!" Tonton replied instantly, "I must go. I cannot stay anymore."

"Please stay . . . please," Papa pleaded, now he knew what he had not known before.

Tonton broke down and wept like an orphaned child in a room full of families. Papa felt this; he felt his pain deeply as though it were his own. He turned to Tonton and wrapped his arms around him, and they held each other, these two men like giant rocks worn down by tears that flowed beneath them a stream of water. These two men, who cried not for themselves but for their families; Tonton for the one he had lost, and Papa for the one he was still so lucky to have. How difficult it is to remember, how easy it is to forget.

Later in the evening, by the time Mami had returned home with Jean and Marie, she could tell from the moment she looked at Papa there was a new weight in his eyes. He did not tell her Tonton's story, he respected the fact there was a reason Tonton never spoke of it; not out of a façade or to maintain an appearance, it was because, as Papa now understood, Tonton did not want anyone else to carry the extra weight he too carried. Tonton spared many of this burden; he was an artist, in the way he spared others of a suffering he bore within.

chapter 23

MAMI HAD NOT SPOKEN TO FAMILY back home in a week or so. A week is a particularly long time as Kinshasa moved so fast it would take you a whole week to be updated on the week of news you missed, which meant you would be behind another week, and would have to repeat this endless cycle just to remain informed.

She was on the phone to *Kin* one evening—*Kin* is by default the abbreviation for Kinshasa, it showed who was really from or who really knew the city, it was the heart of the country—being updated by Marthe who spoke about everyone else but herself; she told Mami about how Monique was on the verge of getting married; after a successful traditional wedding where "*ba kangi lopangu,*" or how Micheline had now moved across the country to the east and was living in *Goma,* and how mother, well she spoke less of mother also. Mother had always resented Mami for leaving, particularly so abruptly. Mami was always the sensible one, the one she always wanted around, the one who could have handled things as they changed.

"Sist-a, I have sent you some money through Western Union, one hundred dollars, the code is . . ."

"*Zela, zela. Na zwa stilo.*"

"*Sala noki, eko kata . . .*"

"I said wait,"

"The code is . . ." Mami began anyway, "872-707-324." Marthe repeated each number back to Mami, and then all of them together to be sure.

"You have told me about the whole family," Mami continued "*Ebongo yo?*" Mami asked Marthe, noticing how avoidant she was.

"*Tsia.* What about me?" Marthe replied dismissively, knowing what Mami was trying to do. She quickly shut down Mami's attempted enquiry by saying, "marriage will happen when it happens, but if you really want me to get married, bring me to England, and marry me off personally. If not, then stop asking."

Marthe had always been a kind of loveable rebel, a rogue with a heart; she had a strong side to her that few men dared to handle—and even fewer men knew how—but on the other side of this was a softness, a magic, evoking feelings, like a new moon, like mercury in retrograde.

Jean was in his room. He held his diary in his hands. Each time he held it, he was always in awe at how it seemed to age, as if the diary itself was collecting life experiences and growing older through time. He had only written in it once, but was becoming more comfortable with it. This time he picked up a pen and, without hesitation, began writing what came to him:

I have some questions . . .

Why doesn't anyone tell young people the truth?

Why aren't you allowed to ask questions, but you have to answer them straight away when you are asked?

Why is it only speak when you are spoken to? It's like saying only give when you are being given to. It doesn't make any sense to me. None of this makes sense to me.

Last question . . .

Why doesn't it make sense to me?

He put his pen down and spent the rest of the evening staring at the ceiling, wondering about the multitude of questions floating in his head until he fell asleep.

The following Sunday in church, at the end of yet another performance-like sermon, Pastor Kaddi announced there was an important message the congregation needed to hear, and help if they could. The announcement was to be made by Mama Gloria, who was the church secretary; which essentially meant she either made the announcements, or collected the donations, and more often than not both. The donations went towards paying for the bare and empty hall they rented, which was now starting to fill up as more and more people from the community attended, or toward the occasional food they ate after service. They did not collect much, it was hardly a room full of the world's wealthiest people, nonetheless they gave what they could and it sufficed.

Mama Gloria stepped to the makeshift podium. She was quite a stern looking woman, with a rarely smiling face. She looked old, not old because of her age, it was because of her size; she looked as if she had at least three children, and possibly grandchildren among them. Often in the community, a woman's size would suggest her motherhood, and she would be called *mama mobimba*; a whole woman, as if she could ever be half. Mama Gloria spoke with an old *Lingala*; with an accent referred to as *ya ba koko*; it belonged to the elders.

"*Ba ndeko . . .*" she always addressed the congregation as family, because often this is what they were, or at least, how it felt. Mama Gloria announced there was a new family, a mother and her two children, who had recently come into the country, did not know anyone and were homeless. They were being temporarily housed in a hostel, where more often than not, they were exposed to drugs and violence, and felt completely unsafe, so if there was anyone who had some space in their house, or their heart, to take this family in temporarily, there would be many blessings in store for them. It was always blessings, there was never really anything else, nothing else worthy of being received, nothing else they had to give but nothing much else that was wanted.

Mami sat listening and was immediately moved by the announcement Mama Gloria had made, she felt compelled, as though it was her duty to do what she could, even if she did not have the means. Papa was working extra shifts once again, and although Marie and Jean were also sat listening, she knew it went over their heads. It was difficult enough for them to understand ordinary *Lingala* let alone Mama Gloria's, which sounded as though it had survived colonialism in the 1900s.

Mami went to speak to her after the church service was over. Mama Gloria introduced Mami to the family she had mentioned in the announcement; they were sat inconspicuously at the back of the church all through the service, unknown and unrecognized. Mami was not ready for this, she did not expect to meet them so soon and was nervous in case she came across bearing false hope and carrying a promise she could not keep. She knew too well what it meant to be in this situation and to have hope as your sole possession.

Her name was Madeleine, she looked young, tied her hair with a *kintambala* and wore a very pretty *liputa*. Seeing it, Mami felt as if they could have something in common; as if they could be kindred. She smiled and embraced Mami warmly when they were introduced; she seemed to have all the calm and patience of a woman who had already received what she needed, even though she was still waiting for it. Mami did not catch the name of her daughter, who was hiding coyly behind, however, she could not help but be arrested by the bright-eyed stare of the little boy stood beside her who lifted up his arms at Mami so she could pick him up. She followed instructions, whisked him up and sat him onto her hip. He must have been two or three years old. He reminded her so much of Jean when he was a child, there was also something in him always asking questions; always wanting to know. It was then Mami knew, she didn't know how, or even what, but she knew she had to do something.

They came home after church; it was usually a long bus route—where Mami and Marie would sit at the bottom deck, and Jean at the top, because being caught in your church clothes, with the rest of your family wasn't seen as the cool thing to do—but today's journey was surprisingly fast. It was as if the driver was more concerned about getting himself home than the passengers. She prepared a steady meal of *soso*, *fumbua* and *fufu*, a family favorite, on time for Papa as he arrived home from work. It was much less an ordinary family meal and more so a softening up; she knew if he had eaten, and eaten well, he would be less willing to maintain the faculty of saying no.

Papa said no. He shook his head, quite vigorously left to right, whilst they were in the kitchen clearing the plates; the kitchen was where most of the serious family meetings were held. He kept saying no, but would not look Mami in the eyes. He knew if he did, he would soften and eventually fold to her demand. Papa was surprised Mami could make this suggestion; she knew there was no room in the house, however, such was her nature, if there was room in her heart, there was room in her home.

Mami went to church during the week, which had become rare. In fact, this was her first time although it did not feel this way, it felt familiar, however, not equal to the familiarity of a Sunday church service. Church on a Wednesday evening was much different. The main difference being it wasn't in the bare and empty main hall; it was instead in the small back office, with barely enough space to fit a group of infants, let alone a handful of adults. The second thing, Wednesdays were dedicated to prayer; people came to ask for what they needed and what they could not ask for on a Sunday; it was akin to drinking concentrated dilute juice without the water; concentrated prayer. The only thing the same was Pastor Kaddi's presence; it seemed omniscient and ethereal, truly as if a divine power had been bestowed upon him, even during the week, he was truly a man of God.

As Mami sat on the floor in the small back office—they always sat on the floor for intense prayer; the idea was "the further you lower yourself, the higher up you will be lifted by the Lord"—to join the others who had already begun their prayers. She looked around and saw faces she recognized, but not faces she knew, apart from one, Mama Nadège, who she would have preferred not to have known. In such a small space, it would have been indiscriminately rude to ignore her, so Mami gave a polite, diplomatic nod of the head to her, and sat opposite from her hoping to keep interaction to a minimum, or even less.

Maybe it was the heat from the number of bodies in such a small space or the intensity of the prayers, either way, Mami could feel the temperature rising to the point where small beads of sweat trickled down her forehead beneath the bright multi-patterned *kintambala* she had wrapped around her head.

They sat around in a group, and, beginning with the Pastor, each person said a prayer. Prayers were as short or as long as needed, however, the longer was always seen as better; the idea being "the longer the prayer, the more likely it was to cover the distance from earth to the heavens so it could be heard by the Lord." If what was needed to be prayed for was too personal, then Pastor Kaddi could be seen afterward, and often many did. On this occasion, the prayers were long and intense, so long if you started praying on your knees, by the end of even the first one you were guaranteed to be sat on your side. It was said you could tell a true devout believer by looking at their knees, the darkened patches in the middle showed they spent many hours praying.

Mami's turn to pray came at the point where the fatigue was too much for her, she would have preferred to go home, but she knew why she came, and it was not for herself. Although her prayer wasn't long, it was very fast—her idea was maybe if a prayer is said faster, it can cover the distance quicker—and she said it with intent. The next person to pray was Mama Nadège, whose prayer, much to Mami's surprise, was even shorter. Mami wondered how someone with such a power charged motor-mouth did not manage to last long in prayer, however, she did not mind as the stiffness of her back from sitting on the floor had already settled in.

Pastor Kaddi was last, and he closed the prayer, falling nothing short of an epic supplication. They finished. As everyone gathered their belongings to leave, and after some had left already, Mami noticed Pastor Kaddi having an intense conversation where he hovered over a short, stout, teapot-esque Mama Nadège. They were within ear-shot; nonetheless, Mami could not make out the unintelligible exchange between them. Once she was aware she too was eavesdropping, which is a classic trait of a *songi-songi*, she stopped herself instantly.

Mama Nadège had approached Pastor Kaddi after the prayer meet to speak to him regarding something personal, too personal to be heard by others. She sought privacy. She had asked him to come to her house so he could assess her situation and provide some intervention. Pastor Kaddi often paid visits to his church members, rarely spontaneously, but more often, as requested and required; sometimes to bless the house or pray away any negative situations. They arranged to meet the following day, in the evening.

After Pastor Kaddi finished his shift at the security company—where not many, if any at all, knew he was a Pastor, but always suspected there was something different, or "funny," as they put it, about him—he made his way to Mama Nadège's house instead of going home to Dagenham.

Mama Nadège lived in a comfortably large house in South London; on the borders of Lewisham, which he took well over an hour to travel to, finally mounting the Docklands Light

Railway—the train without a driver that all the children, and some adults, would rush to the front to and pretend as if they were driving—and inconspicuously read his bible to pass the time. Her house was very spacious, for someone who did not yet have children. Her husband, the no-show, was also not present and Pastor Kaddi did not know why. She was married to a West African man; either from Ivory Coast or Mali, or another African Francophone country. No one exactly knew, they could go only in so far as they could place his French accent from the few times he had been heard, which was far less than he had been seen; it was a different kind of African-French accent to her African-French accent, but they understood each other.

Mama Nadège welcomed Pastor Kaddi in and sat him on their large three seater cream sofa in front of the widescreen TV showing an international soap opera with an English family which had crossed waters and transformed itself when it arrived, picking up new words and leaving others behind.

"Pastor, thank you for coming . . . thank you so much," she said graciously, as she poured him a cup of tea in her antique metallic silverware. Pastor Kaddi noticed the silverware, he looked around the room and noticed a number of other items also antiques; the clock, the piano she didn't play, the vase in the corner on the wooden stand, the wooden stand, maybe she wanted to give the house an older feel, as if she had been here longer, much longer.

"No problem, my sister . . ." Pastor Kaddi replied humbly, as if he had already completed a big task he did not want to take credit for. She sat beside him on the far end of the three seater sofa, leaving one space between them.

"My sister . . ." he continued, she noticed this 'sister' appellation and it felt new; special even, outside of the context of addressing a mass congregation, but he called everyone sister, although it did not feel this way to Mama Nadège, not right now.

"How can I help you?" his voice sunk low, deep, and looked at her as though he was looking through her; into her, into something else.

"Well, Pastor, we spoke a little yesterday at the prayer meeting," she spoke shyly, as if there was a reason for her to be shy, "but I did not want to say too much because I know people talk about other people's business in the church."

"Oh, you do not have to worry."

"Pastor, my 'osband and I are having problems. We are trying to have child, for one year, but it is too long. He is fed up. I don't know if something wrong . . . with me. He does not touch me. He says he is tired. He says he has a headache. I know he is lying." She broke down, in a full display of vulnerability only without the tears.

"Oh?" Pastor Kaddi replied and placed his hand on hers to console her.

"There, there, my sister, there is no problem too small or too big for the God we serve," he reached into his bag and placed the Bible he read on the train, sometimes out loud so others could hear, on the wooden table he now noticed was also an antique, "we will do what we know best . . . pray."

He took both of her hands and held them in his, closed his eyes and began to pray. It was a beckoning of the tongue, a summoning louder and louder until it filled the room and made even the antiques tremble. Mama Nadège, eyes closed, listened along and replied to his "hallelujahs" with her "amen."

After approximately ten minutes, or what felt closer to at least a few hours, Pastor Kaddi broke out of prayer.

"This is going to take a lot of work; the prayer must be stronger, with more power."

Mama Nadège did not really understand what he meant by this, nonetheless, she continued in vigorous support for it felt like a serious statement. He reached into his bag and fumbled around for something he could not find.

"Do you have holy water?" he asked, the one he carried in his bag was not there.

"Er . . ." she hesitated, not knowing exactly what made the water holy or not, and whether or not she had it. He noticed her hesitation and stepped back in, "or any bottle of water I can bless and make holy, but it has to be unopened."

"Yes!" she exclaimed, and rushed out of the room to the kitchen, where she chimed and clanged in the background, all the noise she made whilst looking for it. She looked high and low, until she eventually found a bottle from a multipack she kept in the bottom cupboards. She brought one back to Pastor Kaddi who was still sitting on the sofa, with an intense look in his eyes. She sat next to him, and placed the bottle of water on the table next to the Bible. He did not look at it, instead he looked straight at her as though she was the bottle of water, and it was her he must bless.

She sat beside him, a little closer than she was before. He kept staring, and noticed her rotund breasts, sitting up large and perky, disproportionately large for her stout body but oh so inviting. He began to salivate as if he was Pavlov's dog and had heard a bell; the bell was her breasts, the sight was the sound. He took her by both hands, as he had done previously before he started praying, and closed his eyes. He remained silent, no words, no beckoning, and no summoning, just silent. He opened his eyes again, and saw her now staring back at him. He was ravenous; he had a full appetite for the kind of sustenance only she could now provide. She began to pull back hesitantly but he leaned in closer, and closer, close until the space between their lips was only enough for a crack of light to break through. He kissed her, wild, as though he was eating her face, a hunter landed upon a runaway prey. His hands began to explore every contour of her body and removed her clothes, and his, until there was only skin on the cream leather sofa, which he noticed was also an antique, making the kind of sound only bare skin on a leather sofa makes.

Right there, in the deadliest silence, he entered her, thrust himself back and forth into her, like a swinging pendulum, back and forth, having his way, with the certainty and normality of someone who had not done this for the first time. He finished. Without breaking the silence, he put his clothes back on, and left.

chapter 24

Achieving in school changes your social circle and the kind of acceptance you receive. This was something Jean had acutely come to realize; the better he behaved and the better results he achieved in tests, even if the tests were meaningless, the greater the shift from *cool* to *uncool*, from acceptable to unacceptable, from the in group to out.

Jean started hanging around with Chris, the mathematics genius international student, and Jamil, whose father, Jean had come to discover, worked behind the counter at the local petrol station and gave him chocolates and sweets to give to his son's friends. School was a different experience with them. They had fun *in* class, sometimes they went to the teacher after the lesson to ask for more homework or higher level work to do, sometimes they would visit different teachers to ask them if they need help with anything or to complete odd jobs for extra merits, and if there was nothing to do, they would occasionally stay in the classroom completing work, particularly maths; it was no surprise Chris was so good.

Jean found this very new and different. Nonetheless, he carried the burden of judgment placed on him by others, a burden he tried so desperately to escape. In spite of all this, they *laughed*, though, over different things; the *cool* group would make jokes often mocking each other over their appearance or clothes, or girls, or even boys. The *uncool* group laughed over something in the news, when a teacher made a mistake in class, a line in a book they had read, or, and this was the most frequent one, when they would bring in a newspaper they bought from the local newsagents and edit the title or the articles; crossing out certain letters and words and leaving others, so it would have a hilarious new meaning (to them):

Los Angeles Jury Finds O.J. Simpson Not Guilty of Murder.
Los Angeles Jury Finds O.J.Simpson Not Guilty of Murder.

"Angel finds MP Guilty of Mud." Jean read, "how can you be guilty of mud?"

"Only the angel knows, only the angel." Jamil replied whilst Chris giggled in the background.

Jean found out he was rewarded with a place on the school trip to Boulogne. It was overwhelmingly exciting news, particularly as it came to him as a big surprise, which he was highly suspicious of when one day after school Mr. David asked him, Chris and Michael, with the bright ginger hair and thick rimmed glasses, who already had a GCSE certificate in one subject whilst everyone else was barely getting started, to stay behind. Jean, incredibly tense at first for being told to stay behind—old memories came back to haunt—noticed his company and realized either two of the smartest students in the school had turned bad and they were all being told off together, or they were being rewarded for something. They were each handed specially sealed letters containing information of the trip to tell their parents. Jean rushed home, running the entire way waving the envelope in the air, to tell Papa but arrived, crashing through the front door and into the living room, only to find Marie.

"Where's Dad?" Jean asked, out of breath. Marie looked up, taking her eyes away from the page of the book she was reading.

"Out." She replied abruptly like an adult resenting the interruption.

"So where's Mum?"

"Out."

"Are you home alone?" Jean asked. Marie refused to answer this question as if it were something beneath her.

"Again." He grunted as he realized. It was her turn to ask questions now, so she came at him with a flurry.

"What's wrong with you? Why are you so out of breath? And what's that you're holding?" Marie asked, noticing the way he was clutching onto the envelope and struggling for breath.

"This?" Jean hoisted it into the air.

"Are you in trouble again? Is it another suspension letter?" She laughed at him.

"This . . ." he ignored her remarks and confidently repeated the same motion, "this is the permission letter for the rewards trip to France."

"Look at you, well done . . . I guess. It took you long enough."

"It doesn't matter how long it takes as long you get there in the end. This is what truly matters."

It was a few hours before either Mami and Papa arrived home. It was a Wednesday evening and Mami had continued her recent habit of attending the mid-week prayer sessions at the church. Papa was working late. Tonton was out.

Marie had already taken herself to sleep; she did not, unlike most children, wish to stay up late and often reiterated the benefits of sleep; how it helped regulate the bodily functions and something else Jean had already stopped paying attention to by the time she said it.

Mami was on the phone when she walked through the door. She was not speaking loud, there were no echoes of *"eh-hein"* through each room, so the phone call was local and not to Kinshasa, but from the way she gripped the phone tight to her ear, it was clearly important. It was Mama Gloria, the church secretary.

Jean rushed to the door when it opened, envelope in hand, thinking it was Papa. He was disappointed but happy to see Mami regardless, he tried to wave the envelope in her face and she nodded, however, the importance of the conversation—it was always an important conversation when Mami was on the phone, or so she made it seem—superseded his achievement. Jean waited patiently until Mami finished.

"What is it?" Mami asked, annoyed by his tirelessness.

"Read the letter." Jean replied. He handed it to her all the while smiling his wide-stretched smile. Mami opened it. The English came to her slowly like a film with a bad plot she did not have the patience to see to the end.

"Just tell me what it says," Mami said, then gave the letter back to him.

"I did really good in school and I got rewarded with a trip to France!" He answered excitedly, awaiting an equally enthusiastic response.

"Well done." Mami replied as though it was something he did every week. Jean felt dismissed but not defeated. Nothing could eradicate this feeling of exaltation running through his blood.

"Can I go?" He asked excitedly like a boy half his age. Mami hesitated to reply; she mumbled incoherently under her breath an answer neither yes or no.

"Mum?"

"It is best to ask your father." Mami finally answered.

"Okay."

"But it is late and you have school tomorrow. You need to sleep."

"Don't worry mum, I'll wait for him." Jean insisted and pleaded, until finally she acquiesced to his demand. Jean left the permission letter on the dining room table, and waited for Papa on the sofa, watching TV and all the shows he did not usually get to watch, until he feel asleep right there, long before Papa even arrived. He remembered waking up on his bunk bed in the middle of the night, but was too tired to seek an explanation as to how and so he went back to sleep until the morning.

The permission letter occupied his mind through the entire day, and whether or not he would be allowed to go. His fate rested in the hands of Papa, the ultimate household decision maker who, often times, whether or not he said yes to something depended not on the achievement or the activity but the mood he was in.

Jean had never been awarded for anything, at least not outside of sports. Papa was never too impressed with his sporting achievements; sports day, football team, borough football team, he was indifferent to. This was Jean's first academic reward, and it filled him with unequivocal pride and boosted his self-esteem to the size of a mountain.

Jean came home to find Papa asleep on the sofa in front of the TV blasting news from another part of the world. He looked at the letter and it was on the table where he left it, no indication of whether or not it had been opened and read, let alone touched. Papa snored loudly, really loud as though he were a vacuum with powerful suction. It disturbed the whole house. And as much as it annoyed Jean, he was scared to wake him. So instead, he tried to be as loud as possible; dropped his bag on the floor, stomped through, until eventually, he turned the TV to full volume until Papa was startled into waking.

"Hello Dad" said Jean, acting like he barely noticed him, whilst he sat on the sofa adjacent following his usual after school tea drinking ritual.

"Hello . . ." Papa grumbled a reply, "*Boni classe, eleki bien?*"

"School was good." Jean replied. He fell silent; nerves consumed him as he hesitated, "Dad?"

"Yes." Papa replied almost falling asleep once more.

"Did you read the letter?"

"What letter?"

"The letter on the table, about the trip."

"Mm-mm."

"Shall I get it for you?" Jean asked. Papa lifted his head slowly as if it was weighted down and nodded yes. Jean got the letter from the table and passed it to him. Papa began reading.

"To the parent/carer of Jean Ntanga . . ." He laboriously read the letter, in the fourth language to lay its mark on his tongue, and it sounded like the wounded running an uphill obstacle course with a weighted backpack.

"Oh!" Papa shouted excitedly in a high pitched voice. "Congratulations, my son! A trip to France," he chuckled to himself in elated bemusement "look at what you can do when you try!"

"So can I go?" Jean asked excitedly.

"Eh?"

"Can I go on the trip, Dad?"

Papa was slow to reply, he shifted on the sofa from a slump to an upright position. His entire demeanour had changed in the space of a few seconds; he went from full smiles, front teeth showing as straight as ever, to serious faced and eyebrows crossed.

"Jean . . ." Papa spoke, his voice now much lower in register than the excited tone before. Jean felt confused because the conversation had the heaviness of when he had been in trouble at school; however this was the complete opposite situation.

"I can't go?" Jean asked, anticipating.

"No, it's not you can't go. And it's not I don't want you to go . . ."

"So what is it? The money? It's too expensive?" Jean asked pre-emptively, anticipating. Papa did not answer. He waited out his reply as though there was a push and pull of letting it out and forcing it back in happening in his mouth.

"No. You cannot go because . . . we don't have passports." Papa told Jean, which sounded as if he was a doctor informing a patient of the diagnosis of a chronic illness.

"I don't have a passport?"

"No. None of us do; me, your mother, Marie . . . we cannot go anywhere. We are refugees, son."

"So I can't go . . . I can't even go on the trip?"

"Sorry, my son."

"I always thought we never went on any trips anywhere because we don't have any money, not because of this." Jean replied sounding dejected.

"Yes, that too, but we would have found a way. You have worked hard and you deserve this."

Papa said, trying to reassure him.

"Dad, can I ask you something?" Jean asked, with a croak in his throat, voice breaking, falling apart like an abandoned building with no foundation to hold it up.

"Yes, of course."

"What is a refugee?"

"A refugee is simply someone who is trying to make a home."

part II

chapter 25

Pastor Kaddi gave another one of his electrifying sermons, however, this time something was different; it was not the choice of his words or how he spoke them, it was not his vivacity or energy, or a lack of; he was still sweating vigorously at the end, nor was it the new electric blue suit he bought; it looked as though it was solar charged, the way it drew in light from the sun, and shone. Something was different about Pastor Kaddi because he did not have with him his black leather-bound Bible with gold engraved writing on the front which he usually waved through the air during his sermons.

Mami noticed this as she sat in church taking notes of his sermon and the scriptures he referred to and recited from memory. Pastor Kaddi did not use another Bible; he had often said that particular copy was holy and blessed and considered the relationship he had with his bible a marriage; he dared not touch another. But for the life of him, he could not remember where he had left it.

Mami came to church with Marie. Papa was working a late double shift, and Jean was given the rarer than a blue moon allowance of staying at home as he claimed he did not feel well, which, ordinarily would not be enough of a reason, but given how hard he had been working and how un-visibly, though internally, upset he was about the trip, Mami decided to let him. Mama Nadège, the *songi songi*, gossip queen, was also not in church, which Mami did notice, however, not for the reason you miss someone because you feel their absence, rather for the reason you don't miss someone and you're relieved from the burden of their presence. She had not seen her for a while; naturally there were rumors, the predominant one being she had fallen sick or was unwell, and the scaremongers insisted she had been deported. After the church service was over Mami went to speak to Mama Gloria, the church secretary, and continued the phone conversation they had previously. From a distance their conversation looked light-hearted and amicable; however, between them it was as serious as a meeting of governmental officials.

Mami had told Mama Gloria she would take in the newcomer Madeleine and her two children into her home. Although it was a decision Papa was against, and they had previously agreed it was for the best not to, her heart superseded the decision as she felt too compelled to help in any way she could after seeing Madeleine and hearing the same announcement week after week after week.

Mama Gloria had spoken to Madeleine during the week and had told her the news, which she was happy to hear not only because of where it was but who it was. Mama Gloria also told her to bring all their possessions with them as they would be going after church on Sunday. When Mami saw they had barely a suitcase between the three of them she was certain she had made the right decision to help them no matter how much it impinged on their aspirations of a normal life. The rest of the congregation also supported in what little way they could, some giving clothes and a small amount of much needed collected money able to see them through.

Mami, Marie, Mama Gloria, Madeleine and her two children, squeezed into Mama Gloria's red two-door Nissan Micra where the smallest child had to sit across two people's laps at the back and duck down anytime there was sign of a police car passing by. She was one of the few women who drove a car in the church, if not the only one. It was a rare sight but Mama Gloria had been able to access things the others saw as unobtainable because she had been here a little bit longer, and knew the system a bit better. Some, usually the embittered, would say it was because she was married to an English man who did things for her and not anything she did for herself. There were also those who could not exercise their faith, and refused to believe any man, let alone an English man, could marry a woman as serious and as grumpy as her.

It was not a long drive home to Mami's. On a Sunday evening the roads were clear as people usually choose to make the most of their remaining weekend time by spending it at home and preparing themselves for the Mondays they hated. When they arrived home Jean was in the living room watching TV. He had his diary clutched in his hands, which he stuffed into the seat of the sofa and stood when he heard the front door open and Mami announce "allooo!" as they walked in. He met them at the corridor and was taken aback by the number of people he saw waiting there. It was like a surprise birthday party for the birthdays he did not really even care to celebrate. He recognized Mama Gloria as the lady in church who stood on the podium and said things he never paid attention to, however, he did not recognize the new faces.

"Jean, *wapi Papa?*" Mami asked.

"He's not home yet." Jean replied, face demanding an explanation. There was a short silence. Mami tried to figure out the best way to tell Papa the news when he came home: food. He was always calmer, thus more likely to accept, after a home-cooked meal.

"This is Mama Madeleine. Say hello." She said.

"Hello." Jean greeted her coyly.

"And this her children . . ."

"Christelle," Madeleine's daughter introduced herself and smiled but her face did not change, her cheeks did not lift as one would expect, but she smiled nonetheless.

"My name is Glody," the little bright-eyed boy also introduced himself and walked toward Jean with his hands lifted in the air so he could be picked up. Jean obliged.

"They will be staying with us for a while." Mami said.

Jean looked over at Marie and stared at her asking the question he was not bold enough to protest out loud. Marie was indifferent to his reaction, not because she did not care but because she knew this was not the moment for them to have an opinion.

"Mama Madeleine and Christelle will stay in Marie's room and Glody will share with you."

Jean would have felt indignant, but the satisfaction of seeing Marie share her room in the same way he had had to all this time overrode the indignation. Also, the little bright-eyed boy made him feel calm; he made him think of how it would be to have a younger brother, someone he could be an example and role model to, and he welcomed it.

Although Tonton's presence was still felt, he was at the home much less these days, spending more time out than in, for reasons none of them sought to question.

After a few moments of showing them around the small flat and the inescapable formality of eating a meal together no longer as guests, Mami showed Mama Gloria out and they both thanked each other profusely, each in abundant appreciation for the sacrifice the other had made.

After a hectic remainder of the evening cleaning, pulling out mattresses, new bed covers and sheets, unpacking a large suitcase and finally crashing on the sofa, it was late and everyone else had gone to sleep. Mami waited for Papa to come home. When he finally did arrive home, he found her sleeping on the sofa. They spoke briefly. Mami told him about the latest house guests. He was not surprised, in fact, he did not even react as if he was being told anything new. Although she was pleased, Mami put this down to Papa being tired, rather than him already being prepared because he knew it was only a matter of time.

Over the next few weeks, the new family and the old family (including Tonton, who would still stumble home late at night, loud enough to wake Glody from his slumber) was slowly coming together to form a new hybrid family more comfortable with each other's presence in the house. Papa was the one who seemed to react the most alienated by it all, he would often spend hours in his bedroom, leaving Mami, Madeleine and the other children in the living room to accommodate each other, either because he wanted to give them more room to enjoy what limited space was available, or because he resented it all. Mami noticed this; his distance, how he spoke less, and showed his perfectly straight teeth even less so, and particularly, how he was much more tolerant of Tonton, how he did not chastise him for his late night entries, or empty bottles and cans left lying around. Mami noticed all of this; however, it wasn't noticed by everyone else as they always assumed he was tired from work, which was always a good excuse for not wanting to engage.

Jean and Christelle had been speaking more and more, much to Jean's surprise. Regardless of the language barrier, built up between them as high as the Inga dam, there was still a flood of conversation; Jean spoke mostly English now, and understood French whilst his Lingala decrescendoed into the background like the end of a beautiful song. Christelle spoke Lingala, she spoke as if she had been, for a long time, watering the seeds planted on her tongue. Her French, too, was fluent, and often he would have to tell her to slow down, but her English dragged as if it were hurt. "I . . . want . . . drink . . . tea," she would utter laboriously but ever persistent. Between the two of them, they made it work, and where there wasn't anything being said, Glody was able to fill the welcomed silence.

When Jean was busy hoisting little Glody into the air whilst Christelle watched, he said "Glody is so much fun. I would love to have a little brother," to which Christelle, out of the blue, replied, "he's not my little brother," and after offering a long pause for Jean's heart rate to return back to normal she added, "he's my son." Jean's jaw shattered into little pieces inside his mouth but on the surface he simply looked back at Christelle with a blank face. He did not know how to react. He wasn't sure how old Christelle was, she had a youthful face not yet worn from the sorrows of the world. He assumed they were roughly the same age, give or take a few years, both teenagers nonetheless, both worrying about the same things in life; making friends and being liked by them, school, not being annoyed by parents, having the latest games or trainers to maintain coolness. Not necessarily in this order, but at least they would both as teenagers be concerned about it. He did not realize Christelle would already have to worry about the future of another human being who she had brought into this world. He tried to imagine himself as a father. He stopped instantly.

Nonetheless, although Jean was shocked it made sense to him. He realized how often Glody would run to Christelle instead of Madeleine, or how over-protective she was of him, and how it had to be something more than sibling love, because he knew he had not cared to the same degree for Marie. He did not externally react after hearing this, even though on the inside he was exploding with the question: *how?* Nonetheless, he knew it was his place not to ask questions, there are some paths not all feet are meant to walk, and on some paths, no feet at all.

Whilst everyone else was either at work or school, Madeleine and her children mostly stayed at home. She was very useful, often cleaning and sometimes cooking, trying to provide as much home labor as possible to substitute for the rent she could not pay (and would never be asked to), as a thank you. They were without papers, and after a battle of being moved from centre to centre, temporary housing to temporary housing, to no housing at all, with strangers who spoke not their tongue or knew none of their culture, moving in with Mami and the family felt the same as being welcomed back into their own home.

chapter 26

ON SUNDAY THE ENTIRE FAMILY ATTENDED church and arrived early. Mami accompanied by Marie as usual, Papa made sure not to work so he was square and stiff facing forward, Jean was present in body but absent in thought—he would have preferred to be playing football with friends and the new extended family Madeleine and her children also came. Even Tonton was present, though he sat at the back of church in aviation sunglasses, head tilted back onto the wall, which made it difficult to tell whether he was awake or asleep; those who knew him, which was everyone, knew that he was sleeping.

The church service was as full as they had ever seen it. It was as though the entire congregation had received a letter summoning them to court, and had all turned up to church to exercise their faith, in need of miraculous reassurance by the Lord. Even Mama Nadège, who had not been seen for a while, made a surprise but welcomed return. Although she did not sit right next to Mami, the seat she usually occupied often with intent, which was now taken by Madeleine, she sat a few chairs down in another row, close enough to be noticed. However, she was not sat alone. She came with her husband, the West African man who was usually a no-show and was heard much less than he was ever seen. Mami looked over and smiled at her, and Mama Nadège gave a half-hearted smile in acknowledgment, as though it had been forced out of her, as though she suspected she had been spoken about.

It was time for the opening hymn, and everyone stood to sing. Mama Nadège was slowest to stand, Mami noticed her movement was stiff from the back and the knees, not because of her size, although this would have been an easy assumption to make, but because of a burden she was all too familiar with.

"*Aza na zemi?*" Mami pointed with her head, and whispered to Madeleine who was sat next to her. Madeleine was none the wiser and assumed it was just her weight."*Aza munene,*" she replied.

The congregation sang the opening hymn, during which Mami spent most of her time adjusting to get a better look. Finally, when Mama Nadège rested her hand on her stomach, and stroked it lightly, Mami knew it was not an indication of her hunger: she was pregnant! And heavily so. Mami gasped so loud from the surprise it took in all the air around her, causing the other members of the congregation, even Madeleine and Marie sat right next to her, to look over suspiciously. Mami turned the gasp into a cough as if there was something stuck in her throat, and everyone looked away.

Pastor Kaddi had a much calmer demeanour in his sermon; it was as though what was once the crashing wave of the ocean against a rocky shore became calm water flowing smoothly under a bridge. He spoke about having compassion and forgiveness in your hearts, and being considerate of the struggles other people go through. He read from one of his most beloved chapters. He read because he had retrieved his black leather-bound Bible, with gold engraved writing on the front, which he thought he had lost to the world. He read from the book of Matthew, Chapter 6 verse 14 – 15:

For if you forgive others their trespasses, your heavenly Father will also forgive you, but if you do not forgive others their trespasses, neither will your Father forgive your trespasses.

Mami took notes as she tried with all her efforts not to be distracted, as though she were a mediocre student with a short attention span, but she could not help it; the excitement of Mama Nadège's pregnancy, of which she was certain, there was no doubt, overwhelmed her. She kept frequently looking over, angling her head for a better view.

Pastor Kaddi requested the congregation to engage in collective prayer. He asked for everyone's participation; he asked for them to close their eyes, and from their hearts forgive those who had wronged them so it could be cleared to receive the blessings promised on to them. The congregation followed and proceeded to close their eyes in prayer, even Mama Nadège's husband, who was heard much less than he was seen, closed his eyes. Mami closed her eyes too and pleaded deep inside herself for her cries to be heard. She opened her eyes, and looked over at Papa, who was sat in the opposite seats, with his eyes closed. Jean was sat at the back of the church with his head bobbing up and down resisting sleep. Mami would have been upset with him, but she cleared her heart and forgave him also.

After Pastor Kaddi's heartfelt sermon, Mama Gloria came forward for the announcement. She addressed the congregation as family but spoke as if she was the voice in the supermarket inconveniently disrupting a peaceful shopping experience to tell a staff member to report to checkout. There was a moment of compassion, in keeping with Pastor Kaddi's message, when she spoke endearingly of the warmth and love shown by those who were able to help Madeleine and her family, who now had somewhere to stay. The congregation applauded the news, and in the midst of the moment, Mama Gloria and Mami looked at each other, in clandestine, with a fondness and appreciation only they knew.

Mama Gloria went on to make another grand announcement. She asked Mama Nadège to stand, which she did in a visibly labored fashion—her belly now protruding through the long cardigan she wore on top of her *liputa*—and announced Mama Nadège "*aza na zemi*," to which the entire congregation erupted in rapturous whooping and joyful singing. Mama Nadège shyly smiled and raised her hand, then sat back down as labored as she did when standing.

After the church service was over, and people stayed behind to socialize and eat food; today there was a humble serving of *mikate* and *makemba*, Mami, unable to contain her excitement, went over to speak to Mama Nadège, who was having her celebrity moment of constant adulation and praise, whilst her husband stood idly in the background similar to a security guard or an umpire in a rather boring sport.

"Mama Nadège!" Mami shrieked out whilst stroking her stomach, "Congratulations! So this is why you were away. Why didn't you tell me?" Mama Nadège mumbled nervously and did not really offer Mami an answer.

"I was so worried when I did not see you for a long time," Mami continued excitedly, "No Wednesday prayers, no Sunday services, but you come back and you are pregnant. I am *so* happy for you."

"Thank you, Mami, thank you." Mama Nadège replied, with only a few words. Mami was wrapped in so much excitement she did not even notice how little Mama Nadège spoke.

"And congratulations to you too, sir." Mama extended the gesture to the husband, who nodded, neither accepted nor rejected it, and continued to stand idly in Mama Nadège's shadow.

"So is it a boy? Is it a girl? How many months?" Mami rushed on not giving her a chance to reply. Before Mami could throw in another hailstone of questions, Pastor Kaddi kindly interrupted and very happily greeted them—after each church service, he went around to personally shake the hands, hug and greet each member of the congregation—and wished Mama Nadège *"Felicitation!"* which he boomed from the top of his voice, as though he were beginning the service once again, and hugged her warmly. Pastor Kaddi turned to Mama Nadège's husband, the West African man. They both looked at each other with feigned interest, and he again wished him *"Felicitation,"* in a much more reserved manner, as if someone had turned down the volume of his voice. Mama Nadège's husband smiled and nodded. Pastor Kaddi turned to face the small group around them, whilst speaking to Mama Nadège and her husband. Papa and Mami stood side by side listening.

"This is a blessing," Pastor Kaddi repeated, no less than three times, "a blessing from God!" he boomed, pronouncing the Word with an extended *o* in the middle, certain and proud.

"He has given you a blessing as a testament of your faith, for you never stopped believing."

"He's such a good man," Mami whispered to Papa who was daydreaming into the distance, "listen to him speak."

"May we all receive such blessings from the Lord, Hallelujah." Pastor Kaddi concluded.

"Amen!" Mami burst out spontaneously in response consuming the rest of the group around, including Mama Nadège's quiet reply, which tried to hide itself as if an embarrassed child sitting in the corner.

chapter 27

M ONDAY AFTERNOON BROUGHT AN EXHAUSTED JEAN home from school. It was not due to fatigue from sports, or from participating in anything particularly strenuous. Nothing beyond taking part with the games Chris and Jamil would play, taking something of each other's and running away with it until they were caught or pulling away each other's chair before they sat down. Jean was tired because of how little sleep he was getting from having so many people in the house; every day was like a loud social gathering.

He came home to find a surprisingly calm house; Mami was preparing food, Marie was in her room, Papa was at work, this was usual, but the calm came from Madeleine, Christelle and Glody not being there. Tonton was out.

This was the first time he had been in the house without them since they had arrived. He had gotten used to their sounds— Glody's happy laughter and shrieks of joy when he raised his arms to be lifted up and down, Madeleine's chatter with Mami in the kitchen, and Christelle's often silent observant presence. He did not mind their presence, but the reminder of how it

felt to have peace and a little more space came sweet to him as though it were an unexpected gift from a stranger.

He slumped onto the sofa, with his school bag and shoes still on, and switched on the TV and began watching the show of the young boy with the magic watch with the ability to stop and start time as he wished. He would use it to save people—a child who was going to get run over, or stop burglars robbing a house, which, Jean thought, was all commendable but were it him he would have used it mostly to stay in bed a little bit longer in the mornings.

His quiet moment was disturbed. Mami came into the living room and told him to *"Telema!"* and place his belongings in his room. Madeleine and the rest came home, and the wave of noise came flowing back. Jean did not know where they had come from but from how they were dressed and the slow steady walk with which they entered the house, it seemed important. He did not say much, Mami met them at the door and dove straight into conversation.

They had returned from a meeting with their immigration lawyer several bus rides away. A young looking man, which made Madeleine suspicious of his experience and ability to fulfill his duties. His name was Mark and he wore a dark blue suit one size too big for him, but at least he wore a suit. He was accompanied by a translator named Anne-Sophie who had a light tinge of red in her hair and her most distinguishable features were the glasses she wore hanging off her crooked nose.

Mami took Madeleine into the kitchen, and closed the door behind them. She was clutching a wad of folders and files to her chest as if she was a student going to class. They spoke for a long time in the kitchen, but had forgotten to switch on the light so whilst the sun was setting, it made their conversation appear twice as serious; it looked as though they were plotting a clandestine operation underneath a sky with streaks of gold.

Jean had returned to his room and was lying on his bed, half way falling asleep, when he heard Mami bellow his name

summoning him, "Yes, mum!" he replied loudly, and mumbled under his breath annoyed because he knew he was being sent somewhere. Jean found it frustrating when Mami summoned him because he knew she would ask him to do things she could easily do herself—pass the remote, go to the shop, or look for something she had lost.

"*Lata*." She said, telling him to go and get dressed, which meant he was being sent outside.

"Okay." Jean replied begrudgingly. He followed instructions, got dressed and came back to the kitchen.

"*Mema oyo*," she dumped the A4 folder into his arms, "*Kende ko sala photocopie*," and gave him the money. Jean sighed and eventually went, however, he saw it as something she could do herself and so he brewed with resentment.

He slowly walked to the local internet café with the huge *Dahabshiil* sign on its window, which everyone assumed was the name of the shop. It was owned by a Somali elder who was there every hour of the day. Everyone called him "Uncle"—maybe it was because of the familiarity of his demeanour; he felt like a relative. The internet café would, in the evenings, double up as a meeting ground for the elder Somali men, who would sit chewing *khat* and retelling stories only their ears and hearts could understand.

Jean walked in and the man smiled showing his slightly stained brown teeth, welcoming him for they had gotten familiar with each other the many times he came after school to use the computers. "Internet?" he asked Jean with his distinctive east African accent.

"No, photocopy." Jean groaned in reply. The man laughed in a hoarse tone—his voice was worn from adjusting to the cold weather and the combination of whiskey in the evenings and coffee he drank in the mornings. He knew how much Jean despised making photocopies, reason being, they took so long and he always got the pages wrong. Jean was counting how many pages there were, so he could see how long it would take, when he noticed a few words pop out and grab his attention from one of the pages. He felt as though if he looked and read what was written, he would be breaking someone's trust, but the feeling of curiosity overpowered him. He saw Madeleine's full name, and age; she was younger than Mami. He started reading.

Kinshasa prisons are not the same as Western prisons, the heat, the smell, no windows, no sunlight, and there you sleep on the floor, and it is damp because it is where you go to the toilet. I was in prison for at least eight days until I stopped counting. My daughter was with me, a few cells down, I could hear her. I do not know why they arrested us, maybe for wearing the wrong clothes, maybe because they thought we had money. All I know is the city was on fire and les Soldats were dogs, I can still hear the echoes of their chants, "MPR egale servir, se servir, non;" serve others, do not serve yourself.

I used to sell bread, sometimes they would harass you, because you are a woman, make you give them money, or something more. At night it was the worst. There was no noise—nobody moving, no sound meant people were tired, or sleeping, or worse. This is when it would begin: les Soldats, prison guards, policemen. I did not know who. It was dark, they all had the same uniform, the same face, the same smell, same intention. They come into your cell. You could hear their boots, creeping, even the cheap leather their shoes were made from squeaked. Then the clink of metal; the key going into the keyhole and opening the cell gate, then the clink to close it again. Every night was the same. The first time is when you scream the loudest, hoping somebody can hear you, hoping somebody comes. Nobody hears. Nobody comes. Each time you scream a little less, a little quieter, until your screams are silent. I also heard my daughter scream. I had never heard her scream before.

Then one day, they let us out. My daughter was sitting waiting for me. It was the first time I saw her since. She looked at me with eyes as though the living thing inside of her had stopped breathing. We went back home but it was not the same. There was nothing for us there. And in these months, my daughter's belly started to grow. But she became blank, empty, staring into the nothing in front of her. It was not the same when our family in the village found out. For a long time my daughter did not touch her son, so I nursed him. For a long time she would sit and watch him, and sit and watch, never taking her eyes off her child. He became my child. It was a shame on our family. Then one day my husband . . .

Jean could not read any further. He felt as if he had left the room and was being held in the same prison, the same time, he could feel it, the heat; trickles of sweat crept down his forehead like tiny spiders, and the smell; he breathed it in, the taste rested on his tongue and his stomach turned almost causing him to throw up. He suddenly remembered where he was. In the shop. Uncle. *Dahabshil.* Photocopier.

He felt as though he had been standing there for hours. He watched the light from inside the photocopy machine pass through as it whirred into action. He looked around frantically; everyone else carried on as normal whilst he remained over-whelmed from this out of body experience where, for the first time, for a moment, it was as though he went into the body of another life and became them. Someone he knew.

After Jean's deep breaths returned to normal, he finished photocopying the rest of the sheets of paper, preferring to look away than to acquiesce to his curiosity and read again. He paid and walked home, steps a little slower than before but this time, for a different reason.

Later that night, Jean could not sleep. He lay in bed sweating profusely as though he was laying in the open sun. He felt like he was no longer in his room, but in Kinshasa, in the prison, the imagined sound; the screams and the stomping boots, echoed in his head and through the room. He wrote in his diary that night:

I don't know who I can speak to about any of this. Every time something happens, I think it is just one small thing, but it gets worse. And I have no way of doing anything about it. It's scary. I feel as if I'm watching all these car crashes happening on the path I'm traveling, and all I can think about is when will we crash? It's not a question of if we will crash, but when. I know it will happen one day, and this is a scary way to travel through life. Or maybe it has happened already, and I didn't know about it? There is so much I don't know. And again, I have so many questions. I want to ask my Dad or Mum about this but I don't think I can. I am scared.

Unable to sleep, Jean got out of bed and went to the kitchen for a glass of water. To his surprise, he found the lights on and Marie in the kitchen by the sink also filling up a glass of water.

"What's wrong?" Jean asked.

"Nothing," Marie replied, "I just can't sleep."

"Me neither."

"It's just so noisy in there, I hate sharing a room." Jean chuckled at her complaints for finally she was beginning to understand how he had felt all these years, "Madeleine snores so loud, she is so annoying, and Christelle . . . ugh, always getting in the way."

"Don't be rude!" Jean snapped in defense.

"I wasn't trying to be rude, I was just saying . . ."

"Well, don't."

"I just meant how it's hard because there's no space."

Jean let out a groan, which Marie sensed had nothing to do with what they were talking about.

"Are you okay?" She asked, showing concern.

"Did you know we were refugees?" He cut straight to the chase.

"What do you mean?"

"Refugees, like, you know when . . ." he hesitated.

"When what?"

"Basically, we don't have papers . . . to stay in the country."

"What does that mean?" Marie's voice started to crack.

"I don't know, it's kind of scary and no one talks about it."

"How?"

"Like, didn't you hear what happened to Mum's friend at church? She was deported. And no one said anything. That could happen to us. We could be sent back."

"No! Why would you say that?" Marie's voice sounded heavy with emotion.

"But that's just what could . . ."

"No," Marie interrupted, "it's not going to happen to us." She did not want to imagine, let alone hear the rest of his sentence, lest it tempt fate, "Please, you have to promise me, please." Tears flowed down her faced as she hugged Jean so tight as if to stop him from going anywhere, "Promise. Promise," she repeated. He hugged her back, and held her, realizing how deeply he cared for his little sister, and how their bond grew deeper with the new awareness they both had of themselves.

chapter 28

AFTER A DRAMATIC START IN BRUSSELS; mostly because of Phelix and his, quite literal, shortcomings, Papa eventually settled as quietly and comfortably as his introverted personality allowed him to. He, more and more, learned to see things in advance before they happened, choosing to stay in his room and read than to head on a night out, often into a cold night, when invited by Phelix. He still, nonetheless, carried a stick where his books were, just in case.

It was almost always Phelix who insisted they go out to a party or a club, Claude and Paul, always in a pair, were only going because of Phelix, but their indifference to partying, and then to Phelix, eventually grew until even they were looking for other options. Some nights Phelix would arrive at Papa's dorm, with the pair, knocking "*Tock! Tock! Tock!*," insisting they go out for a drink—a drink to him, and a drink to them, meant two different things—and they would eventually wind up staying in Papa's dorm room, knees knocking, crammed like sardines in the small space between them, having serious passionate discussions on world affairs.

They could not ever seem to agree on any issues—religion, society, history, politics. As students, they saw the world according to their subjects: science, engineering, sociology and art, Papa and Phelix often coming together, against Claude and Paul. And when Paul would say something the rest considered too abstract and idealist, such as "everybody should be free to love whoever they desire regardless of race or gender," they would interrupt and say "Oh! It's because you're an artist, the real world is not this way!" as if there was a separate world he was living in.

There was, however, one thing they all agreed on most of the time; women. They exchanged stories of lament and longing, conquest and concubines, heart break and hope. Paul usually spoke the least on this; Phelix would speak incessantly, with longing and adoration, about *Reni*, who the others had already forgotten, and other girls, the kind of girls he liked; Claude spoke of love as though it were some kind of social experiment, placing himself in the midst of the multiple identities he assumed; and Papa lamented, not really ever knowing why, over Mami, but was ever so cautious as not to reveal her name. It was as if he missed her, in a way he could never admit but also never reject; it was a reoccurring dream he felt each night but would forget by the morning, the feeling of his eyes adjusting to the brightness of dawn after the darkest of nights. She was the light that broke the sky, the same light breaking him.

Koko Patrice was there to meet Papa at the airport when he landed back in Kinshasa for the first time. It was a long flight. Papa fell asleep and woke several times, sometimes over land, sometimes over water, each time regretting looking out of the window because it ignited the fear of heights he thought he had left behind in his childhood. When he did land, the first thing he remembered was the hot Kinshasa air. It rushed into the airplane and swept over his body. This is how home felt like; a familiar warm embrace.

Koko Patrice waited for Papa whilst leant over the back of a smooth grey-silver Mercedes car, with sparkling chrome wheels and jet black tyres. Papa found it odd to see *Koko* this way, leaning on someone else's car. He looked like someone he did not know, someone he barely recognized; could he have really changed this much in a year?

As Papa approached, and *Koko Patrice* realized he was there, he placed his bag next to him, not knowing quite how to greet or be greeted. *Koko Patrice* gave him a firm hand shake, as if he was trying to grind his knuckles into dust. To any lookers on, it appeared to be a business client being picked up for a meeting rather than father-son who had not seen each other for a lengthy time. It was only when *Koko* picked up his luggage and placed it in the boot that Papa realized the new Mercedes was his. It wasn't new, new, but new enough to look as if it should belong to someone else. *Koko Patrice* got in the car and motioned to Papa, "*Kota! Kota!*," who in turn stood there frozen, staring, in shock and awe. He settled into the soft leather seat of the car, and noticed how pristine the interior had been kept; not a single speck of dust. He watched *Koko Patrice* as he drove with both hands clamped on the steering wheel, eyes straight ahead, leaning forward as though it was his head controlling the direction of the car.

They drove from *N'djili* airport along the long straight road of *Boulevard du 30 Juin*, to make their way home to *Bandal*. Papa noticed how the streets were so much livelier than where he had just come from. There was an inimitable energy and movement, a dancing of the bones, a rush in the blood, and a peace flowing through the river of the mind. This is how home felt like; a familiar peace.

There was a long period of silence, an expected silence. Papa and *Koko Patrice* hardly spoke when he was in another country let alone when they were together. Conversations were often one way, and instructional; *Koko* reminded Papa what he was not allowed to do, or informed him of the money he was sending to support him, all received with a gracious reluctance. They spoke three times in the year Papa recalled; when arriving, in the new year to wish each other "*bonana*," and when he was coming back home.

Koko Patrice broke the silence.

"*Olingi voiture oyo?*"

"*Oui, eza kitoko*," Papa replied, hesitant and confused as to why his father asked him about the car, as if he had just seen it. He suspected there was something else to be said, something greater.

"*Mwana na ngai*," *Koko Patrice* continued "*oza ko sala malamu, bravo*." Koko congratulated Papa on how well he was doing. The unfamiliarity of praise from his father stunned him, he was more used to being instructed, reprimanded, than praised.

"*Makambu ezali ko changer na mboka oyo . . .*" *Koko Patrice* continued but abruptly ended there, adding nothing else. Confused, Papa looked around at the streets through the window he had rolled down to let the not-so-fresh Kinshasa air in. He contemplated what *Koko* meant by this, "things are changing in this country," he was looking, however, he could not see. Everything still appeared to be as he left it.

The Congolese students who were studying abroad, in Belgium, France, and even in countries as far as Germany and Romania, came back home around the same time for the summer holidays. For the next few weeks, there was lots of excitement surrounding them. They would meet to share stories and tell each other of life under foreign skies, not really meeting with others who had been abroad but more so, with those who had stayed home. They spoke as though they were explorers, travellers, who had left and returned bearing an important message as if it was found by the ocean, written on papyrus and sealed in a glass bottle, or engraved on two stone tablets and left by a burning bush on top of the mountain. It made them feel special. The same feeling when you leave to go and find yourself but return only to see you were there all along.

Papa avoided this. There was no big homecoming for him. No other students for him to share stories with. No family to come around and make him the warm home cooked meals he longed for whilst he shivered in the cold of his dorm room in Brussels. It was just him and *Koko Patrice*, and he often stayed at home whilst *Koko* went to work, not at the bank but somewhere more important, to which Papa had not paid attention to when *Koko* told him and instead nodded along, whilst simultaneously daydreaming, in the middle of the rare occasion of a conversation. He often daydreamed of Mami, thinking of her, where she was and how she was doing. He felt consumed by the irony, although he had returned and closed the distance there was between them, he did not feel much closer to her at all.

On some days, he would leave the house and roam the streets, venturing to where they first met, lurking, passing so many of the other students, some of whom resembled her, reminded him of her, but it was never ever her. He would sometimes spend all day in the shop where he knew she used to go and buy bread, waiting for her there, much to the annoyance of the vendor, who, at first, was suspicious of this young man, waiting for hours in the shop then always leaving without paying for anything, until he came to the conclusion there must be something wrong with the boy; a diagnosis of chronic loneliness and nowhere to go. He dared not to pass by Mami's house. She lived in a compound with high gates and a guard in *Gombe*. She was the daughter of a military man; their house was not a house you just passed by on your way to somewhere, it was the destination.

It was agonizing knowing they were so close yet so far away, it unnerved Papa to think of her this much; was she thinking of him? If she was, why hadn't she made the effort to reach him? He thought how she could be thinking the same thing, and it all became a complicated maze they wandered aimlessly through. He did not see Mami. Not in the shops. Not on the street. Not for the entire summer. And slowly, she started to fade into the back of his mind as on old memory does.

It was a few summers passing until Papa saw Mami again. A few more years of European winters and African summers, a few more years of the growing silence between him and *Koko Patrice*, a few more years of the longing; the waiting in the shops, on the street, each time shorter and shorter. But nonetheless, when he did see her, it was as though seeing her again for the first time. It was as though she was a new woman who he had already known.

They ran into each other at the *Zandu*, the central market where, it seems, the entire city of Kinshasa went to buy their food; the *kwanga*, *pondu*, *makemba* and their fancy *liputas*, usually of the best *super wax* quality. It was a busy place; a traffic of human bodies, creating a beautiful explosion of sounds and colors.

Papa was walking through the many rows of the market, where mostly the women sellers sold their fruits and veg to earn just enough money to take care of themselves and everyone who depended on them, when he noticed someone who he thought was Mami. He was certain it was her. He followed the woman around, walking behind her, from a distance, as she shopped and collected her food in a bag, until eventually, when he was certain it was her, absolutely certain, he approached her from her blind side and accidentally bumped into her clumsily, knocking her bags to the floor.

"*Yo mpenza!*" Mami turned around and shouted, louder than he had ever heard her raise her voice before, until she turned around and saw it was Papa, and a quiet fell upon her, warm rain over a forest tree; "*yo,*" she now said softly, lowering her head. Papa raised her head, lifting it from her chin with his index finger. She was beautiful, more than he had known. Her beauty had grown as if it were something being nurtured and well taken care of, like a plant, a flower, like something which grows from the earth. She smiled. Her dark eyes resembled two marbles containing a myriad of galaxies, and her cheekbones were thrones upon which deities sat. She looked at him, eyes darting back and forth to the different parts of his face. She was getting to know it once again. His face had also changed; he had a thick, jet black moustache now, and an afro, big enough for it to be an afro but still small enough so *Koko Patrice* would not impose another instruction on him and tell him to cut it off.

Papa picked up the bags he had knocked over, and gave it to her still smiling face, as they walked off together, in seemingly synchronized steps, out of the *Zandu* to the busy *balabala* filled with traffic.

"So, *docteur* . . . can I call you *docteur*, yet?" She said, smirking. He laughed too, remembering how he enjoyed her humor, her wit, her sarcasm; and how much he had missed it.

"Not yet. I've just started, but soon you will be calling me doctor."

"You still don't look like one . . ." She stepped back, looked him up and down, and noticed he took up more space in her eyes than he did last time, he was eating more and sweating less, his arms looked bigger, as if they too could carry her the same way his eyes did.

"And what does a doctor look like?" Papa replied, in an exaggerated unimpressed tone.

"Well, not like you." This time she laughed, and he knew she was laughing at the flared jeans he wore and the open collar shirt.

"How is Brussels?" she asked, returning to a manner of sensibility.

"It's okay. It's cold. They still treat you as if it is 1880s, instead of 1980s, but it's okay," Papa replied very matter-of-factly.

"How is Kinshasa?" he asked. Mami did not answer the question; she simply looked at him cunningly. She knew he was not asking to know, he was asking as if to remind her he had left and she had stayed. Mami found this ironic as all the students were always keen to return during the holidays, but even more keen to remind people that they were away.

"How are *you*?" Papa asked, this time more genuinely, with a desire to truly know. He was aware of how he had grown, how his experiences had changed him—from the late nights drinking, and the fights, to the late nights of reading and solitude—but he did not know how she had grown, how she had changed; if there was something slowly dimming the light inside her, which is what happened to so many.

"I am fine . . ." she replied hesitantly. He stayed quiet, saying nothing, looking at the floor as they walked as if not accepting this as enough. ". . . You know, just the usual, family pressure, and circumstance not allowing me to do what I want to do."

"What do you want to do?"

"I want to be a teacher."

"A teacher?!"

"You seem surprised?"

"Surprised? No. It's just you don't look like a teacher."

"Very funny! I see you are using your head for a sense of humor instead of growing a sorry excuse for an afro. You look like *Sassou*, your hairline that is."

"I do not look like *Sassou-Nguesso*," Papa denied, although he knew it was a little bit true. "Seriously though, a teacher? I didn't know . . ." he continued.

"You never asked . . ." Papa waited in silence, as he knew she was right and he had no retort, "Men never ask. The world is always about them and what they're going to do, and the women they're going to choose to be their sidekick."

"Gosh, you're starting to sound like your sister."

Mami cut her eyes at Papa with the sharpness of a samurai sword.

"*Touché*. I'm sorry . . ." he cleared his throat dramatically, "Tell me, Mami, what is it you would like to do?"

"I would like to be a teacher. I would love to work with children."

"I think you would be a fantastic teacher."

"Really?"

"Yes. I have already learned a lot from you."

"How? What I have taught you?"

"A lot of things, but the most important of all is you have taught me patience." Mami waited for Papa to continue. "Yes, patience; the best things are truly worth waiting for." Papa looked at Mami with the same longing he once knew, the longing he thought he had forgotten. The longing that she too had felt.

"Well, I'm glad you learned . . ." she paused, a sadness swept over her eyes, "I wish it were easier though. My family insists marriage is the most important thing for me now; I must find a husband, and prepare myself to be a good wife, and mother . . ."

"So have you found one?"

"Found what?"

"A husband . . ."

"No!" She replied sternly, "I do not care for a husband. There are things I want to do with my life."

"But you are thinking about it, no?"

"Yes, of course, all the time, because all women stay awake, late at night losing sleep thinking about finding a husband," she was now skipping ahead, mocking theatrically in a sing-song voice, getting the attention of on-lookers, as they continued to walk down the street, "Oh, husband? Where is my husband? Where will I find my husband? Will he be street cleaner? Or a seller in the Zandu? Oh, husband? Where will I find you? Maybe he will be a businessman . . ."

"Or maybe he will be studying abroad to one day train to become a doctor!" Papa shouted ahead at her. Mami stopped immediately. She turned back to look at Papa with squinted eyes, as if he had handed her a plan she needed to evaluate before approval. She continued walking, slowly, until he caught up.

"Well . . ." She began once again, with her softest voice, resonating in all its magic, "it was nice to see you again."

"It was nice to see you too." Papa replied. There was a long pause between them, each waiting for the other to say what they were too prideful to say themselves. It was Papa who eventually lost his nerve and said he wanted to see her again.

"It would be nice." Mami replied, happy he had acquiesced to his feelings and not let pride win over love. They made arrangements; a week, a time, a place and parted ways.

"See you," she whispered, contentedly.

"*Kende malamu.*"

chapter 29

LITTLE HAD CHANGED AT HOME FOR Mami, apart from the furniture resembling what they were seeing on their colorless television at the time. The family -Marthe still as resistant and steadfast as ever, Marie who was elusive, and Monique and Micheline who were busy emulating their father, *Koko ya Mobali*; and *Koko ya Mwasi*, his wife, who still never spoke over him— were together in one way but fragmented in another. The sisters were still divided, Mami and Marthe, ever responsible, with the others still pursuing their more youthful endeavors. None were yet married (each for a different reason) and all were living at home which you never really left until you were married but it was never asked what happened to those who never did.

Mami came home in the evening to find Marthe already there, which was a rare occasion these days, in their shared room, lying on the bed staring at either the glossy US magazine she held in her hands or the ceiling above her; both providing equal entertainment.

"You look different . . ." Marthe quickly stated the moment she saw her. Mami, who crash landed onto her mattress, not so much ignored the statement, she just paid it no mind, wishing not to bring further attention to herself.

"Hey, don't ignore me . . ." Marthe rolled up the magazine and threw it at Mami, missing terribly, as it deflected off the bed and landed on the floor.

"*VOGUE* . . . Red Hot! What next? Fashion and beauty." Mami read the cover title with a heavy tongue, "why are you reading this?"

"Because it belongs to the others." She already referred to the sisters as the others, never as sisters, and even rarer by their names, "and I am trying to figure out what in their godforsaken brains would make them want to read this."

"The woman looks pretty though . . ."

"The woman looks as if she is secretly plotting the revenge murder of her husband of twenty-six years who has been cheating on her with his secretary who is having his baby." Mami burst out laughing, "Just look at her, look at her eyes," Marthe added.

There was a knock on the door, and before the knocking ended, the door swung open and in came Monique with her hand out looking straight at Marthe.

"*Nini?*" said Marthe.

"The magazine!" Monique replied, in a tone suggesting there was no other possible reason as to why else she would be there.

"I don't have it."

"You took it."

"Here it is . . ." Mami interceded, preventing a full scale sister to sister conflict. Monique snatched the magazine with her brightly colored nails and, instead of leaving as she usually would, sat down and joined them.

"So what are you talking about?" Monique asked. Marthe and Mami looked at each other with confusion, as if to question whether what was just happening was really happening.

"Oh, you know. The usual thing women talk about: how corrupt the government is, how they swindle and steal all the money and how to lead a political rebellion against the state and give power back to the people."

"Ugh, you are so boring. All that politics talk. You should really be talking about that guy she's been seen around with." Monique pointed her head at Mami, who attempted to look as unassuming as possible. Marthe was left with her mouth wide open, gasping in surprise.

"What? Everyone is talking about it. I thought you knew." Monique added, then stood and swiftly exited, striding confidently as if to say *my job is done*. Mami huffed when she left as though she had been grossly inconvenienced.

"So that's why you didn't answer my question."

"You didn't ask one." Mami replied.

"Oh, you knew what I meant, I said you look different. I knew there was a reason why."

"It's nothing. And how do you know anyway? You really believe her? The girl who goes from *Limité* to *Ngaliema* to be with guys whose real names she doesn't even know."

"Listen, I am a woman. I know these things. I am also your sister."

Mami let out a huge sigh as she listened to Marthe.

"I haven't seen you this way for a while, I can't put my finger on it, not since you were asking me silly questions about boys and sex."

"I did not!" Mami replied, embarrassed and in full denial.

"Ah, so it is a boy."

"How do you know?!" Mami exclaimed. Marthe looked at her with you-should-know-better-than-to-ask-questions-you-already-know-the-answer-to eyes.

"Fine, if you're going to behave this way. Yes, it is a boy if you must know."

"Do tell."

"He's back."

"Who?" Marthe asked with curiosity, and Mami looked back at her with the same eyes.

"Ooooh!" Marthe realized with surprise, the longer the "oh," the greater the surprise, "Not only is it a boy, it is the same boy. The boy who I used to lie about and cover for you those years ago. I always wondered what happened with him, after you stopped asking me to cover for you, I never cared to ask. I was just glad to not have to do all the extra work any longer."

"Thanks!"

"Don't get me wrong, I'm happy he's back. He was alright. I actually thought he had gone because father had found out and sent *les Soldats* around to his house to pay him a visit."

"Not a funny joke to make."

"Who said I was joking?"

"So what happened?" Marthe continued.

"I saw him today, at the *Zandu*; he looked so handsome, he's really a fine boy." Mami replied.

"Okay, slow down, before you do anything hasty like let him impregnate you before he marries you."

"I would not be so silly."

"Oh, it's so sweet, *elikia ya bolingo*, love's hope. So when will you marry?"

"I don't want to marry him!"

"It would be sweet if you did. But what about all those men who come to father to ask for your hand in marriage? They'll be heartbroken."

"The same men who you've been running away from for years?"

"I don't want to marry. You do. There's a difference."

"Well I'll just have to tell father to return the crocodile shoes and the fancy suits."

"Don't forget the cheap wine . . . although, mother would have probably already drunk it all."

"When *will* you marry though, big sister?" Mami said with compassion, showing concern, as if there was something wrong with her.

"Contrary to what people think, not all women are simply waiting around to marry. Marriage is a prison. I have seen it. I don't want to spend the rest of my life waiting for a man to come home, too tired and exhausted to pay attention to me, after a long day at work and a long night of paying attention to his mistress!"

"Do you always have to be so negative?"

"Do I always have to speak the truth, you mean? Yes. I do."

The following week Papa and Mami met as they had arranged. It was a Friday evening. The sun setting from above made it seem as though orange lava was flowing through the streets of Kinshasa below. There was a different kind of heat, not from the sun, but more so from the bodies set to be colliding after the sun vanishes to shine light on the other side. The workers would soon be turning into partiers, and would go on until the sun appeared again.

Papa was nervous Mami would not show. There was no way of knowing whether or not she would; he could not call her, he could not visit her house to make sure she would be there the next day, nor much else. He certainly could not pick her up. He relied solely on faith, throwing a prayer to the gods, which, when she appeared wearing a *rouge bourdeaux* patterned dress covering the entire length of her body, holding on to each curve as if it was hanging on to the edge of a mountain, onto dear life, he knew his prayers had been answered. She arrived whilst the sun was leaving; it was as though she had come to take its place.

He met her in *Koko Patrice's* new Mercedes, parking right next to her, as she waited on the sidewalk looking down both sides of the street frustrated she could not see him. He jumped out of the car, and opened the door for her, waiting for her to get in, paying no mind to the very surprised look on her face.

He kissed her, cheek to cheek, and trembled at her touch. Papa noticed how tense he was, driving both hands clamped on the steering wheel the same way *Koko Patrice* does, so he decided to relax a bit, slumped his shoulders, leaned back in the seat a little bit, occasionally looking over at Mami.

"Why are you smiling?"

"Impressive." Mami replied.

"This? Thank you, I guess."

"You must be doing well for yourself."

"Well, not quite . . . I don't want you to think it is mine. It isn't."

"Really?" Her tone was sprinkled with sarcasm.

"It is my father's."

"I see."

"I don't want you to think I have money or anything. I am poor."

"So why did you come by car and not by foot?"

"Didn't you say it was impressive?"

"Yes, I said it was impressive. I did not say I was impressed."

They went to a bar called *Jeunesse Africaine* in *Bandal*. Papa pulled out a chair for Mami and watched her as she gracefully descended into the seat. They sat beside each other, on the patio, looking out onto the street. There was a cacophony of sound, a mix-match of activities, from the honks of the passing cars, and the yells of the men who had been drinking since the afternoon, to the boys carrying scraps of metal in a wheel barrow to sell, to the policemen who relaxed and chatted on the street corners.

"So is this the date we were meant to go on . . . ?"

"We were much younger back then, we couldn't really go on dates. At least not with your father and all of his . . ."

"I know. All we did was go on long walks."

"Sometimes that's all it takes to know whether or not you can spend the rest of your life with someone."

A young looking waiter, who appeared as though he could be one of their friends, came to politely ask, leaning in, with the utmost hospitality, *"quelque chose a boire?"*

"Une Coca-Cola, s'il vous plait?" Papa replied.

"*Coca?*" Mami asked, surprised and looked at Papa as if there was something wrong with him.

"Yes." He replied, confused.

"Why *Coca*, you do not drink?"

"No," he shook his head slowly to the left and the right.

"No alcohol?" she reiterated.

"No," he said once more, head still shaking slowly left to right. "Why?"

"Why, what?" Papa could not comprehend her surprise. The waiter who was also still stood there, leaned in, watching them back and forth like a tennis match.

"Why do you not drink?" She asked, as if it was an urgent question she needed an answer to, "like those men?" she pointed to the groups also sat outside on the tables opposite, who looked as though, from all the empty bottles on their blue plastic table, they could have drowned each other in a pool of alcohol.

"Well, I cannot speak for those men," he looked over again, pausing, then continuing, "but I hear it has been said, a man growing up either sees his father and drinks, or sees his father and doesn't drink. I saw my father, and did not drink."

Mami did not know how to respond but sat there taking in the depth of what Papa had said. He often spoke this way, she remembered, saying a lot whilst saying not much at all. It seems, this time, since his departure, he had learned to do this even more elusively. She thought carefully about what she should drink.

"*Et toi Madame?*" The waiter now asked with impatient politeness.

"*Une Coca-Cola.*" The waiter brought over two bottles of Coke with ice—in this heat, ice was a delicacy—and served them and quickly disappeared as if not wishing to serve, or even see, them again.

The enticing rhythmic music of Congolese rhumba played in the background, flowing into the air, setting the mood perfectly for the unfolding future they both wanted to walk into.

Ebale ya Congo, ezali lopango te, ezali nde nzela.

It did something for you, the music, made you feel as if the was a stirring within you only one other soul could feel, and you felt it together, there was magic.

Papa's favorite band was OK *Jazz*, more so, they were the entire nation's favorite band, however, Mami did not care much for them, or for other music; she did not care much for what was considered worldly entertainment due to her faith.

As the night went on they found themselves sitting closer together, although neither of them had moved. It was as if there was a natural magnetism, a gravitational pull of two forces beyond each other, of which they knew nothing. Papa looked into Mami's eyes, and realized the feeling within him had not changed; he did not know all those years he had thought of her warmness in his room, in a foreign city too cold for his heart, was slowly bringing him back to this day. He kissed her. Their lips locked. Soft. Hers had grown as if she had been speaking of great truths whilst he was gone. And just like a great truth, a revelation of a thing once unknown, it was comforting, and always arrived at the right time, never a moment too soon.

It was a great risk to kiss this way, a statement even, for anything could happen, anyone could see them; Mami's father could be passing by with his *Soldats* and Papa could wind up in prison until her father's anger simmered down. It wasn't unheard of, and would not be the first time, but Papa was ready and daring, a little braver than before, a little bolder; life had hardened him, made him stronger and a little less scared.

chapter 30

"IT IS GETTING LATE." MAMI SAID as they sat under the night abound with stars and a bright full moon, "I should be getting home. Marthe doesn't want to start covering for me again."

"I can't believe she ever did," Papa laughed at the sudden onset of old memories, "but you're older now, you should be allowed, no?"

"You know how it is. Plus, it makes no difference in my family. No ring. No . . ." she placed her fingers over her lips.

They walked to the car; Papa walked to the driver's side as Mami stood by the passenger side of the car waiting, until he realized and walked the way back around to open the door for her, "thank you," she smiled politely. They drove off.

"All this time, why did you not at least write to me?" Mami asked, curiously.

"So your father's *Soldats* could open the letters before you did?"

"You've made a fair point."

"I could ask you the same thing."

"I did not know where you lived, how could I have possibly written to you?"

"But you thought about it?"

"Yes." Mami admitted, after a long pause, as if she had admitted defeat.

"Why don't I show you where I live, so next time you will have . . ."

"But what about your . . .?" She interrupted him nervously.

"Do not worry," he eased her, "My father is away on business, whatever business he occupies himself with now which he happens to tell no one about. He won't be back for a while."

It was a drive the same length of a *Zaiko Langa Langa* song before they arrived at the porch of Papa's house where they parked the car. There were no lights on in the house, only the dim light of the street lamp reflecting off it, and where there were no more lampposts it was pitch black; an absolute darkness with no shape or form.

"This is it."

"Nice house. I think I know this street."

"Yes. *A Solongo*."

"Would you like me to show you inside? It will only be for one minute."

"Okay. But I cannot stay any longer."

They walked toward the house and Papa quietly opened the front door, in the slowest possible manner, paying special not to make it creak as it usually does.

"This is it: home."

"You have a lovely home," Mami said, noticing how neatly and intently in place everything was, from the books on the shelf to the display cabinet of fine china, "but why did you switch the lights on?" she asked, "do you not like the moonlight?"

Papa looked at her with an understanding he could not have reached on his own. He switched off the light, walked back and took her in his arms. They fell, into each other, onto the sofa behind them, softly, lightly, floating, like leaves in the autumn, a petal of a flower, or how the sun falls into the horizon. Arms entwined like how space is with time, they kissed and each moment their lips met became a memory; he, of things he never thought possible, her of dreams she was waiting to come true. He lowered her dress, and felt the soft of her skin on his; smooth, velvet, like all the soft things invented by nature. Mami stood up. She looked at Papa with a silent message seeking greater comfort than the living room sofa. He understood and led the way. They walked up the stairs, all the while their hands remained held, fingers locked at the tip. Each step felt like a climb for a more breathtaking view, higher and higher, until they both arrived.

They lay in bed, looking out of the window that invited the moonlight in to enchant them into a spell of light sleep and heavy breathing.

"Do you believe in love?" Mami asked.

"*Bolingo* . . . ?"

"Yes, love."

"Well," Papa hesitated, unsure of how to reply to a question he had never been asked before, "it's not that I don't believe in love, or even that I do believe in it."

"What do you mean?"

"I mean, love exists. It's not something you do or don't believe in, that's like saying if someone believes in the sun?"

"Do you?" She laughed lightly at her own humor.

"I think love is the most powerful thing in the world, but the way people see it is wrong."

"You are right. Too concerned with nice things, romance; flowers, and chocolates."

"When really, love is . . ."

"Like the sun."

"Like the moon."

"Like flowers and chocolates," they both burst out in shared laughter. Papa now sat up looking at Mami lying beside him.

"But *bolingo* is powerful, by its very definition." Papa spoke now softly "*linga* means love, and *bo* means plural, or collective, so to love is not just an individual act, it is one of two people, yes, but also of the family, the community, of the people, the collective; of all of us."

"I mean, when I think of my love for you, I . . ." Papa continued with his monologue.

"Wait, your love for me? You love me?"

"Yes," Papa replied, slightly confused, "do you not love me?"

"*Eh, na ndimaki te.*" And in her disbelief she reached up and kissed him, "of course I do."

They kissed once again, and in their kissing gave each other back to themselves, like a cup of water flowing from empty to full, empty to full, empty to full.

It was late. Papa switched on the corridor light as they came down the stairs. Papa let out a huge gasp, which would have been louder had the air not been sucked out from his lungs from fear. There, sat by the table, next to a small candle-lit lamp reading the wide newspaper he did not read, was *Koko Patrice*. Papa's heart was beating so loud it echoed through the walls in the house. His trembling hand fumbled around the light switch. Mami stood timidly behind him. *Koko Patrice*, glasses at the tip of his nose, peering beyond them, let out a low grumble somehow asking a question Papa knew he needed to answer.

"This is Mami." Papa answered, voice shaking.

"*Bonsoir Monsieur,*" Mami quickly added, with a polite voice.

"*Bonsoir.*" *Koko Patrice* replied with a resounding voice like the bottom string of a bass guitar, "*Elle est votre petite amie?*" He asked with gross curiosity. Papa nodded, his head moving up and down, like a yoyo, with fear.

"*Aaaah,*" *Koko Patrice* roared with excitement, "*elle est jolie,*" and opened up his arms to hug her warmly. Mami reciprocated, and from behind Koko's back, gave Papa a glaring stare piercing through him. Papa was shocked at *Koko Patrice's* calm reaction. He had no idea how to interpret it, but it all, no doubt, seemed a meticulous calculation. Mami very politely, and graciously, excused herself and Papa left with her to drive her home. They walked back to the car.

"You said he will not be back for a while!"

"I am *so* sorry." Papa replied, panicking. "I thought he wouldn't. I had not seen him for two days."

"And you said I am your girlfriend?"

"I know. I am very sorry."

"But why are you apologizing?" Mami replied. His face was classically bewildered.

"Unless you were lying . . ." She continued.

"No . . . no, er . . . I wasn't." Papa stuttered uncontrollably.

"You should never apologize for telling the truth."

They quickly got in the car, neither of them bothered with the formalities of who was going to open the door for whom, and began to drive.

"Did he know you took the car?"

"No." Papa replied, whimpering. Mami burst out with laughter. "My father is going to kill me. Tomorrow will be my death day."

"Don't worry, I hear it's not that bad." Mami continued to giggle in the background.

chapter 31

AFTER A FEW SUMMERS, SCHOOL IN Brussels had now become an unflinching challenge for Papa. It intimidated him like a bully in the playground edging ever closer. As much as he enjoyed the studies; in fact, it was the classroom where he felt most comfortable and would go willingly as if it was an escape from real life, it was everything else outside class which was really testing him. His life became an unsteady diet of tomato soup and white bread, and perhaps, on a good day, a baguette. Papa was losing weight but it was easy to disguise during the cold winters where the lost weight was made up for with extra layers of clothes.

Papa tried so hard not to turn to *Koko Patrice* for support with an allowance, however, his stubbornness was not as strong as his hunger. Also, Phelix, who heavily relied on his Minister of a father for regular allowances, did not help with his constant squandering of money on drinks, food, clothes and the kind of women he liked. The students had lost their scholarships. After a myriad of protests against a government who claimed that the correlation between the exponential growth of their

221

pockets and the decline of public funds was merely coincidental, they were left to fend for themselves. Papa was now reluctantly continuing and surviving through the allowance sent to him by *Koko Patrice*; it felt as though he were a teenager once again, under his father's dominion.

"I am pregnant." When Papa heard these words from Mami, he almost vomited the tea and jam and butter baguette he had eaten for breakfast on what was supposed to be a calm Sunday morning. He had to cover his mouth to stop himself from retching. It sent a tremor of worry and anxiety through his entire body, from the bottom of his flat arch-less feet to the last curl of hair on the top of his head, and destroyed the peace of mind he thought he had.

They say you see your entire life flash before your eyes when you die, but for Papa it flashed before his eyes at this news; he imagined *Koko Patrice's* reaction, his school career, and the entire future he had worked so hard for rain on him as if it were heavy red-brown bricks which he could only protect himself from using an umbrella. It's not that Papa did not want to be a father, it was always something he dreamed of, it's just the news came at him faster than a speeding train which he was facing tied with ropes by the ankles on a track. He collapsed back onto the bed in his small dorm room and dropped the desk phone, which he had installed not long ago and now used it to speak with Mami every two weeks on a Sunday, and the curled wire snapped it back and it banged loudly off the wooden desk and dangled off the edge.

Papa regained consciousness; he did not know how long he had passed out for on the bed, it felt like a whole night's worth of sleep, but the sound of Mami on the other side shouting "*Allo! Allo!*" woke him back up quickly.

"Are you sure?" Papa picked up the phone again and asked Mami.

"Yes, I am sure. I have seen enough pregnant women in my life to know I am growing a baby, and not just getting fat!" Mami replied frustrated.

"I am sorry. I am simply scared."

"You are not the only one."

"Have you told your family yet?"

"No." Papa gasped in shock.

"You mean they do not know?" He added.

"I said no," Mami replied in an irritated tone, "what do you want me to do? Call my father in for a meeting and have a parade to make the announcement? He will have your head delivered to him first class on a plate."

"Do they not see it or . . . ?"

"I am not far along. They cannot tell. But I know Marthe is very suspicious, she wonders why I go to the bathroom in the middle of the night so often and spend so much time in there."

"So what will we do?" Papa breathed a huge sigh; a gust of wind entered his tiny room.

"You will do nothing." Mami replied. "You will carry on with school and finish your studies."

"I cannot continue with school. I am the boy's father!"

"Excuse me, the boy?! How do you know it is a boy?"

"Is it a boy? I've always wanted my firstborn to be a boy."

"Why?"

"It is tradition; me, my father, my grandfather, my great grandfather, we are all firstborn boys."

"Well, I do not know what it is. It could be a girl. I want it to be a girl."

"If she will grow up to be like you, I would be happy either way."

After a conversation lasting longer than any other time Papa had ever spoken to Mami on the phone, they eventually hung up, and Papa's once thunderous, beating heart, filled with blood rushing through his veins like water through a fire fighter's pipe to put out a fire, began to settle, and his lungs regained the calm breathing he knew once before.

Papa returned to Kinshasa. Nobody knew. He had saved the money *Koko Patrice* had been sending him, which was supposed to support him for the rest of the year, and bought a plane ticket home; of course not only a plane ticket, he also bought some nappies, small baby clothes, and other necessities. And, a treat for himself, his favorite of *pain au chocolat*, which, after a long diet of tomato soup and bread, tasted like experiencing some kind of heaven. He wondered when, if at all, he would next be able to enjoy anything such as this, so he made sure to treasure the moment. The remaining money he kept tucked away in a dark, worn, black leather bag, deep in his suitcase, for good measure.

For the first time ever, Papa landed in Kinshasa with no one to meet him at the airport but the people who hustle to carry your luggage, without asking, so you can pay them some loose change for them to release it back to you. He took a taxi back to the house. The driver did not say much; he wore a hat and had a face suggesting he spoke only of serious matters and nothing else. As they drove down the long road of *Boulevard du 30 Juin*, Papa began to see what *Koko Patrice* meant when he said "*makambu ezali ko changer na mboka oyo;*" things were changing in the country, and it was not for the better. Papa understood. Maybe it was because he too would now be a father; everything changes immediately at this point—the future becomes much more immediate, or maybe, after all of the many years he had been away, going back and forth, now was truly the first time he had come back to stop and look properly. Papa wasn't sure but whatever the reason, he saw what he could not see before and it troubled him how much worse things had gotten. How the poverty became more visible, more present—there were more men by the roadside, selling things, hanging around in shabby clothes, some on a hustle, some with no hope, little boys on the streets, dusty and dirtied, young girls who were already mothers, carrying children on their back too whilst they worked, and some of the buildings he once knew had become dilapidated and resembled discarded bodies without the souls that once lived in them.

Some of his friends spoke about it too, particularly whilst they were in Brussels—it was safer to do there—they increasingly discussed the state of politics and government in the country; how *Le Maréchal, Mr. Président's* regime was a corrupt dictatorship and how they would one day bring the change needed for the people, for the country. Much of this conversation evaded Papa; he often found it indignant hyperbole from the elite class; the sons of ministers and wealthy businessmen who would one day take their fathers' places.

What was more shocking than the state of the city in decline was the *désespoir*, the hopelessness on people faces. There was a change of temperament in the city, among the people; a heated temperament was beginning to bubble into the air as though a rage waking from its sleep.

Papa stepped out of the taxi and walked the path to the house carrying his luggage. It was late afternoon and so he did not expect *Koko Patrice* to be home. He hesitantly walked in through the front door because he had become so accustomed to *Koko Patrice's* magician-esque appearances out of nowhere. *Koko* was not in. Papa took this opportunity to re-settle and prepare himself for *Koko Patrice's* eventual arrival. The evening had arrived and eventually the night; *Koko* had still not returned home. Two days had passed and Papa had still not yet seen *Koko Patrice*. This simply made the anticipation of telling him the news grow bigger and bigger, to the point where even the thought of telling him made Papa feel anxious. Every sound resembling footsteps or a car driving by, made Papa so nervous he would feel nauseous. He spent the entire two days in the house only feeding himself a steady diet of *ntaba* in the evening from the roadside cook who he would shout his order at from the window.

On the third day, after sunset, *Koko Patrice* came home to find Papa sitting in the living room, as though he was waiting for him. It was a kind of role reversal, as if he was now the father and *Koko* was the son. Papa looked as *Koko* walked past and saw him stop in a startled manner. He quickly processed it was his son in the living room, and not an intruder, nor anybody else. *Koko* was always good at masking his reactions or how he felt; he had a stoic response to everything.

"*Bonsoir.*" *Koko Patrice* spoke in a calm, baritone voice echoing throughout the whole house, or at least, in Papa's head.

"*Bonsoir.*" Papa replied with composure, keeping his cool. There was a tense faceoff between them, implicit and unspoken but well known, and strongly felt. Papa was keeping calm and not letting the fear overwhelm him for he knew he had to explain himself, and *Koko* knew too well he was owed an explanation for his presence.

"*Qu'est ce qu'il y a?*" *Koko Patrice* asked, removing himself from the authoritative figure he was and showing concern once he noticed how tense Papa was. After a prolonged period of silence, Papa began explaining how he had left school to return to Kinshasa permanently, during which *Koko*'s facial expression changed from calm to a mouth wide open in shock: a frothing indignation, stoicism lost, almost foaming at the mouth, trying to contain his rage. As Papa continued to tell him how Mami, the girl he had met (because *Koko* had already forgotten), would be bearing his child. *Koko* approached Papa in slow movements, which did not scare Papa because he had already accepted the possibility of certain death as his fate, and sat on the chair beside him. His only response was "*Eh!*" followed by bellowing laughter. This confused Papa; almost angered him. He was so scared to tell him his news, had he known the reaction would be laughter he could have saved himself all the anxiety. However, *Koko* did not laugh for long; "*Yo!*" he pointed at Papa with a thick, stiff, wooden looking finger shaking from an uncontainable anger. The next words out of his mouth were "*Mema ye awa,*" requesting Papa to bring her to the house, and Papa knew from this moment on, there was no turning back.

chapter 32

"WHAT?! YOU'RE PREGNANT!" MARTHE SHOUTED IN shock. Mami had finally confessed, after being subtly harassed for weeks when Marthe had noticed her odd behavior.

"Yes." Mami replied, very matter-of-factly.

"Is it with this boy?"

"Yes."

"I knew you were having sex!"

"So?" Mami blasted out, "Like you wouldn't know about sex. You're hardly the Virgin Mary . . ."

"Well, I'm not the one who is pregnant, am I?"

"Shh! They'll hear you." Mami growled. "This isn't helping. What am I going to do?"

"You have to tell father!" Marthe insisted.

"How?"

"I don't know. How does he not know already? The man has had five children and still can't tell when a woman is pregnant."

"He cannot tell because he was never there for any of them."

"Typical man." Marthe responded in disgust, indifferent to

the fact this man was also her father, "and where is this boy who you have been having sex with?" She continued.

"He's here, he has come back home."

"From *poto?*"

"Yes. *Azongi mboka.*"

"For good?"

"*Nayebi te.*" Mami shrugged as she could not give a response to a question she did not know the answer to, and in the exact moment her shoulders came down, she broke into tears. Marthe, going from harsh over protective big sister, to warm and caring in an instant, hugged her warmly and reassured her everything would be okay.

Shortly after, with the support of Marthe, Mami told *Koko ya Mobali*—the father, the military man who was always in uniform—told not just him but the sisters, and *Koko ya Mwasi* too, all together, in their grand living room one evening. Father's reaction was as expected; he began shouting so loudly through the entire house even the guard came storming in and stopped in absolute silence when he saw it was *Koko ya Mobali*. He demanded to know who the man responsible was. Mami refused to tell him, she saw the rage in his eyes, and heard the thunder in his voice, and feared it would find its way to Papa like a fire ravaging everything on its path.

Koko ya Mobali said she must leave the house. In his eyes she was no longer his daughter; no daughter of his could allow such dishonor to be brought upon the family name, particularly from someone of no position in society. The sisters tried to defend her, not Marthe for she knew it would be to no avail, more so Monique and especially Marie, the youngest, who felt like she was losing a part of herself she was yet to get to know. Nonetheless, *Koko's* stubbornness was totalitarian. He could not be moved. Maybe it wasn't so much he didn't expect this from any daughter of his, it was more so he didn't expect it from Mami; she was the most sensible, the smartest, the one who was meant to follow the path as it was laid.

Though his words stung Mami, she had nonetheless antici-
pated it, therefore it made dealing with the consequences a little easier. It was during this time she realized something, what
Marthe had been saying all along, she realized how mother never
spoke over father; she always remained silent, in her position, in
her place, just as Marthe had said. In the presence of *Koko ya
Mobali*'s apoplectic rage, Mami could see mother's eyes and how
they had the same feeling she felt, however, she remained muted
by her fear. This is something the other sisters too had learned,
as they sat silent, watching.

"*Yo oza zoba! Escroe!*" Mami released her fury like a volcanic
eruption back at her father. She could no longer contain herself
and refused to live in fear as her mother had done all her life.

"I am your daughter, and this is how you treat me? You are
not worthy to be my father; you are not worthy to be a man!
And, you are a disgrace to that uniform you claim to be so proud
of; *servir, se servir non*, you are a coward! You speak of serving
others but you only serve yourself!" She heaved and spat on the
floor, then ran out of the left room in tears. There was silence in
the air, the kind only heard at a funeral—a mourning, a remembering of things.

Though it overwhelmed each of the sisters, they knew if any
of them could handle something as big as this, it would be Mami;
everyone had their weight to carry, their burden matched their
strength and somehow Mami had always been more equipped
for life than the others.

Koko Patrice on the other hand, had only one question to ask
Mami and Papa when he met with them together, "When will
you marry?"—it was not a question of *if* but *when*—to which
Mami and Papa looked each other with startled faces; it was
something neither of them had actually yet considered; Papa
was too busy worrying about the future and trying to readjust
his entire life, and Mami was in too much shock from the dras-
tic effects of familial abandonment. Papa took the initiative

and responded saying it will happen soon, which only ignited *Koko Patrice's* anger more, which he quickly had to bury. Papa explained to him how Mami's father—who, from the family name, *Koko Patrice* knew of but did not know personally—had sent her out of the house and excommunicated her from the family so Mami had asked to stay with them. *Not while you are not married. If you can do the action, you must accept the consequences and deal with the responsibility.*

Papa heard these words and it cut him open as if they were flying daggers thrown at his chest. He almost felt, rather, he knew, if Mami were anyone else, with any other name, the answer would have been different, however, *Koko Patrice's* belligerent pride knew no limit.

Papa found a place for them on the other side of the *commune* and paid for it with some of the money he kept tucked away in the dark, worn, black leather bag in his suitcase. It was a drab and dreary place; the worn front door looked as though it instead belonged in front of a shed than a house, there was no furniture inside, save the sofa with the faded three-leaf flower pattern, a muted wall color not resembling its original look, a square room with white walls no longer white, and a flat mattress they slept on tucked into the corner. Electricity was sparse, on a good day. Papa spent each day searching for work, which came in all forms but mostly in the form of selling crates of beer. This worked out well enough for them to get by because, unlike the other merchants, he did not drink his own supply.

As the months passed and Mami began to show, her stomach now protruding beyond the loose *boubou* she wore to try and cover it, the normalcy of their situation began to settle in. It was as though her being pregnant was an indefinite state and neither her nor anyone else knew when it would change. The baby came on a Sunday morning weeks before it was planned, in the darkest hours of the night before the sunrise. Papa woke to the sound of Mami who moaned and groaned in significant pain and discomfort. They were being driven by their neighbor Jean-Louie, who had been woken by Mami's panicked screams, and decided to drive them through the empty streets to *Hopital Ngaliema* looking back, over his shoulder, talking needlessly along the way.

Papa was with Mami the entire time not knowing exactly what to do—though one would think he should be informed by his prior aspirations—whilst he watched the nurses and the doctor deliver the baby, but still, being present, being ever present, he felt was the least he could do. She had given birth. The doctors kept Mami and the baby in hospital. It was a few days, though the wait felt as long as the term of pregnancy itself, before Papa was able to see both mother and child together. He did not leave the hospital, not to eat or wash, or even seek comfort. It was a boy. Mami held on to him tightly and swayed him side to side. Papa's eyes swelled with tears until they strolled down his face. The little boy grabbed Papa's finger and wrapped his hands around it, "Look," Papa said, astonished at the sight, "he has such big hands."

"We'll name him *Jean*." Papa suggested, "*Jean Kongo Mulendo Ndiantola Ntanga*, after my grandfather." Mami happily smiled and accepted. The doctors decided to keep Mami, and the little baby Jean, in for a few more days for monitoring. During this time, word of Mami giving birth had got out to the rest of the community; nobody knew how because neither Papa nor Mami had told anyone, or even wanted to. Nonetheless, they began receiving visitors. Some were expected—Mami's friends who she had known from school or in the local area. And some weren't, such as her big sister Marthe. However, although it did surprise her, Mami should have known it would be her and only her who would deny father's orders and come to visit.

"So this is my nephew?" Were Marthe's first words, as she held Jean and bobbed him up and down. She looked at Mami, looked over at Papa and added, "He's so pretty. Luckily, he resembles his mother more than his father." Papa smiled wryly in response and overlooked Marthe's comment, allowing her this one opportunity to get something off her chest and say something subtly sardonic for all those times she did not and could not, before she knew it would get this far, and intervene the way a big sister needed to.

"I brought someone with me to see you, but she wasn't sure if you would let her."

"Who?" Mami asked, perplexed.

"*Kota!*" Marthe shouted out in the direction of the door, and in walked Marie, the youngest sister.

"Aaw," Mami held out her arms and they held each other in a loving embrace. She looked at Marie with a question in her eyes that she already knew the answer to.

"They wanted to come," Marie answered, "but we could not all come together. Eyes are everywhere; *ba songi songi.*"

Mami sighed. Her heart felt heavier. Although she understood, she would have loved for her sisters to be bold and dare to break free from the crushing grip of their father's dominion. Nonetheless, it was nice for them to be here, in spite of it all.

The same night, Mami and baby Jean were given the all clear by the hospital staff and they were due to leave in the morning. When the morning came, the nurse entered slowly through the double doors leading to their room and brought a visitor in with her. Papa and Mami both stared in a stunned silence—she, waiting for Papa to react, and he, unable to. They stood still only to be interrupted by the wailing of the little baby in the background.

"*Bonjour.*" *Koko Patrice* said. He was dressed sharply; there wasn't a single crease in his short sleeved double breasted suit with the handkerchief in the pocket, "*Bonjour et felicitation!*" he said graciously with the eloquence of a man whose tongue had never spoke ill of anyone.

"*Merci.*" Papa replied flatly. Mami stayed silent; Papa spoke on behalf of both of them now. *Koko Patrice* walked over to Jean with outstretched arms and lifted him, to which Jean responded by quietening himself and offering a gurgled smile. He walked around carrying the baby in his arms as if they were the only two in the room, lifting him up and down and pointing him to the city life passing by beyond the window.

Koko Patrice placed Jean gently back into the arms of Mami, who began holding and swaying him. He took off the hat he wore matching his suit, held it to his chest and began to speak.

"I wish to extend to you . . ." he hesitated, "an invite to stay at the house . . ."

"Your house?" Papa interrupted.

"Our house—the family house. I would be very happy for you and your family to stay." *Koko Patrice* finished speaking and gulped as if he had swallowed his pride, which had the density of a golf ball. Papa heard his offer, he knew there was an apology in there somewhere, but it would be asking too much for him to hear both. He momentarily contemplated on the proposition.

"No." He gave a short, stunted reply. Papa could feel Mami staring at him; there was a warm burning sensation he felt on the side of his neck, which he knew was her stare. He did not look back. *Koko Patrice* exhaled deeply; a haunting disappointment loomed over him.

"Let me at least drive you to where you are going."

Papa did not reply; the omission of a response was enough to show he had accepted the offer. He could not bring himself to actually say "yes" and take anything else from *Koko Patrice*; it seemed pride was enough of an inheritance.

They drove through the streets of Kinshasa in *Koko Patrice's* grey-silver Mercedes in the direction of the other side of the *commune* of *Bandal*. Papa asked *Koko* to pull the car over one street away from where they were staying; he did not want to leave to chance the possibility of an unexpected visit, similar to today, though he knew *Koko* could find them easily if he really wanted to, and he did not want him to see how they were living: bare and broken. They said their goodbyes, short and stunted.

chapter 33

THEY CREATED A MAKESHIFT COT FOR Jean to sleep in the corner of the room with the mattress on the floor and where the white walls were no longer white. They slowly began to settle into the house. Although it was not permanent, for now, they had to make something of a home out of it, so whilst Papa was out on the streets working, selling what he could, Mami slowly began to transform and bring back to life a place lying in a deep comatose state; flowers, a small table, pictures of family, anything she could find to give this space a feeling, a personality. So much time had passed, and in this time, they started to slowly settle into life as a new family.

Papa came home from work one evening. The worn front door was ajar. It creaked open and closed, blown by the wind. He felt startled; a bolt of electricity ran from the bottom of his feet to the top of his head alerting him to danger. He crept in.

"*Allo!*" Papa called out. No reply. He slowly pushed the door. It opened in a lethargic motion and creaked even louder than before.

"*Mami?*" He bellowed. No reply. "*Jean?*" he called out; as if he could answer. Still no reply. There was no sound. It was dark and he could not see a thing; he thought the electricity had cut out, it often did, which was no surprise; having no electricity was worse when it cut out during the climax of a tense period, a football game or the ending of a movie. Papa walked in, creeping, and bumped the muscle on his shin bone hard onto an edge; the table.

He thought he heard movement; footsteps and shuffling, distant and coming closer, from another room. Footsteps approached from outside.

"*Allo?*"

"Who is it?" Papa roared back before the voice could finish. It was Mami. She held Jean. She switched on the light.

"What are you doing?" She asked, and then let out a high pitched scream, which stretched her lungs, when she saw the room. It was ransacked. It looked as though the attempted interior design; flowers, a small table, pictures, had been personally rearranged by a tornado. Papa gasped, threw his hands onto his head and held them in despair. He looked around, everything they had slowly accumulated had been destroyed to pieces, the small table chipped, the sofa with the three-leaf flower print showed itself ripped open, the glass of framed pictures lay smashed covering the floor.

"What happened?" Mami asked, in a state of shock.

"*Ba yibi biso.*" It was at the moment Papa said they had been burgled he truly came to grasp the severity of what had happened. He ran into their room and flung open the suitcase.

"It's gone!" He said reappearing.

"What is?"

"The money."

"What money?"

"I had money saved for us I kept in the black leather bag in the suitcase. It's gone."

"So we have nothing?"

"Nothing." He let out an exasperated breath, "nothing but the money I have earned today," he pulled out *1500*

Francs—approximately £1.23—out of his pockets and threw it on the floor. He went and sat on the sofa, which was now ripped and barely resembled itself, with his head in his hands.

"*Mama-e! Ba yibi biso.*" Mama exclaimed, "How can they do this?" She held Jean on her hip, who, by now, had gone from silence to wailing as he could sense the distress in the room.

"I'm not surprised, *débrouillez-vous pour survivre,* is what the President said; make ends meet to survive. People have no choice."

"What will we do?"

Papa knocked on the door three times, loudly. It was less of a knock and more of a pound with the side of his fist; it echoed. A thumping bass drum. They waited. It was night time, late, so they did not expect a speedy response. With no money to take a taxi, or any other form of transport, they had walked. They packed their bags earlier the same night; it wasn't much, everything they really wanted to take with them could fit in one suitcase. Anything else wasn't worth keeping. Three more knocks. Papa insisted on knocking, although he had the key. He wanted their presence to be known, to be felt; he wanted to disturb whatever peace had been settled into, since theirs too was disturbed.

"Ah." *Koko Patrice* feigned surprise when he opened the door and saw them, "You have arrived," he added as though he had been expecting them all this time. This bothered Papa, it bothered him because they both acutely knew there would not be any other circumstance, but an extreme one, for him to return, and *Koko Patrice* had not even bothered to ask what happened; he had no intention of doing so either. According to *Koko,* he had won. Mami politely said hello without saying hello as they walked in, and *Koko Patrice* responded charmingly, kissing her on the cheek and cooing at his grandson.

Each passing year brought an unsteady decline; a whirlpool of descent, deeper into an unknown. It was not just in the city, though there it was felt the hardest, it was across the country; from the villages where news spread fastest via word of mouth and people still walked miles for the nearest anything, and the towns where the radios were the gate keepers of the latest information, where what was publicly televised never reflected the reality of how people felt.

It was a time of uncertainty and in these times people only lived in one of four states. The first was fear, for after many years of witnessing a great widened downfall such as increased violence on the streets; women attacked, children abused, people being robbed, all merely for survival, and having to pay one thousand times more the price for a loaf of bread, you no longer fall, rather you are thrown, never knowing for tomorrow. Second, anger. Because after the fear subsides—it never really goes—a rage awakens within you and you are forced to make a decision; either live and die this way, or fight for another. After this, is hope, which is usually reserved for those with either an intense belief in a higher power or with means to escape and leave the situation; most only had means for the former. The fourth state was the one governing you; and it was heavy, with the power to crush bones into dust.

There were those who were old enough to be familiar with this experience, they had already lived through it with the *old power*, who claimed to bring *civilization*; taking what was there, making it hollow and filling it with emptiness. They did not think they would be living through this again; the breaking of the chains, the lifting of a burden, the climbing of the mountain, so soon, and with one of their own. For those who had not yet lived through this, there was something in them that believed another way was possible; it was in their blood as though they too had lived it before and had fought for something new.

Le Maréchal, Mr. Président was due to give a public address in front of dignitaries, distinguished guests and ordinary people alike. The trumpets played to welcome him, and the faces, the many floating faces, the many floating faces exuding fear or fandom waited and watched; eyes emboldened with anticipation for the man they had revered for so long. The man who, according to legend, held a mysterious power given to him by a *marabou* or *nganga* that no one could take away from him other than those from whom it was received; many also believed he had acquired this sacred power and ordained himself as the Almighty.

Le Maréchal, Mr. Président, the man who had renamed himself *The All-Powerful Warrior Who, Because of His Endurance and Inflexible Will To Win, Will Go From Conquest To Conquest, Leaving Fire In His Wake,* the man who, upon first seizing power, displayed his force by hanging three bodies on display for daring to oppose him. The man who established one party rule, a totalitarian iron fist gripping around the necks of the people struggling to breathe, his fanatics and their chants, *MPR egale, servir, se servir, non,* serve others; do not serve yourself, whose echoes reached far and wide. *Le Maréchal, Mr. Président* approached the podium and stood before it, in thick rimmed glasses, ornamented in a befitted black and gold uniform; with the lapels glowing from a brilliant gold, and began speaking whilst holding an expression of power and self-assuredness trying to mask over the concern and uncertainty only he knew he was feeling inside.

"*Très chers compatriots, nous voici pour la troisième fois aux rendezvous de l'histoire . . .*" He began and spoke, not with the charisma they once knew, not the charm, or the eloquence, but with rigidity; he read each word as if they were repetitive notes on a sheet of music with no melody. The anticipating crowd of people sat in a deadly silence and listened to his words. He said what he wanted to say, they waited for what they wanted to hear; neither of them moved.

Le Maréchal, Mr. Président continued speaking as he began, however, some way through his long, drawn-out, hyperbole came a breaking where he spoke of a change to come with a different voice, more compassionate than ever; more human.

His words were taken, by those who heard, as a crack of light in the darkness, medicine to the sick; a healing of open wounds. "*Comprenez mon emotion,*" he added, which was followed by the sounds of a thousand rapturous hands clapping, the chanting of his name and an ovation. They swallowed his promises, his vacuous and empty promises, like poison to the thirsty, fed to them like starving children with no food. Promises are made when intentions are not honored; be weary of the man who feeds you promises.

chapter 34

KINSHASA NO LONGER EXISTS; IT'S *not a city anymore. Soon, at this rate, it's going to be a village.*

The city was on fire. Clouds of smoke rose up into the sky catching the bullets ripping through the air; gunshots in the background were heard so frequently it gave the feeling of normalcy, like the sweet melody of musicians busking in the street or fireworks let off in the distance during autumn. There was hysteria. People had lost all sense of control, lost all sense of order, particularly those who were meant to be maintaining the control, maintaining the order.

Les Soldats, heavy booted and armed, stomped through streets, stomped, sometimes each step cracking necks, breaking bones, cracks of backs followed by screams. They created their own order; it followed no order but its own disorder. It could not be stopped, not even by *Le Maréchal, Mr. Président.* His known force was no match for the soldiers for they were his force, and they stopped listening to him and created a new force built on the backs of the resentment, rage, and regret. Homes were broken into; any visible sign of wealth taken. The shops where people once bought their bread and had shown amity to the local owner, were now broken in; smashed glass and burnt doors. The soldiers started and the people followed. They stole anything and everything they could carry, and they burned what they couldn't. It did not leave much but the destruction of a city lying in its wake.

Mami was at home with little Jean, who had now grown big and would usually be running around, however, on this occasion, he was sensibly calm and quiet as if he too could feel something different in the air. Mami gave him one of *Koko Patrice's* books from the shelf to read; *Koko* often read to him, and Jean was always calmest in these moments, he was his most free. *Koko Patrice* was away. He spent more and more time away, they did not know where exactly—it was never the father's responsibilities to explain his movements to the children—however, he remained in contact when it was necessary, for him. Mami had eventually managed to convince Papa to return to Brussels for university to finish his education; they saved enough money for him to go back—much of the saving was actually *Koko Patrice's* giving.

Papa was defiantly reluctant, "I have a child . . . and I have *you*," he said; unsure on how to refer to her who was still not yet his wife. Nevertheless, Mami insisted, and strongly so, saying, "I will not let myself and our child be the reason you dropped out of school and then one day look at me with disdain and your child with resentment. If you will fail your education, it will be your own doing."

So whilst the city was burning itself alive, Papa had no choice but to clutch the phone to his ear to speak to Mami and watch the images from the Belgian news channels he always used to avoid.

The mania continued to spread throughout the city, for hours, days, weeks. Nobody really knew or counted, but it happened for a long a time. It was worse after sun down because nothing was seen. There was only the invisibility of darkness, which only heightened the fear of mania reaching you; *Les Soldats*, the thieves in the night, getting closer and closer, and if it hadn't yet reached you, you knew it was alarmingly close, gaining on you, hot on your heels like a rabid dog with teeth like a shark.

Mami felt nervous because it was just her and Jean in the house, there was no one else to help or protect them; she could not, and still had not gone back to her family, nor could she go anywhere else. From their open window in the living room they could hear the cacophony of blistering bullets and searing screams, setting a deep fear into their hearts. Each night the noises got louder and louder, closer and closer.

Mami was sat with Jean; in between the blissful ignorance of a child's world and the harsh reality of an adult's, she had to navigate between both, and all the traveling back and forth left her exhausted. The phone rang, and before the first ring could sound Mami answered as if she knew the instance he would call.

"*Allo?*" she said, nervously.

"You have to go." Papa spoke with urgency.

"What do you mean go? Go where?"

"You have to leave Kinshasa."

"Leave Kinshasa? And do what? Go to the village? Are you out of your mind? There are *Soldats* everywh . . ."

"No! You have to leave the country!" Mami did not respond; she remained mouth wide open, gasping in shock, uncertain of what Papa was suggesting.

"It is not safe for you there, alone."

"I have Jean."

"I'm being serious. Please. I am very serious."

"Where will I go?"

"Come to me, here, in Brussels."

"*Mama na ngai,* Brussels?! *Eh!* Who told you I want to go to Brussels?"

"It is not safe in Kinshasa!" Papa said now shouting down the phone panicking, as if he was trying to urgently communicate something Mami could not understand.

"I know this. I am here." Mami shouted back equally frustrated.

"It will only get worse. Please . . ."

"I do not wish to leave Kinshasa. Going to Brussels was the choice for you, it is not mine. I do not want to . . ."

"Please, you and Jean will be safe here. You will be with me." Papa's voice was cracking, as though he were about to cry, which lead to Mami sobbing herself. Jean looked up from the book he was reading, and came to sit on Mami's lap and wiped the tears from her eyes.

"I am scared . . ." Mami said, her voice breaking into tiny little pieces, "I am too scared to leave. I am too scared to stay."

"Please, come to me. Things are going to get worse. This is the beginning of the end; this is what *Koko Patrice* had been talking about."

There was a long silence between them whilst Mami sat thinking; the nearing sounds of the trouble outside came sweeping back in.

"How can I leave with no money? What do I need to do?" Relieved by her decision, Papa let out a huge sigh, his tension eased but only slightly.

"You see *Koko's* car?"

"The Mercedes?"

"Yes. You need to sell it."

"What? How? I don't even have the keys."

"There is usually a spare set in the first drawer of the cupboard to the left of the dining table . . ." Mami did not move and Papa knew this although he could not see her, "go and check," he prompted.

"You want me to steal your father's car and sell it for the money?"

"You are not stealing it, not if you're being given the keys."

"It's still stealing!"

"Are they there?"

Mami replied by jingling the keys to the phone. Papa cheered in the background.

"You can sell it. You will get a few thousand dollars at least. You can use it for . . ."

"Slow down! What about *Koko Patrice?*"

"Don't worry, I will deal with him."

"You are also forgetting one *big* problem, where will I find someone to buy the car?"

Papa went silent. He had no answer. He did not know who or where she could sell the car, he just saw the money before the deed had even been done.

"Don't worry, I will find a way." Mami said reassuringly. After a few moments, once they ended the conversation, Mami picked up the phone to make another call. The phone rang several times as she waited patiently.

"*Allo*, Marthe?"

Anything they couldn't steal, they burned, which wasn't much. The streets were scattered with bodies.

There was banging on the door. It startled Mami from slumber. She awoke and looked frantically for Jean and found him sleeping on the sofa beside her. The banging continued. She peered through the curtains to see who was at the door and saw nothing but pitch black darkness outside. The electricity was cut off so there was no way to tell who was at the door. There was also no way for whoever was at the door to tell if there was anyone inside. Mami wondered whether or not this was a good or bad thing. The banging continued, this time so loud Mami could not tell whether it was the fear in her heart or the person at the door. She cautiously approached the door. Turned the handle, and opened it.

"What do you mean you're leaving?!" Marthe burst into the house.

"Shhhh!" Mami replied, quickly bolting the door shut.

"Don't shush me; I'm your older sister!"

"Jean is asleep." Mami whispered, pointing to the large child curled up in the foetal position on the sofa with his thumb in his mouth. Marthe's demeanour instantly changed. She always softened up at his sight, she held him in her arms as if he were her own child. She was amazed at how Jean had grown, how quickly the years had passed from when she held him in the hospital, to now a large boy, whose head was too big for the rest of his body. Around her, there was nothing he went without. She sat down beside him and lightly stroked his head, wiping the accumulated sweat on his forehead from the heat, whilst his deep breathing raised and lowered his chest. She then stood, went to the drawer and lit a candle, placing it gently on the table.

"Marthe, I'm pregnant."

"Again? How?" Marthe replied in shock. Mami looked at her as if she should know better, "I meant how long?" Marthe corrected herself.

"I don't know, a couple months or so maybe. I've been too stressed out to think about it."

"Don't worry, it will be alright."

"You always say that."

"I say it because I mean it." Marthe said, trying to reassure her worried sister.

"Why is it so hot, can you open a window?"

"Why don't I just send out an open invite for the rioters instead?" Mami replied frustrated. Marthe ignored her sarcasm, too enamored by Jean's blissful sleeping, "I'll take him up," she said and picked him gently as he murmured softly under his breath and wrapped his arms around her, laying his head on her shoulder, long legs dangling down. Marthe returned after a few minutes and sat next to Mami on the sofa who had made them some tea to drink. They sat in a still silence drinking deep into the night.

"You're leaving."

"I have to. You've seen how things are here, I have no choice."

"I don't blame you. I'm just saying it because I can't believe it. You're leaving. You *and* Jean." Marthe started sobbing heavily. This was the most emotion Mami had ever seen her express, it felt surreal; as the eldest sister she always had to be the strongest, the most serious, the most like father, the person she tried most not to be; it left Mami in awe, in many ways she was like him, but not at all.

"I need your help, though . . ." Mami continued.

"I'll do anything. What do you need?" Marthe replied sniffing whilst she wiped her tears.

"I need you to help me to sell a car."

"A car?"

"Yes. The Mercedes."

"What? But isn't that . . ."

"Yes, it is his. We need to sell it to get the money to pay for the tickets. Otherwise we will have no way."

"Right." Marthe replied in a serious tone after a moment of deep contemplation.

"I don't know where to go to sell it, but if we get enough money for it, you can come with us . . ."

"*Te!*" Marthe exclaimed, "*te*" she said again quietly whispering, correcting her former loudness, "I must stay."

"It is too dangerous."

"No. I cannot go. You must go, not me. I will stay. My family is here. Everything I have is here. We cannot all leave. You have a child, a family, a future you can make something of," Marthe insisted, "and I will help you. I know where we can go."

"I love you, *ma soeur*." Mami replied. They hugged and held each other longer than either of them had ever held each other before, this time not knowing if it was the last.

On a pas l'espoire. We have no hope.

The next morning Mami and Marthe left Jean with the neighbors, arousing a little suspicion, and hurriedly left to go to the car.

"Where are the keys?" Marthe demanded. Mami gave it to her.

"You can drive?" she asked, as she watched Marthe power around to the driver's door.

"What are you waiting for? Get in!" Mami, who was stood stunned to stillness, quickly followed instructions. She got in and watched Marthe start the car, screech it and speed off while she put on her seat belt.

"Where did you learn to drive?" Mami asked, shocked, considering what *Les Soldats* would do if they caught her driving; women were not afforded such privileges.

"When you grow up the firstborn daughter of a military man, you inherit his arrogance and stubbornness. There were just some things I would not accept being told that I was not allowed to do simply because I am a woman." Mami laughed at Marthe's boldness. None of the other sisters could have done this, only her. Not even Mami herself. She looked at the intense look of focus and determination on Marthe's face and had to fight back the sadness from creeping in; the sudden realization she will soon not be able to reach out and hold, not be able to see her sister's face so closely, overwhelmed her.

Mami did not yet know where they were going. She placed all of her trust in Marthe. As they drove deeper and deeper into the city, the aftermath of the destruction became more and more visible, more apparent. Whole buildings were burned through, charred from the fire, some still letting out an air of smoke. The windows of looted shops were smashed in and huge panes of glass littered the streets. They drove past a man in the distance, lifeless, sitting on a chair with a bandage, leaking blood, wrapped around his head; where he had come from, where he was going, no one knew. Mami wondered if he had been helped, and forgotten, or worse yet abandoned. There were bodies, lifeless bodies, lying on the street like they had fallen in to a permanent sleep, a dreaming of some peace. Mami tried not to look at the bodies. Instead she looked up, up to the sky. It was the only thing that had not changed; still the same bright blue, the same golden shining sun, she reached up to touch and felt the window caress her arm.

They were now in the safe area, where not much of the damage had reached. They passed a group of Belgians and French, who were being escorted hurriedly into a truck, getting ready to return to their country for their own safety; it is one thing to endure your own suffering, but another to endure someone else's. Seeing them, Mami realized that her leaving and their leaving was not of the same kind.

They arrived at a large compound, just past the other side of the city. There were private armed guards outside. Mami looked alarmed, worried even. However, whatever was happening in the city was not happening here. There was a peace here, not the kind your soul goes in search of, nonetheless, still a peace different from the destruction they had just seen. Marthe got out of the car and walked to the guards outside the compound. Mami watched her approach them with a confident familiarity and begin to speak to each other inaudibly. One of the guards left, leaving Marthe pacing up and down restlessly, and returned two minutes later and finished the conversation with a serious nod of the head to Marthe who returned to the car as they opened the gates.

They drove over to a spacious court yard with a smooth L-shape tiled red brick floor. Mami had not seen such an audacious residence for a long time. She looked to the left, whilst Marthe parked right in front of the house, and noticed a number of cars, of which she counted three or four; they looked as though they had not been driven before, as if being driven was not their purpose. A guard sat on a dusty chair in front of the cars, with a bucket, and cloth, and the shining bright wax polish of each car suddenly made sense.

They entered the house, "follow me," Marthe said, as if Mami was going to wander off in a different direction like a child. They walked up a floor of stairs. Every ornament was in pristine condition and perfectly placed like a curated exhibition. They entered a room.

"Ahh, BONJOUR," boomed a voice beyond, from someone Mami had yet to see. He appeared and kissed Marthe on each cheek to greet her, grabbed her in a peculiar place and held her a little too close for Mami to be comfortable with seeing. The man who owned the voice was shorter than both Mami and Marthe. He was round and bald; sweat from the heat trickled down the top of his head to the layers of fat rolled up on the back of his neck, which he wiped with a white cotton cloth as he went to sit down after introducing himself without the utmost charm.

"So, you have come." He spoke, still loud. His voice did not match his appearance, maybe he had to shout to make up for all those years he was not heard by everyone above him.

"Yes, Prince. You know why I am here." Marthe replied.

"Yes. Yes, I do." He scoffed, as if expecting something else. The more he spoke, or even moved, the more familiar he became, nonetheless, Mami still could not figure out from where. She remained sitting quietly in her seat as if she wasn't there. Prince stood, looked long and hard out of the window and then sat back down.

"How much do you want for it?" Prince asked.

"How much are you offering?"

"What kind of business is this? You want the buyer to name the price?"

"I am giving you a chance to get a good deal."

"How can this be a good deal if I do not know if what I am investing in will be there tomorrow?"

"$5000 dollars." Stated Marthe. Prince scoffed at her sugges-
tion, as if he was insulted.

"You know it is a good deal. And you know I am good for it."
Marthe replied.

"I know what you are good for!" Prince roared and pointed
his stubby finger at her and slowly lowered it."Why have you
come now? And why are you in such a rush?" He continued with
an air of suspicion.

"Why are you so hesitant? Since when do you ask this many
questions?" Marthe cut back at him.

"I'll ask what I like."

"Just get it over with; you never usually last this long with
anything else."

He scoffed at her reply to show his disdain, bitter because he
did not have the wit for a retort of his own.

"You need me, don't you?" He spoke again, with a secret confidence.

"Yes," he chuckled, "you need me. You are leaving and you
need the money. Just like the *mindele* and everyone else, you are
leaving." He burst out with laughter louder than the voice he
spoke with.

"Fine!" Marthe huffed.

"Don't worry. I understand. Kinshasa drives many away, but
you . . ." he interrupted and pointed his stubby finger at Marthe
once more, "you cannot leave."

"Er . . ." Mami attempted to interrupt, scared, feeling her
chances of leaving slipping away.

"Shut up!" Marthe quickly silenced her.

"I just want to say . . ."

"Not now." Prince silenced Mami.

"Well done!" Marthe continued, and applauded slowly and
sarcastically, "you have figured out our plan, genius, now you
can give us the money for the car so we can get out of here."

"Ha! I'll do no such thing."

"I'm not going to sit here and . . ."

"SHUT UP!" They both roared at her this time.

"You'll be going nowhere . . ." Marthe looked at his stubby fingers pointing towards her.

"Now, Prince, my Prince, why are you behaving this way? Are we not friends? Are you not a business man? I am bringing you a good business deal."

"You are not going anywhere, until I get my money."

"What money?"

This is where Mami remembered this man from. Many years ago, he had paid *Koko ya Mobali* the dowry money, and insisted *Koko* keep it—which *Koko* did—even though Marthe had no intention of marrying him. It was the crocodile man, with the crocodile shoes.

"You know what money I am talking about." He replied bitterly.

"Why would you let such foolishness ruin a great opportunity for business? I saw you looking at the car, think how it would add to your collection. What kind of business man are you?" He stood again to look out of the window, "Come on Mami, let us go, this man is wasting our time." Marthe kissed her teeth and reached over to drag Mami, who was now a ghost of her former self, so they could leave together.

"Wait . . ." He sat back down and continued, "I want the car, but not without the money I am owed."

"Fine!" replied Marthe as she returned to sit back down, Mami followed behind, "you can have your money."

"So, I will take away what I am owed. This is my offer." He took a pen, wrote down the amount on a piece of paper, and slid it across the table to Marthe.

"$3000?!" Marthe exclaimed.

"Take it or leave it." He replied sternly. Marthe looked over at Mami and saw the pleading in her eyes. She had been so caught up in the game with this man, she had forgotten what this was really about.

"Fine. We'll take it."

He went to the window and whistled, and one of the guards appeared in the room within a moment. He whispered in the guard's ear and moments later, the guard returned with a large sack of cash.

"Three thousand." He counted the money in front of them, and placed it in a leather bag.

"You can keep the bag. Consider it a gift." Marthe smiled wryly, dropped the keys on the table, picked up the bag and left, with Mami following behind.

"Have you gone mad?" Mami erupted as they left and walked out of the compound far away enough from anything.

"Listen, I'm sorry. I had to, the man is so stupid. He doesn't know he just used his own money to pay off his own debt which he owed to himself. Foolish."

"We nearly didn't get the money."

"Don't worry, we got it. I did not mean to make you panic. I know if I would have told the truth he would have just tried to manipulate us even more. Now he thinks both of us are leaving, he can finally stop looking for me."

"Come little sister, let us go home." Marthe walked as though she was marching, and carried the bag behind her shoulder whilst Mami followed nervously behind.

Deep inside the hearts of each and every one of us, we are all always reaching for a place that we can call home.

"I have the tickets." Mami clutched the phone tighter than she had ever held it before.

"When do you leave?" Papa replied.

"In two days." They both simultaneously exhaled as if they had been holding their breath for days. In this tender moment, they held each other, and thought of some far away ethereal place in the future, where they could be together.

"*Koko Patrice* still has not yet returned, I am worried for him."

"Do not worry. He will be fine."

"Are you sure?"

"Yes, I have spoken to him," Papa knew all too well they had not spoken but he did not want Mami to worry any further, "he will be fine. He will return soon."

"Okay." Her heart settled, even if only momentarily.

"You have to tell me the exact information about when you arrive. I will wait for you and Jean at the airport." There was a knock on the door. Mami answered, and let Marthe in who she was expecting. She ran in to pick up her favorite nephew and whisk him in the air whilst Mami finished her phone conversation to Papa.

"Are you ready?" Marthe asked.

"How do you even get ready for something like this?" Mama let out a labored sigh.

"Have you packed anything yet?"

"What do I pack? It is one thing to leave to go on holiday or for a trip when you know you will be back, but what does it mean to pack never knowing when, or even if, you will ever return?"

They embraced and held each other close as if lamenting over each time they never did, how each time was never long enough, whilst Jean stood in the middle of them looking up.

"Don't worry, little sister, no matter where you go, I will always be there for you."

Mami nodded in response, as Marthe wiped the tears streaking down her face.

"I will come with the driver to pick you up at 8 p.m. to take you to the airport."

"Have you told father?" Mami asked. Marthe did not reply, unable to look at her, she looked aimlessly at the floor.

"The sisters know. They wanted to see you, especially Marie. But I told them to stay. It is too dangerous."

"You did the right thing." Mami replied, though it still did not alleviate Marthe of the burden she felt. "It's okay," Mami added, "it would make no difference. Everyone is just waiting for me to get married and do everything properly, so things can be back to normal. It's a shame; we worry more about honoring the family name, than we do about honoring the people in the family.'"

They spent the rest of the day together, singing, laughing, eating, and remembering.

8 p.m.

"Are you ready?" Marthe asked as she entered the house. Mami nodded and produced a large suitcase. Mami was dressed in a beautiful bright blue and yellow patterned *liputa*, with a white blouse and hair wrapped in an equally stunning *kintam-bala*. Jean was ready, dressed in his finest trousers, shirt and tie combination, which made him resemble someone many years his senior. Mami wanted them to look their best for whatever may come.

"Is that it?" Marthe asked.

"What else can I bring?" Mami replied. "The most important things cannot be packed."

They left the house without looking back and entered the truck. The driver, the same man who used to go out and buy them snacks and other things not meant for them when they were teenagers, waited patiently and nodded at Mami holding in both a smile and a tear as if the joy of seeing her again battled the pain of watching her go. They sat at the back, whilst Marthe and the driver were up front.

"Is this father's truck? Why did you take it?"

"I figured if we had a military truck, nobody would ask us any questions."

They drove along the streets of the city Mami once called home, and watched as the destruction from the nights before haunted all of the memories she had come to know. The air was tense, hot and humid, not from the dense traffic or the Kinshasa sunshine which had set but from the uncontainable volatility lingering in the air. After a long drive, they reached *Boulevard du 30 Juin* and slowly proceeded up the long straight road to *N'jili Airport*, when traffic wound to a staggering halt. They could see a queue of cars up ahead into the distance and faint outlines of people in the darkness, all accompanied by a cacophony of sounds; the shouting of commands.

"What is it?" Mami asked fearfully.

"I don't know." Marthe replied. She tapped the driver and motioned him out of the car to go and check. He opened the door and stepped out. He returned less than a minute later.

"*Bakangi nzela.*" the driver said.

"*Ba nani?*"

"*Les Soldats.*"

"What's happened?" Mami asked, unable to hear their conversation. "They have closed off the road. They're checking all the vehicles."

"Who?"

"*Les Soldats.*"

A deep rain of fear washed over Mami and submerged her into a sinking silence. She pulled Jean down onto her lap, hiding him from view. Marthe looked back at Mami's jittery panic, "don't worry, it's going to be alright," she tried but her attempt at reassurance went awry.

"Can we not go back around?" Mami asked.

"If we leave, they'll see us, and if they see us, they'll . . ." Shouting erupted in the background breaking them into a silent fear. It was loud and echoed around them as if all the men had surrounded the truck. It became louder, more aggressive. Three gunshots ripped the air. Followed by another succession of gunshots, too many to be counted. It was impossible to tell whether it was at people or not, but the shouting was enough for panic to rise. Mami held onto Jean tightly, wrapping both arms around him, squeezing out his breath.

"*Baluka! Baluka!*" Marthe shouted at the driver, and he spun the car, quickly manoeuvring it out of the traffic and speeding off in the opposite direction.

"What are you do . . ."

"We have to!"

"What if they come after us?"

"We have no choice."

As they drove back down the long stretch of road, in the rearview mirror, they could see a truck approaching them at full speed. *Soldats.* The truck approached like a monster in the night, the front lights beaming like beady eyes, and it's camouflaged olive green coat with cracks like crocodilian armor. They pursued in heat. *Les Soldats* edged up right behind the truck and were now bumper to bumper. Two gunshots from the chasing truck fired into the air from the waving AK47 in the shadow of the night.

"Drive!" Marthe shouted at the driver who looked consumed by fear.

"What are you doing? Just pull over." Mami pleaded.

"Never!" Marthe insisted, "we have come too far." The driver attempted to pick up speed but the truck began to splutter like someone running out of breath. Marthe pointed up ahead to the driver, so stuck in his frantic driving he could not understand, "*Kota awa, kota awa,*" she repeated at the top of her lungs screaming, until he realized the left turn she was pointing to and at the very last second took a sharp turn into the side road, which almost toppled the car over as it lent onto the two side wheels suspending them in the air before it came crashing back down. Mami hit her head on the window. Jean thumped into her and began wailing. She tried to quiet him.

They went down the back roads, turning left and right, left and right guided by Marthe, until they were somewhere Mami had never been, unsure whether they were still being followed. The driver brought the car to a screeching halt.

"Get out!" Marthe shouted and jumped out of the truck.

"What?!" Mami said exasperated, panting out of breath, "get out to go where?!" she shouted in panic.

"Don't worry, I know someone here. If they find the truck, they will not find us."

They got out of the truck; Mami, out of fear rather than trust, and began to walk down the back road into the insidious darkness that consumed them as if the ocean was the night and they were swimming through; drowning, quickly running out of air. There were no lampposts here, nothing to light their path but the dim glow of the moon. It was too dark to even tell one house from the next but Marthe led the way, and the rest trotted closely behind. She stopped in front of a door with an ambiguous sign on the front Mami could not understand.

"Where are we?" Mami asked.

"Shh. I know a *Nganga 'Nzambi* here who can help us." Marthe replied. Mami was unsure, she felt a growing uncertainty but she followed as there was no other option. Marthe knocked on the door three times, unusually near the bottom, the sound was low and hollow. Footsteps shuffled from behind the door. It creaked open. A short man in a dark suit hurried them in. He led them through the tiny hall of their makeshift church into a backroom.

"This is Pastor Samy." Marthe introduced them all to each other and for a moment, the calm and peace they knew once before had returned, even if only for a moment.

"There is no way to the airport Pastor . . ." Marthe continued in her own conversation.

Mami watched her, watched her older sister reveal parts of herself she had no idea existed. It was as if she had gotten to know her more in the last few days than the last few years.

"Come with me." Pastor Samy said, as he led them to another place behind another door out to another road.

"*Zwa*" he gave Marthe a set of keys from his pocket, and pointed to the small dusty white car parked beside, "*Nkende nzela ya sima*. It will be safe that way."

"Thank you!" Marthe replied zealously, whilst Mami broke down in tears in the background.

"I can't do it. I can't go." Mami wailed.

"What do you mean you can't go?!" Marthe roared at her like a chastising parent to her child.

"It's too much. It's too dangerous."

"No. You must go." Marthe held Mami by the shoulders and looked her deep in her eyes.

"Your life is no longer here, *ma soeur*. I love you, but you cannot stay." They locked arms and held each other like they could never let go.

"Wait . . ." Pastor Samy shouted. They froze. "You cannot go yet. We must first follow tradition." He pulled out a small grey-ish clear plastic bottle of water from his pocket. Marthe got down on her knees and the rest followed. Pastor Samy bellowed an incantation from the depths of his diaphragm into the air of the night. He finished. Marthe placed her hands out, one palm atop the other, and he poured the water into her hands, she drank some from her palm and splashed the rest over her. Mami, the driver, and Jean followed and did exactly what they had seen. Pastor Samy continued by spraying the water onto the floor, pouring a libation, and then over the car.

"Your path is blessed, *na nkombo ya Yesu*, go in peace." They stood and rushed to the car.

"What time is the flight?"

"It is at 10 p.m. We have less than one hour." Mami answered in a panicked voice.

"We'll make it." Marthe said, in her most determined voice, "Go, go, go!" she roared at the driver, who started the car, revved it and drove off leaving tire marks along the road. They followed the direction Pastor Samy had suggested and, it was as if by a miracle, the pathway was clear.

They drove along the road, reaching top speed in a car appearing as though it could not do another mile. Mami sat panting in the back of the car clutching Jean who, despite everything, was calm. They arrived at the airport, paying off the security guards who tried to make a little extra cash by taxing a few dollars on anyone who was entering and leaving. The driver skidded and parked as close to the entrance as he could. Marthe grabbed their suitcase and ran in front to find the way for them, whilst Mami and Jean ran behind. There was no time for goodbyes. Marthe gave her sister their suitcase and watched them rush into the life waiting for them ahead.

chapter 35

"I HAVE GIVEN YOU TWO CHILDREN, and *still*, you have not honored me as a woman."

Mami looked at Papa suggestively as though she was trying to communicate a hidden message. He understood, nonetheless, he feigned obliviousness to benefit his cause.

"If you're going to say something," Papa replied, "it is best to just say it."

"It is not for the woman to say, it is for the man to know."

"But no man is born knowing, even the wisest man must be taught."

"Then let time be your teacher, not even a fool would wait this long for a lesson his classmates understood long ago."

"Then it is understood. I have every intention of honoring you." Mami smiled a subtle smile at his response, "I always did."

A few weeks after they were first introduced to the church after Mami's chance meeting with Tonton, Papa decided to honor her. He saw it as a sign, that the time was right. For so long, everything had taken him away from tradition and maybe this was something to bring him back.

It was on a Wednesday evening, in place of what would have been the weekly prayer session. Pastor Kaddi led the service. He wore a shining brilliant bright cream-white new suit, white shirt, white tie, with leather white crocodile shoes. He was dressed as if he had floated down from a cloud just for the service, and was due to return shortly after. Papa was dressed in a dark blue suit with an orange tie, and Mami wore a blue and orange *liputa* ensemble to match.

There were only a few witnesses, as required for a union to be made holy; Mama Gloria, in all her sternness, attended to register and record the event, there were two members of the congregation who also attended unaware the evening prayer session was cancelled because they did not pay attention to the announcement in Sunday's church service, nonetheless they stayed. Jean and Marie were left at home, one to look after the other—which way, depended on who was asked—unaware of the occasion they were missing. They assumed Mami and Papa were already married and never asked; they never dared to assume otherwise.

Sitting on a chair at the front was Tonton dressed in full *sapeur* mode, the most electrifying colors; a kaleidoscopic outfit which made him look more glamorous than the bride and groom, he looked as though he would marry himself if he could. Tonton felt it was his duty to attend. He would not have dared miss this for anything else; he felt partially responsible for the union as it was he who had introduced them to the church. Amongst others, he would extend this responsibility and claim it was he who had introduced them.

"We will read," Pastor Kaddi began animatedly, "from 1 Corinthians chapter 13: 4 – 8" he continued with a soft compassion in his voice even he had not heard before; "Love is patient, love is kind. It does not envy, it does not boast, it is not proud . . . love never fails."

"Brothers and Sisters, we have gathered here to witness . . ." he continued, then gave a most heartfelt declamation on the wonders and purpose of love, "It is not something you fall in, it is something that you rise to. Love is what you do, but more than that, it is who you are, who you have been before you were *you*." Following this, Papa and Mami made their declarations of I do, for better or worse, good or bad, until death them do part. He honored her, as he had intended. Husband and wife.

"Oyoki sango?" Mami rushed into the living room where Papa was watching television. Jean was in his room with Glody, Marie in hers with Madeliene and Christelle. Tonton was out.

"What news?" Papa replied inquisitively.

"He is gone!" Mami shrieked.

"Who?!"

"Le Maréchal, Mr. President!" Mami roared, waving her arms everywhere in hysteria. '

"What?!" Papa was overwhelmingly shocked at the news. "Is it over. Is it really over?"

"Yes!"

"How?"

"A *coup d'état*. It happened today."

"Today! How do you know?"

"I am on the phone to Marthe now! She just told me." Papa frantically searched the five channels they had on television to find some kind of breaking news report or information; there was nothing. He switched to *TV5*, the only extra channel they could afford, which kept them up to date with what was going on in the *francophone* world.

"Bonjour Messieurs et Mesdames, aujourd'hui le 17 Mai 1997, il y a eu un coup d'état à Kinshasa, Zaïre. Le Maréchal, Mr. Président . . ." the broadcaster delivered the breaking news.

"There is trouble in the city," Mami continued, "people are on the streets, there is mayhem."

Papa sat there with his mouth wide open unable to take in this unexpected news, whilst the voice of Mami, shrieking at the top of her voice, filled the house. Madeleine, Christelle, and even Glody, leaving Jean behind, all came pouring into the living room as they heard the commotion. The rest of the family now stood as if spectators, watching something occur they did not know. Marie was always quickest to respond to any noise or excitement.

"What is going on? Mum?" Marie asked, as she peered into the living room and rushed in.

"I don't know if this is good news or bad news . . ." Papa said worryingly.

"Why is there so much noise?" Jean came running into the living room shortly after.

"What do you mean?" Mami asked Papa, confused by his response.

"I mean, we do not know what will come next; more war, more conflict, more fighting, or will there be peace? Will there ever be peace? We do not know."

"Helloooo . . ." said Jean, restlessly.

"Thirty-two years! Thirty-two years! Do you not remember?" Mami retorted, frustrated.

"Of course I remember!" Papa burst out. "How could anyone forget?"

"So why are you worrying?"

"Because I am scared, I do not know what will become of our country. If we will ever be able to return. If we will ever know peace."

A silence fell in between them as they both ran away to visit the memories in their hearts they buried deep with them.

"Mum, Dad, what has happened?" Jean asked, breaking the silence.

"There has been a coup. *Le Maréchal, Mr. Président*, is no longer in power, he is not the president anymore. *Ba bimisi ye.*" Papa replied, his voice still sprinkled with fear. Madeleine, upon hearing the news and seeing the report, broke out of her statue-like stance that stood watching the TV, and fell to the floor, shrieking and sobbing. She pulled the *kintambala* wrapped around her head, and threw it to the floor, and began clutching at her hair. Jean and Marie stood frozen, shocked at her reaction, though Jean understood, or rather knew what they did not know he knew; he remembered what he had read, and what this moment may mean to her, however, to actually understand, was something that would come to him later. Mami and Christelle rushed to Madeleine, both held her by the arms, and helped her to the sofa. Glody too started crying, he could sense the pain and uncertainty in the room, and it scared him, as the news scared them.

"What does this mean?" Jean asked, he was now worried for he too felt their worry, their pain.

"The coup?" Papa replied.

"No, what does this mean for the country?"

"I do not know. Nobody knows. We cannot predict the future. All I know is violence begets violence, so come what may, this is only the beginning."

chapter 36

IT WAS THE DAY OF PAPA'S court hearing. He had asked for the time off from work so he could attend, however, he did not say it was for court; he instead told them he would be taking his daughter to her doctor's appointment. He hated having to use Marie as an excuse; however he refused to be criminalized further for simply trying to survive. He would have much preferred to be spending time with her, even if it was at the doctor's.

He wore his best suit, his only blue suit, but with black shoes, a white shirt and a dark red tie. The suit was made from a dark blue cotton material he had inherited from *Koko Patrice*; he had it for years and it fit him as if it was personally tailored from Saville Row. Papa wanted to give the best impression he could. The suit made him look as if he had another name, another face, a different story other than his own.

Papa went to court by himself. He did not want Mami also having to go through the same intense worry, though he knew she would be just as worried, if not more, left at home. He arrived at Highbury Magistrate's court at 9:30. His hearing was at 11 a.m., however, Papa wanted to make sure he would not be late as he did not exactly know where he would be going or what it would take, so he ended up getting there so early and the extra waiting time only further increased his anxiety, raising his blood pressure beyond 140.

He sat in the reception waiting, an exercise of patience, as he watched the other court attendees flow in and out for their respective cases. They were all different. Papa expected to see hardened criminals, intimidating men who feared nothing and stared at you with eyes not there. Instead he saw everyday people, people who he could have passed on the street or come into his shoe store whilst he was on his security shift. The most intimidating people he saw were the men in robes, the judges; they were the decision makers who held his fate in their hands, they held the most power. They walked as though they breathed a different air to everyone else, as if certain they would not also meet the same mortal fate as the rest.

Papa waited impatiently, not moving from the bench he sat on in the reception area, until his name was called, which they mispronounced; "En-tanga." This would usually bother and frustrate Papa, "Ntanga . . . all together" he would insist, and always made sure to Jean and Marie to do the same, to correct anyone who mispronounced their name, but this time it felt so futile, and so he said nothing, as if his voice had been taken from him.

He entered the court room; it was empty. The grandness of it all overwhelmed him, as he stepped into the booth and was brought the Bible to take the oath. The judge wore a white wig, which covered his thinning grey hair beneath. He peered through his expensive glasses hung on the edge of his thin, long nose, as though it was sculpted onto his face, to read the case file in front of him.

"Mr. *Ntanga*" the judge pronounced it properly, much to Papa's surprise—maybe there had been another *Ntanga* who he had known—and began to speak with an English Papa could not understand.

"You are required to pay back the total sum of taxes unpaid for your second job which you failed to declare. Furthermore, due to your immigration status, you will be assigned a probation officer, who, hereby, will be responsible for the assessment of your case and the final outcome."

He banged the gavel and the court session was over. It lasted two minutes, and though Papa was not sure what it meant, he left with another piece of paper with details of where he was supposed to go and the person he was supposed to meet.

The probation officer was a man not too different from Papa. He looked kind, amicable, held a pleasantness suggesting he enjoyed quiet activities such as reading and talks of the world. It made Papa feel as though, perhaps, in another time and place, a reversal of roles or change in situation, they could have known each other; could have been friends. He introduced himself as "Peter Markham" and shook Papa's hand firmly but showed a friendly smile. His office was not as intimidating as the court room; nonetheless it still held a power of its own. Papa sat waiting to be spoken to.

"Mr. N-tanga . . . did I pronounce it correctly?" He asked. Papa was surprised. They had not ever asked before, they never usually do.

"Yes." Papa replied.

"So I see here . . ." the probation officer continued whilst flicking through a folder of files, "we have an issue of declaration of work, which, given your immigration status, is a very serious issue." Papa carried on listening, nodding to show he understood.

"Can you explain to me what your current situation is?" the probation officer asked, his voice had a melange of routine professionalism and genuine concern, which made Papa feel a little bit more comfortable.

"Sir, I have a wife. I have two children. I am working as security guard, and I do not have enough money for them, for everything. So I am working now in the mornings too, as a cleaner."

"Why did you not declare the work?"

"I do not know . . ."

"Did you know what you were doing? That you were intentionally avoiding this declaration?"

"No." Papa replied, after a long, drawn out, pensive silence.

"I need you to be honest with me. Well . . ."

"Sir," Papa interrupted, "my son is in secondary school; I want him to do well. I want him to get education. My daughter, too, is very bright. We do not even have a computer at home. I have to give them £1 to go to an internet café only for one hour. And I cannot even give them every day. I wanted to save more money for this."

The probation officer sat quietly, listening, staring intently into the eyes of Papa as he spoke.

"You do realize because of this I have to make a decision and this could have an effect on not just you, but your family. You could have your application for status rejected, meaning you would be deported." He gave a flat, thin-lipped horizontal smile.

"This is why there are rules, and why you must follow them. Do you understand that?"

Papa felt a fear strike his heart he had not yet felt before from another man, it wasn't a physical fear—he was used to those, that he knew how to manage—it was a deeper fear; a fear something could still take his life but in a different way. Papa sat still, trembling.

"Do you smoke?" The probation officer curiously asked.

"No." Papa replied quickly.

"Do you drink?" Papa shook his head in response, as though he had lost his voice from fear.

"You don't drink." The probation officer sounded surprised. Papa shook his head once more. The probation officer sighed a deep breath, and sat forward, interlocked his hands with his index finger pointing upwards placed over his lips as though he was holding back something he was supposed to say.

"I must make a case assessment. I have to make a decision . . ." he continued, and spoke a bit slower as if going against himself, "in the meantime you will be required to sign in with me on a monthly basis until your case is resolved. Do you understand?"

Papa understood. He understood it meant more waiting, more uncertainty, more anxiety and sleeping not knowing what tomorrow may bring. He understood it meant his life was not in his hands, his future was being decided not by a god, not an omnipotent, almighty power who decided the fate of all, not by any divine being or a supernatural force, but by people, by a person, who bled and breathed as he, a person who did not know him and who he did not know.

When Papa arrived home Mami was waiting for him with such eagerness she met him at the door once she heard his keys jingling from outside.

"*Balobi nini?*" She asked nervously, fearfully.

"They said I have to wait." Papa sighed and Mami groaned in frustration simultaneously, "they need to make a case assessment."

"What did they say will happen?"

"They said I could . . ."

"No. Don't say it . . ." Mami burst out in shock.

"It will be okay."

"What will we tell the children?"

"We do not tell them. It will be okay. It will be okay." Papa said to comfort Mami, and repeated, as if to convince himself of something he was not sure of.

chapter 37

J EAN HAD STARTED HIS GCSE EXAMS. He was amazed at how
much time had passed, and so quickly. How much he had
seen, and how so much had changed. The GCSE years were
serious; they were made to seem as if they decided your fate as a
human being. This was when even the most badly behaved children changed their act and became concerned with their prog-
ress and results; not all of course, but most. For Jean, however,
he had always been at this stage, regardless of what pressures
swayed him from one side to another, he was always reminded,
by Papa and Mami, in one way or another, education was para-
mount. Though he did not yet truly understand why, he wanted
to fulfill something he knew would make him worthy in the eyes
of his father. Also, he implicitly knew due to him arriving much
later than everyone, he was always playing catch up; where they
could afford to walk or stroll, he had to sprint and cover so much
ground just to be at the same place as them, and still be left
behind.

"What do you want to be when you grow up?" Mr. David
asked him, hoping to guide Jean in the right direction. It was

a question Jean could never really answer. The other children spoke with certainty about their career paths and what they aspire to be; doctor, lawyer, teacher, football player, mechanic and so on. However, for Jean, he did not so much think about what he would like to be, he thought about what he would like to see, and where he would like to go; he wanted to one day go to France, to go on a trip he would not need to ask anyone permission for, where he did not have to worry about any kind of document or papers and whether or not he had the right one. He also knew he wanted to help people, people such as Madeleine, and Christelle. However, he did not know which profession or career this came under, so he often did not give a reply. And when he was pressured to say something he would mumble under his breath and shrug his shoulders as though he was not concerned.

It was difficult for Jean to study at home but he made the most of it; though now instead of playing video games he spent most of the time when he wasn't studying, writing in his diary. Not only were there almost twice as many people in the house as before, meaning it was twice as loud—and it was already loud enough as it was—one of them was a small spider-boy, super hero imitating child who, at any given opportunity, would be scaling their bunk bed as if they were climbing frames in the playground whilst Jean was trying to study. A three bedroom flat shared by enough people to field a baseball team, with three generations between them, wasn't exactly ideal but it worked, and Jean felt more determined than ever before to make something out of it.

It was weeks before Jean would find out his GCSE exam results so he spent most of his days either playing football with the rest of his friends or being deservedly lazy at home; laying on the sofa watching television, or on the desktop computer Papa had finally managed to buy for them for their learning, but even more so as a consolation for all the other things he could not offer. Marie was now settled in secondary school, her exceptionalism showing no signs of slowing; however, the family did not pay attention to it the way she wanted them to because to them, it was expected, normal; as though she had been in secondary already. In their minds, they were waiting for her to graduate from university, BSC, MSC, PhD, therefore all else until then was simply introductory.

Marie and Jean had gotten closer and shown more maturity and mutual support, however, Marie was always quick to remind him no matter what his results were, she would do better, to which Jean did not contest because he knew it was true, but not only that, he wanted it to be. Madeleine and Christelle found familiarity among the family and were increasingly settled at home, comfortably. Even Glody, the rambunctious child with endless energy, was referring to it as *home; I want to go home, is there food at home* and *there's lots of people in my house*. It made everyone smile, in a warm way that also made them wonder. Tonton still spent more time out than in, still extravagant, still constantly inebriated, still trying to forget. Still always remembering. Mami and Papa persisted as usual, somehow trying to manage everything in this new land they were still getting accustomed to as well as the old land they had left behind. And in the midst of the storm, they still stole quiet moments of peace to carry each other through. Mami continued her part-time job as a dinner lady in Marie's former primary school; however, as it was summer, she too was on a holiday, although it was reluctant because during this period, she would not be paid which meant phone calls from Kinshasa were harder to take and promises had to be delayed. Papa spent more time out of the house, working his morning cleaning job and security day job, taking as many hours as he could in extra shifts, to the extent his manager was convinced if the store was open twenty-four hours, Papa would work all twenty-four; he was never late and never called in sick. However, he still had to attend to sign in with his probation officer as his case was still pending. "Still pending!" He would air his frustrations out when speaking to a worried Mami as they tried to hold their nerves, and their family, together; there was no easy way of telling them one of their parents may be deported, so they felt it was best not to tell them at all, unless that day came. So they both hid it really well, in order for the children to carry on as normal. However, even though she tried, from the day the brown enveloped arrived, Mami felt nervous about every single one after and would defer the responsibilities of opening them to Papa, even when he was not there. It was not so much the actual cause or the authorities; it was the uncertainty, none of which they had any control or influence over. It was placing the entirety of your existence into the hands of someone else, someone who did not already know what weight they carried, for them to decide whether to take some away or to add on more. Nonetheless, they carried on the only way they knew how; with hope. Always with hope.

Jean walked to school for the last time. It was a slow walk, much slower than usual. He took in the moment, knowing nothing was going to be the same after. School was opened from 8 a.m., for those who were eager to get their results, and some arrived this early; of course Chris and Jamil were among the very first. However, Jean strolled in around midday, he had slept in, not wanting to waste a day waking up early if he was not obligated to. He had told Mami and Papa he did not have to be in school until 12 p.m., and they were none the wiser, but also, he did not want to interact with the other students and bask in their successes or failures with this school, it was more so the failures—he knew they would all be consumed by.

As he walked into the school entrance, he noticed how empty it was, the open space calming his nerves. There was a parent of a child he barely spoke to sitting by the benches consoling them and offering support; tears meant disappointment, and disappointment meant failure so Jean steeled himself, but could feel his heart sinking with each step. He walked into the reception, and saw the smiling face of Mrs. Butler. "Hello Jean," she greeted him enthusiastically, as if she too had just received her results. It still amazed Jean how she was able to remember everyone's name.

"Hello, Mrs. Butler." Jean replied, failing to match her enthusiasm.

"Come alone then, did you?"

"Yes." He offered no explanation. She flicked through the box of envelopes with her quick fingers and neatly manicured nails.

"Ntanga, isn't it? With an N?" she asked and smiled, handing him the envelope. "Yes." Jean answered, smiling back at her as he took it nervously into his hands. He walked across to the waiting area and sat down where he had sat down when he first joined the school. A brown envelope. He opened it. Gripped the paper tightly with each hand as it trembled in the air. His eyes glared looking through it.

"Jean," a voice interrupted from above, "so good to see you."

Jean looked up and saw Mr. David greeting him with a smile. "Hello, sir."

"Are you happy with your results?" Mr. David asked, his question layered with positivity. He never asked whether or not the student passed or failed, his focus was always whether or not the student felt fulfilled; whether they felt they did the best they could and were happy with their efforts. Jean took the paper and handed it to Mr. David. He watched his eyes move left to right as he read the letters written on the paper.

"Well done, Jean! I knew you could do it."

"Thanks, Sir."

"This is brilliant. Five A to Cs; Two Bs in English, B in Maths, B in Sociology, C in Science, whoa, really well done. It's not just about what you got, it's about where you started. Also, you got what you needed for sixth form, and who knows, maybe after you'll go to university."

"Maybe." Jean replied, contentedly. Mr. David stood there

beaming, more excited than Jean was, as if he was the architect of a grand design that had finally been erected.

"I'm going to go now, sir." Jean said, not really wanting to be in school any longer than he was obliged to. Mr. David walked with him to the gates.

"You've done really well, Jean. I hope you know you have a lot to be proud of."

"Thanks, sir." Jean nodded, his eyes revealing the words he felt he could not say.

"By the way, did you ever write in the diary I gave you?" He asked, curiously.

"Nah." Jean replied, "I didn't need to," shrugging it off.

Jean arrived home to find everyone waiting for him, apart for Madeleine and Christelle who were out somewhere he did not know.

"So . . . ?" Marie asked with excited anticipation as he walked through the door. Jean ignored her and walked straight into the living room where both Mami and Papa were sat watching television. Papa quickly picked up the remote and muted it.

"*Boni Jean, eleki bien?*" Papa asked in a calm voice enveloping his anxious curiousity. He took the envelope out from his bag and held out the results paper, Mami quickly reached up and took it from him, read it thoroughly and then passed it to Papa.

Papa looked at the paper deeply, engrossed himself in it, as if he was reading an exhilarating story he could not pull himself away from.

"What does this mean?" He asked.

"I passed, Dad. I got one A and five Bs."

"*Eh?*" Papa replied exasperatedly, "what is this, five Bs?"

"Yeah, I passed."

"What did you pass with five Bs?"

"I got five A to Cs . . ."

"Stop lying. You didn't get five A to Cs, you got 5 B to Bs," his voice roared loudly, "B, what can you do with B?" He took the piece of paper and hurled it across the room back at Jean with force, as he watched it rustle through the air and land on the floor in front of him. Jean picked it up slowly and dejectedly, and retreated back into his room where he found Glody playing on the bed. Jean sat down next to him and the little boy leapt on to him grinning ear to ear.

"Are you okay?" Glody asked as he noticed Jean's demeanor.

"Don't cry." Glody added as he moved his face closer to Jean's and saw the tears down his cheek, "It's not good to be sad." Glody then wrapped his small arms around Jean and hugged him closely, not letting him go.

chapter 38

IN THE EVENING, PAPA HAD RETURNED to work, Madeleine and Christelle had still not arrived home, and Mami was in the living room watching television with Marie, so Jean decided to go out unnoticed. It was still as bright as it had been during the day, however, the temperature was starting to settle from a musky warmth and cool itself. He walked the ten minutes it took, through the main high street, which was now filled with bodies spilling in out of bars, until he arrived at James's block, the grey high rise upright building resembling a long block of Lego. *Number 73.* He rang the buzzer and waited patiently. Whilst he was waiting, someone came out of the door of the building to exit and let him in. "Lift's not working, mate," the man said, "you might want to take the stairs."

"Thanks," Jean groaned begrudgingly, he was not prepared to walk up twelve floors. He knocked on the door, not loudly this time, but quickly, quietly. He wanted to be heard but was not trying to make his presence known. For the first time, he noticed the color of the door: blue, a bright blue, something between the sky and the sea. There was no answer. He knocked again as he had done before. He waited, patiently. There was no sound this time; he could not hear a television in the background, or the shuffling of footsteps on the carpet. Silence.

He walked out to the balcony and noticed how high up he was, how beautiful the city looked as it contrasted the sky, lighting up as if it was coming to wake whilst the sun set in the horizon, covering it like a canopy. Jean's breathing slowed. He calmed himself. Still looking out into the distance, he climbed up on to the edge of the balcony and sat down, placing both his legs on the other side facing outwards. He looked down. Felt the wind caress his face. And kept looking, down, down, down.

"Jean," James appeared, "what you doing?" Jean was not startled, he expected it, hoped for it even, for him to appear; someone, anyone, but most of all him.

"I came to see you."

"Really?" James responded, surprised.

"Yeah. I didn't see you today."

"I went in early hoping to avoid everyone but they were all there early, too."

"Must have been annoying. I went in late. How did your results go?"

"Okay, I guess. I was only missing one letter to spell out *dumb*, though." Jean did not know whether he was supposed to find this funny or not.

"What did your parents say?"

"Not much. My ol' man was happy I made it this far, and my mum made us some tea and crumpets."

"How did yours go?"

"I passed. I got five A to Cs."

"Ah, well done, man! I knew you would, you were always the smart one."

"Thanks." Jean replied as if the air in him had been let out like a flat tire.

"What did your parents say?" James asked.

Jean froze and went silent. He did not provide an answer. James did not seek one.

"I'm tired. I'm just really tired." Jean finally said. James was quiet, knowing all too well what he meant, knowing all too well what he felt. They remained in their reflective silence looking over the city, watching it fall into a long peaceful sleep.

Jean woke up feeling heavier than he did the day before, heavier than he had ever felt. It was as though someone had slept on top of him, a much larger body, through the night, muting his voice and leaving him flattened and stiff-jointed. He struggled to get out of bed, but eventually managed to muster the strength to plant his feet on the ground and lift himself up.

It was morning, he was not sure what time, but it was bright enough so the glare through the kitchen window hit him right in the eyes. The house was silent, everyone was still sleeping, apart from Papa, who Jean thought would already be at work until he appeared from the bathroom dressed smart in a white shirt, red tie and the dark blue trousers with the pleat down the middle.

"*Bonjour*, Dad." Jean greeted him first, as it was customary for the child to do, to which Papa soberly replied "*Bonjour*." Jean was curious, he knew Papa could not have been going to work, but he never saw Papa dress up this way for anything else other than a wedding or a funeral; he also knew it could not be either, as it was Friday, but more significantly, as Mami was not present—and she was always present for both of those. Jean stood in the corridor watching Papa frantically pace around the house with an absent-mindedness and panic, unusual to what he had ever seen before. It worried him. Although he stood in front of him, Papa manoeuvred around Jean as if he wasn't there. Jean wanted to ask, but did not know how. His mouth was muted out of fear for no child questions their father, even if out of love; it was the unspoken rule.

"Papa, where are you going?" Jean found the courage to ask as Papa passed him to enter the kitchen, words spilling uncontrollably out of him as if bile from his stomach. It made him feel queasy to ask, but he had done it.

"*Nini?*" Papa replied, looking at Jean in a bewildered manner. Jean did not reply, instead he remained immobilized by fear.

"What did you say?" Papa added impatiently.

"I was just asking where you are going."

"Don't worry. You don't need to know."

A silence fell between them that neither of them were comfortable with. Papa continued frantically pacing, dropping his plates into the sink forming a clutter of cups and cutlery dirtied from the tea laden with sugar, and crusts of bread with leftover jam.

"Is something wrong?" Jean asked worriedly. He stood in front of Papa, blocking his exit out of the kitchen. Papa looked at him as though he was contemplating something profound.

"You don't need to know." He answered, and shook his head, moving past him out of the kitchen bumping his shoulder. Jean did not know whether Papa answered the question he asked or the one in his head. Papa walked into the living room. Jean followed. Papa sat on the sofa and put on his shoes. Jean remained standing.

"You said I don't need to know. I want to know!" Jean said, raising his voice.

"*Eh! Tika!*" Papa almost shouted before he realized he would wake the house if he did, "*Tika.*" he growled. He stood up. They stood face to face.

"No, Dad, I won't leave it. I want to know." Jean insisted.

"It is not for you. You are a small boy."

"No, I'm not. I am sixteen, Dad. Sixteen!" Jean roared at him. Papa twitched; a trigger went off. He raised his hand up, open palmed, fingers thicker than branch stubs, and swung it at Jean. It whooshed through the air. He stopped it before it reached

Jean's face. He pointed a finger at him, hand shaking, finger trembling. He looked at Jean, and noticed how tall he now was, how they now stood eye to eye, and how much it was like looking back into the mirror at himself when he was a child. He imagined how he would have reacted to something like this back then; what he would have known, what he could have known. He slowly lowered his hands and placed them on Jean's shoulders, "Son, I love you." Papa said, eyes red and filling up like an overflowing well, "I might be deported."

"WHAT?!" Jean let a shout loud enough to wake up all the sleeping heads in the house. Papa tried to quiet him with a gentle *shh*, and pat of his shoulder. "What do you mean deported?! Why didn't you tell us?" Jean asked, voice broken with worry.

"The authorities . . ." Papa attempted to explain.

"Why did you not say anything? You should have told us." Jean interrupted, shouting, voice broken with worry.

"I wanted to protect you, so you did not have to worry the way we worry. So you will not have to feel fear, at every moment, like how we feel."

"Since when?"

"A long time," Papa replied, then continued seeing Jean's face was not satisfied with his response.

"Do you remember, the times we would take you and Marie somewhere and you didn't know? Or some things we did not talk about even if you asked? It was because of this, because you deserved to live as a child and not worry or be scared for your future at every moment, like we always are. We worry for you, we did not want you to worry too." In that moment, Jean felt the weight of Papa's words crush him, as he realized he was a child after all and not yet built to carry this burden now placed upon him.

Papa looked at Jean as if for the last time, a look Jean saw in his eyes yet did not understand. Jean stood there; tall, still, thinking back and slowly saw the pieces of a complicated puzzle come together. Papa walked past him and left the room. Jean heard Papa's footsteps along the floor until the door closed as he left. He went back into his bedroom and collapsed on his bed. Although it was bright outside, it was dark inside the room as if morning had yet to come, as if the night before still loomed. The curtains were drawn and little difference could be made between the darkness under his eyelids and the darkness in the room. Jean lay in his bed feeling heavier than before, staring up into the nothingness surrounding him. He reached for his diary. Reminded of it by Mr. David yesterday, he had taken it to write in when he returned home last night, however, he felt too empty to find the words. This time, there was a weight filled inside him he was desperate to unload.

9 *a.m.* Papa arrived. On time, as requested. Sat waiting in reception with the burdened stillness of a soul trapped in a statue. There was no sound but the tick-tock of the clock above the reception desk; each tick was louder than the tock, each tock louder than the tick. He could feel his throat dry up as if he was trying to gulp down a lump of sand. He remained stiff, square, still, legs together, hand placed on each lap, tick following tock, shivering like when cold air chills the bones.

Jean picked up the diary and opened it, flicking through the pages he had written in already until he found a new clean page. His hands felt the leather, and it seemed as if it too had aged, as if something about it had gathered more life. He picked up the nearest pen and held it as if it was a paintbrush, whilst his eyes opened and closed, opened and closed, opened and closed, in the darkness, trying to draw in the light.

"Mr. Ntanga, he will see you now," the lady with the soft voice kindly informed Papa, "If you could make your way through the double doors." She motioned with her hands, with the finesse of an air hostess.

"Thank you." Papa replied. He stood up and tried to stay sturdy, his weakened legs crumbling from the pressure. His hands started to shake. He struggled to push open the double doors. He stepped nervously through and sat down on the lone chair opposite the desk of his probation officer.

"Mr. Ntanga, thank you for coming," the probation officer spoke sternly, "I do apologize for how long your case has taken to resolve, however, as I'm sure you are aware these matters must be properly investigated."

Jean clutched his pen and felt it tremble in between his fingers. His chest rising and falling deeper, each inhale and exhale a push and pull between fear and hope. His heart beat faster and faster, palpitating; the feeling that comes with losing grip, on a high edge, before the fall.

Maybe everybody feels this way, like they are on their own, like they are fighting an invisible battle, fighting against an opponent who they cannot see, and against whom they cannot rest, but is always there, always attacking, always hitting. And the more you try to be yourself, the more it attacks, so the more you are forced to hide; the rough parts of you need to be made smooth, the loud needs to be quieted, the color made dull, just so you can find some peace, just so you can find some rest. So you hide, you hide in someone else's language; you hide in someone else's clothes, hoping the fight never finds you. No one tells you this. So by the time it begins you are already losing, there is nothing quite like being in a fight you aren't prepared for; one you are not even sure you are in. No one asks for this. No one asks to be told you are not enough, no one wants to be forced out, you only do when you can no longer fit in—but what if you never have? You only feel this way when the battle moves from the outside to the inside, when you begin to be able to name it. It becomes such a deep part of you that to fight against it is to fight yourself, and so you project it onto others, and then force the fight on them instead. We are not born fighting, we are not born hating, these are placed upon us by the conditions of this world. There is a softer nature, more beautiful, more whole, that rests deep in the center of us all from which we emerge. But once we leave, we never return to there.

We are on the outside looking in, looking into ourselves. Looking in not knowing what we see, not even recognizing who we are. We put up barriers around ourselves because we put up barriers around the world. We put up barriers around the world, because we put up barriers around ourselves, sometimes physical, but almost always not. And in the end, we are all looking for the same place: somewhere to call home. Home is somewhere we know, somewhere we trust, and we only know home, as well as we know the people around us. Home is somewhere we can go, even if we never left, somewhere we can stay, even if we had to go. Home is a feeling. But maybe we all feel this way, like we have nowhere to go; always, neither here nor there, always, never knowing where you are from, always, never knowing where you are going, never knowing home. Maybe we all feel this way or maybe it is just the idea of this feeling that scares us the most? Home is where your heart is, home is where you rest your head, home is where you never feel alone. For me, there is no place to call home, nowhere that I belong.

"Mr. Ntanga, we have reached a decision regarding your case." The probation officer spoke, looking at Papa with a blank stare in his eyes.

epilogue

IF YOU ARE LUCKY, YOU WILL never have to remember home through your mother's tears or the rage in your father's voice when it shakes. Home will be somewhere you run to, never away from. It will never chase you away—a rabid dog hot on your heels with teeth like a shark, teeth so sharp you can already feel it cutting into you.

If you are lucky, home will never up and leave you, and up and leave you, and up leave you, to the point where whenever anyone ups and leaves you, it feels like home. You will look for them, as if they are home, because we all need somewhere to stay, even if it is a person; somewhere safe, somewhere warm.

Home should never be to you an abusive ex-lover; it should never beat you down, taunting you, with its beady eyes and clenched fists knowing too well how much you want it and how much you hurt because it hurts you. Though it has hurt you, and you left it, you should never long for it. But you do. You wish to return, to its forsaking arms, to be held once more, by home, even if only for a little while. You try to remember whether you left home, or if it left you.

If you are lucky, its memory will never haunt you when you move on, so you will not have to remember. A city is merely a collection of buildings, and buildings do not have souls, so how can home haunt you as though a ghost? But it does, cold sweat on your forehead as you buckle to your knees. For who else wakes in the middle of the night filled with this longing, both a nightmare and a dream? You cannot tell if home is dying, or if it is you, but you know you are both fighting to stay alive, at times fighting each other.

Home should never break you in two so wherever you go you are never whole; half of you remains where you left it, and the other half is rejected where you arrive. You are a split flat-sided pendulum suspended in the air on each side.

If you are lucky . . . and you were, none of this would have ever happened to you. You should have enough of home to take with you wherever you go, yet you don't. You carry only what was left to you, only enough to fit in the cracks of the lines in your palm, a small streak of hope, and so you hold it tight, fist clenched with both rage and regret.